The Scottish Colourist

The Second Catrin Sayer Mystery

ALLAN JONES

THE CATRIN SAYER MYSTERIES

The Chinese Sailor
The Scottish Colourist
The Falmouth Model
The Carnforth Double
The Powys Deacon
The Stratford Hunter

This book is a Kindle Direct Publishing paperback.
The series is also available as e-books from
Amazon Kindle eBooks and other suppliers

CONTENTS

PROLOGUE
CORRYCHURRACHAN

Malcolm Drummond had stopped at the small café on the outskirts of Fort William to buy coffee.

Yesterday he had interviewed Alexander Gault in Oban, further south. There he had listened to Reverend Gault's concerns and looked at the paintings by the man's father, Alistair Gault. Then Drummond had driven north, to spend the night at Fort William, finding it busy with tourists; too busy, he felt.

Having interviewed Marilyn Thompson and examined several more paintings by Alistair Gault in her home, he had a lot on his mind. Drummond was the Director of Security for the Kelvingrove Museum in Glasgow and the artist in question, Alistair Gault, had worked there as a conservator during and after World War II.

But the drive back to Glasgow took him south on the A82, along the edge of Loch Linnhe. It was beautiful day, the sun was out and he wanted to savour it; to stop somewhere, take in the view and enjoy a coffee and a smoke. The young server in the café had said she couldn't fill his coffee thermos directly; there were public hygiene regulations that had to be followed. But she washed it out and sold him a large coffee with cream in a paper cup. Drummond stood by the shelf with the napkins and sweeteners and filled his flask himself. The cup went into the recycle. Another waste item, he thought.

He left the closed flask on an empty table while he went to the 'Gents' and came back to find a man just handing it in to the server at the counter. She smiled at him and said, "Thank you," then handed it straight back to Malcolm as the man turned around.

"I thought someone had forgotten it," he said.

"Thanks anyway," said Malcolm. "I was over there." He pointed at the sign for the toilets. "Hygiene regulations," he said to them both.

The server giggled.

He continued his journey down the A82 along the bank of the loch and stopped at a lay-by near the village of Corrychurrachan for his promised break, taking in the rippling waters and their reflections.

When he started off again his plan was to drive straight through to Glasgow and home. It was near Ballachulish that his car veered to the right suddenly, went through the guard rail and down the embankment. If it had gone all the way down to the water it may have been a better outcome, as the hillside was steep but not shear. However, it lost momentum in the small pines and bushes then burst into flames as it hit a tree full on. His petrol tank had been three-quarters full and the coffee flask became a charred metal cylinder – the plastic fittings at the top just melted away.

The driver of the large Volvo truck heading north had just passed the vehicle as it plunged off the road. He had caught sight of the whole accident in his wing mirror. He pulled over and ran back as soon as he could but his company-issued fire extinguisher didn't even get close to addressing the blaze by the driver's side. The other side was blocked by undergrowth. He tried to get close enough to open the driver's door, he said to the police officer, but it was impossible; there wasn't a damn thing he could do for the man.

PART 1

PAINTINGS

1 LANGMUIR

Jackton, Scotland. Langmuir looked at the people in the new group assembled for the start of his course. Like earlier trainees they were looking a little relaxed in the presence of what they took to be a mildly pleasant academic, ready for a three-day training course away from the normal working day. By the end of the first day that would change, he knew; it wasn't meant to be relaxation. Every trainee was of inspector rank; all were seeking promotion. The course was entitled 'Senior Management Decision-Making and External Communications', a fairly innocuous 'umbrella' title, which went along with the fact he never provided course materials in advance.

The Police Scotland Training Centre in Jackton, a small village in East Kilbride, was built for the Strathclyde Police Service. On completion it was almost immediately transferred to the new police authority formed through amalgamation of the different regional police services in Scotland.

Besides its weapons-training capabilities it housed other training services, including a series of residential courses for senior management development. Langmuir's course was part of this set. Experience had shown that unless you took mid-level police officers right out of their everyday job, they spent more time doing their daily work remotely on a smartphone than preparing for their own future. In the residential courses, phones had to be switched off completely during sessions; it was a strict rule.

The meeting room door opened and Paul Courtney, a well-known news reporter for BBC Scotland and his videographer, Sharon, came in. They shook hands and talked briefly with Langmuir and sat in the two chairs at the side of the room. Sharon started to check her equipment already positioned there, drawing the gazes of a number of the course participants. She was attractive.

Langmuir knew they could have recorded the trainee interviews equally well with a small Nikon or Canon camera these days, but it would not have achieved the same effect. A large video camera with 'BBC Scotland' emblazoned across the front and a microphone pushed in their face by a well-known investigative reporter made the adrenalin flow.

The course content had just been updated to include the Kinnington Church incident, now a year old. It was such good training material that it formed the first day's module. The incident may have been fast, but its aftermath had been headline material. He owed the new 'day one' material, inadvertently some would say, to the young Welsh policewoman from the Metropolitan Police at the centre of the incident, Detective Constable Catrin Sayer.

He stood up and went to the centre front of the room.

"Ladies and Gentlemen, welcome to this course which some of you asked to come on and some of you were told to attend. If you were one of the latter, you groaned inwardly or outwardly, I expect, but I hope all of you gain some benefit from these three days we have together.

"My name is Fraser Langmuir. I now teach a course in communications at the University of Edinburgh but, as you will find over the next few days, I lived for a number of years daily with the sort of crises and decisions that you will meet on this course."

Langmuir had a resonant, characteristic voice and it was clear that several of the trainees recalled it and started to focus more on the man. They had heard him previously - and not in any university context.

"So far in your careers you have always been part of a larger structure, never the person 'at the top'. Whatever the operational role, you have had a frame of reference, a boss to go to. When the media has asked for information you have said quietly to yourself, 'Thank God the Chief Inspector or Superintendent is dealing with those arse-holes'.

Paul Courtney pulled a hurt face and the group laughed. "Is that what you are, Paul?" asked Langmuir.

The reporter said, "Not by my book, no, Fraser. We inform the public of the facts we receive. They have a right to be informed. We try to do that."

Langmuir continued. "There is a fear of talking to the media. You all have that because, frankly, you are 'coppers'; you fear the personal public exposure and embarrassment; you say that you aren't 'TV personalities' or don't feel articulate enough, handsome enough… whatever excuse comes to mind.

"Add to that none of you are quite sure what questions will be put to you, what you should or should not say and the anxiety level increases. If you are not totally in control, not properly prepared, it becomes overwhelming. So you are glad it is some superior officer who faces Paul and Sharon, not you.

"Well, this time it is you. That is what we are going to take you through for the next three days within this room where it can hurt no-one, including you. No report back to senior managers, no blabbing by you about this course to others afterwards. I want future attendees to come here as unprepared as you lot clearly are. These are the rules we operate by here."

He looked at Paul, "You won't be showing any of this on the BBC, will you?"

Paul answered, "Not of them, no, nor of you, not this time, Fraser."

Langmuir continued, "Our first module is based on the Kinnington Church incident. It was not that long ago so you have all heard about it, gossiped about it. Now you are going to represent Police Scotland to the press on it."

Fraser Langmuir had once been the Press Secretary to the Minister of State for Scotland before his burn-out, quiet resignation and a subsequent decision to teach at Edinburgh University. He knew exactly what these people would be going through in the next three days because he had lived it for real, for a lot longer.

The group was paying attention now.

2 A CALL NORTH

New Scotland Yard, London. "Good morning, Sayer!"

Drizzle, rain and gusty winds had been the order of the last two days in London. Catrin Sayer had been caught in a sudden downpour between the nearby St. James's Park underground station and the Metropolitan Police Headquarters, New Scotland Yard. She had just come out of the women's washroom in the corridor near her work area, the Art Crime Unit, after repairing the damage.

"Good morning, sir," she said, as Detective Chief Inspector Neville Coltrane of the Art & Antiques Unit, the 'A&A', sailed past. DCI Coltrane seems in a good mood today, she thought.

As she walked by the glass wall of DCI Jane Worsley's office she saw that the head of the Art Crime Unit was already at her desk. On her return to her own work station she started up her computer, seeing Neville Coltrane enter Worsley's office.

Catrin got down to her first task of the day as Detective Inspector Keith Marshall, her direct superior, arrived and said hello. He was leaving tomorrow, Saturday, on a week's vacation.

"I see Neville has dropped in on us," he murmured as he eyed the glass wall. He was watching carefully. Marshall had once been a member of A&A, but had left the unit after a difference of opinion with his boss, Coltrane. He had been transferred and promoted to this new-established group, the Art Crime Unit. Catrin had joined almost a year after the formation of the ACU, direct from uniform work in Brixton. That had been nearly eight months ago.

Relationships between the ACU and the A&A units were cordial, a diplomat would say. A&A was the long-established 'big brother' of the two; larger, well-resourced with a big reputation externally in the art crime scene. It was part of the specialist operations in the hierarchy of the vast Metropolitan Police structure.

The ACU had been in place for a little over twenty months and was part of the Serious Crime Command, reporting to Superintendent Jack Taylor.

A&A had a primary mandate and expertise for all art-related crime in the UK. However, ancillary crimes away from the issues of theft or forgery of important art were generally left to the crime units in each regional police service. Sometimes things fell through the cracks, given competing resources and priorities.

Now the ACU coordinated those cases, working at one end with A&A officers, at the other with the regional forces. It required the delicate ability to deal with art-crime information and not tread on regional sensitivities.

Coltrane left Worsley's office and she came over to their small meeting room. With Aina Jinnah, their civilian File and Data Management Officer, the four ACU members went through the departmental routine briefing and update. At the end DCI Worsley mentioned that a new case file may be coming in, to do with Glasgow; she would know later.

"And if I knew more now, I wouldn't tell you anyway. Keith, you need to think about wrapping up and your holiday, not something new."

Worsley had a number of divisional meetings later that day that had been in the calendar for some time, so she left shortly afterwards.

The day went smoothly. Keith briefed Catrin on two cases he had been working on alone so far, to add to her own for the next week. Around 4.30 p.m. he shut down his system, locked up his desk and said his farewells. Aina and Catrin wished him a good holiday and better weather in France.

By 5.30 p.m. the ACU had closed up shop for the weekend.

~~

Catrin was on the Tube to Liverpool Street Station, heading to Spitalfields where she now shared a flat rented by Helen Banks, a woman who worked at the British Library. When Catrin had worked as a uniform officer in Brixton she had shared a place with other police officers in Stockwell. Now based at Scotland Yard, she had decided to keep her life in two centres in London rather than three.

Catrin's 'other life' was tied to her work as an artist, a ceramic decorator with her friend Jean Hughes. Jean was co-owner of a small pottery in the Spitalfields Market called the 'The Cwmbran Kiln' with her partner in life,

Melanie Farrell. The pottery was located a short distance from Catrin's new flat.

Her mobile phone beeped as she arrived at the station. She had a text message from Worsley saying simply, "Call me ASAP."

It rang only once. Worsley said, "Catrin, pack a bag for Monday, for two or three days, please. We are off to Glasgow early morning, so I will see you at Euston at around 7.15 a.m.. We have seats in First Class on the 7.30 Pendolino and will get breakfast on board. I will brief you then."

"Yes, ma'am."

On joining the unit, Catrin had worked out quickly when formality and informality with her various senior officers was appropriate.

Worsley continued, "We are going first to the Govan Police Station at Police Scotland; then we go on to the Kelvingrove Museum. Do you have a laptop or tablet with you?"

"My iPad, ma'am."

"Good, bring that."

So, thought Catrin, something related to the Kelvingrove Museum and Art Gallery is on the radar. She had never been to the building, so this trip was a plus for that. The Kelvingrove was one of the premier museums and art galleries in the country. She had long been interested in seeing the building and the art inside. She hoped she would get time to do so.

Catrin had met Helen Banks at a party held by some people in the Art Market scene. As they talked, it came out that Helen and her last boyfriend, who also worked at the British Library, had just split up so she needed someone to move in with her to share the rent. It had worked out well so far. Helen and Catrin had different lives but were considerate of each other. Catrin was particularly responsive to doing her share of the work to keep the flat clean and neat; Helen was passionate about that.

On arrival she changed clothes and walked round to the 'Cymbran Kiln' in the rain showers, wielding her umbrella.

She had known Jean Hughes since schooldays in Pontypridd where they each had developed an interest in art. Catrin had gone to Aberystwyth University to study Fine Arts and Art History. She had then fulfilled a parallel ambition to become a police officer, much to the disappointment of her steady boyfriend at the time, David Jameson. It had caused a breakup.

Jean had chosen the Cardiff College of Art and Design to train to be a master potter, where she had met Melanie. It was there that both had 'come out' about their relationship. They were partners in both life and business. With financial help from Jean's dad they had opened the 'The Cwmbran Kiln' where they worked and lived together, sometimes struggling financially. Both were content to be in London and part of an arts social scene that had lost the barriers between the 'straight' and 'gay' communities.

"I'm off to Scotland, short notice, on Monday," Catrin announced.

"Where?" asked Melanie, immediately.

"Glasgow."

"Great," her friend said. She picked up the phone and headed over to her laptop. "That will help."

"Help what?" said Catrin, suspicious.

Jean was finishing a slip covering on a tea/coffee service, part of their standard range, a colour coating over the original clay work. It would dry overnight and Melanie would 'sgraffito' the decoration in the morning, carving the pattern with a stylus through the colour layer to expose the clay beneath. Jean would then finish the glazing and final firing of the work.

"Melanie went to that Arts Council session about improving craft marketing, remember? Back before Christmas. Now we have an exchange of our stuff with various art shops. A few in Scotland are on our list. She has been talking with someone in Edinburgh just this week."

"I am going to Glasgow, though."

Melanie said, "They have shops in Glasgow and Edinburgh," as she continued talking on the phone.

Catrin sighed. "I am a gallery-exhibited artist, Madam, not a trucker."

Catrin and Jean had developed a line of ceramic art; vases, bowls and platters for the high-end sales sector, thrown by Jean and painted by Catrin, each one unique in its intricate decoration. They now sold these through a small gallery off the Fulham Road owned by Elizabeth Marshall, her boss's sister.

"No," said Jean, smiling, "you're our friend and would do anything to help us out. It's not that big a box."

3 BERWICK-ON-TWEED

He lived alone just four miles south of the border now in Berwick-on-Tweed, in a small flat that was part of a converted house. John Dalton had not much money after the divorce and the arguments with the government about his pension entitlement, given his years overseas. It was better than going back to his old pursuits and getting more gaol time, he thought. He was sixty-seven; he couldn't do more time inside, he knew.

When Dominic Connolly turned up late-morning in a fancy Jaguar car with a driver outside his house, he recognized him immediately, despite the time gap. Unlike others who may receive such visits, he had no fear. He owed him nothing and had known Dominic since he was a boy. He opened the door and went on to the path in his slippers.

"Dominic, how are you – and the family?"

"Mr. Dalton, sir, I am on top of the world. How are you?"

The tall, powerful teenager had grown into a hefty man, thickening at the waist but still powerful. He wore an elegant suit, obviously hand-tailored. In his heyday John Dalton had dressed well and mixed with enough wealth to know. The Jaguar XJ was immaculate, other than some road dirt on the journey from Glasgow.

Connolly looked at the old man, smiling, and said, "John, could I buy you a nice lunch?"

When the most powerful drug baron on the east side of Scotland invites you to lunch, you don't say 'no' lightly. But it never crossed Dalton's mind. Their families had lived in neighbouring houses in the area of Glasgow known as 'The Gorbals'. Dominic's dad had been his friend. In the Gorbals then, you were polite to your neighbour and hostile to the police.

"I'll need to find out if I can squeeze into my good suit, Dominic. Come in and wait." Dalton had spread a lot at the waist; age; lack of exercise and a prison diet had all contributed to that.

They ate at the Red Lion Inn, Millfield, Michelin rated, at a reserved table in a full restaurant busy with lunch guests. There the conversation was about family, friends and times past. Connolly knew that Dalton was mulling over the proposal put to him on the drive out and he would soon have an answer from the man.

On the journey back Dalton told him he would do it. "The truth is I am just hiding from the world and from life, I guess. I swore I wouldn't paint again though, but at 67, what have I got to lose, really? I just can't do more time, Dominic; I know that."

Dominic said, 'Kevin' to the driver and a large, fat envelope was passed back to him.

"You will need expenses. This is all cash. I don't want accounting or any back. If you need more, let me know, you'll get it. There is also a mobile phone inside for talking to Niall or me or Kevin. Don't use it for any other call, anywhere. But no matter where you are in the world it will reach us. Just keep it charged up."

Dalton nodded. "I won't let you down, Dominic. This one's not that hard."

They were approaching the road back to his flat. Dominic said, "And John, I still want you to think about doing a portrait of Joan, the kids and me; it would be special for us. An artist like you should not have given up painting."

The old man laughed.

"Dominic, I will have to do that, I guess, it would be something I could put my own signature on, at least."

He turned to face him as the car slowed.

"In fact, it would be a privilege. It would be nice to meet your family after all this time."

Dominic said, "Niall will be in touch. As will Kevin about our portrait. Although our youngest, Alison, will be a pain about staying still for that. You will have your work cut out there."

The man whose name could inspire fear in a good part of the population of Glasgow had terrible trouble in controlling his six-year-old daughter. His wife Joan said he indulged her too much.

Later, John Dalton went through the envelope and the documents and saw he had twenty thousand pounds in cash. Also in there was the title to an apartment in a new holiday complex near Cala en Bosc on the island of Minorca, with directions to its location and the name of the local staff looking after it for him. It was his; that was his payment. All he had to do was turn up with his passport and collect the keys.

He started to plan his moves on the work for the

contract. That work and travel would start in Scotland and France, not Spain.

Two days later he took out his new phone and pressed the speed-dial number for Niall Irvin, leaving an innocuous message about needing to make an appointment for some family legal work. An hour later he received a call back. He hardly recognized Niall's voice until suddenly he broke out in 'The Patter', the Glaswegian dialect, and Dalton laughed, "Yes, it's you, Niall, that sounds like you."

"As I was, John," said Irvin.

The cultured tones had returned. They agreed a time and a restaurant in Glasgow to meet up for lunch.

4 THE BRIEFING

At the platform entrance at Euston Jane Worsley eyed Catrin's pull-along small case and the good-sized carrier bag holding a box beside it.

"A present for someone; I will get rid of it as soon as possible," said Catrin.

On board the Virgin Pendolino train they settled down for the four-hour ride to Glasgow, sitting either side of a table for two. Worsley's voice was low but audible.

"DCI Coltrane came to see me on Friday morning to give me a 'heads up', as he put it, of something heading our way," she said. "A report came in that an elderly clergyman had collapsed with an apparent heart attack in front of the Dali painting in the Kelvingrove Museum and Art Gallery. Do you know the work?"

"It's famous," said Catrin, knowing that Worsley's appointment as head of the ACU had nothing to do with any art background. "Salvador Dali painted it in a very classical style, despite being a surrealist painter. It's a painting of the Crucifixion. I haven't seen it in person, though; I have never been to Glasgow, or Scotland, in fact. Perhaps it overwhelmed the man, if he was elderly and religious."

"Actually, it may be anxiety that overwhelmed the man, I gather. He was waiting around to see the museum security director. I have only sketchy details at present."

She was looking at some notes.

"Reverend Alexander Gault was retired. He was the son of a former employee at the Kelvingrove Museum, a conservator there, long since dead. Apparently he had some concern about possible copies or thefts of gallery exhibits. No fraud or theft has been identified by the museum related to his comments, I understand from Neville, so they really don't know the basis of his concern.

"The security director, Susan Hetherington, will give us the background there after we visit the team handling the enquiry at Govan Road. Reverend Gault had wanted to discuss it with her alone, I understand."

She watched Catrin, waiting for a response. Both Worsley and Marshall did this, she noted. They took the training and development of their new DC very seriously.

"Well, ma'am, I don't see why this case would come our way. There must be other elements; suddenly dying in the proximity of a work of art is not a good reason for our involvement. And if it's about fraud, then it is A&A's bailiwick, I think."

Worsley smiled. "You're right. Reverend Gault was killing time waiting for a meeting that had been arranged two days earlier. Given his sudden and untimely demise, Hetherington talked with the police and they upgraded the case to 'suspicious'. One of the analyses conducted by forensics was on the heart medication he carried at the time of his death, to be taken at onset of cardiac pain. It was a dummy pill, a placebo."

People with heart problems don't carry dummy pills, thought Catrin, so it is in our bailiwick after all.

Worsley continued, "So we are going to start at Govan Police Station with a DCI Eric Sinclair. He has the case now. And then we will go over to the Kelvingrove and meet Hetherington."

"Yes ma'am. Thank you for including me on this. I'll get to see the Dali painting, at least," said Catrin.

"And I will get to see the Spitfire Mark 21 hung in the ceiling of the museum. It's a lovely plane," her boss responded.

Catrin remembered that Jane Worsley had told her once that she was a private pilot and shared the ownership of a small Cessna aircraft with a number of other pilots.

She wondered if Jane had mentioned her eagerness to see the Spitfire to Coltrane and held back a smile. Coltrane was an art expert himself and came from a wealthy art family. He was well-connected and an archetypal snob, so he would probably have left her office muttering about the Met putting a woman who should be in airport policing into art-related crime.

Worsley started reading her laptop, her briefing over. "DCI Sinclair is ex-Strathclyde Serious Crimes Squad, near retirement now, I think. I have met him before but we have not worked a case together."

Catrin was aware that Police Scotland was the newly-created national force restructured from the former regional police authorities in Scotland. For a while, its people would all be known as 'ex' somewhere else, she realised.

They were met by a police car arranged by DCI

Sinclair when they arrived at Glasgow Central Station. Worsley asked for them to be allowed to check into the hotel on the way. "Old habit," she said, "we could be in meetings until late and I don't want to find our rooms gone – it has happened in the past."

She didn't say to Catrin that she could also lose her carrier bag, for which the young officer was grateful.

Govan Police Station, formerly known as the Helen St. Police Station, was a large, high-security building, part of a complex of police buildings on the street. It was home to a number of major crime units, including the Anti-Terrorism Unit. The police car drove them in and they had their identities checked. Catrin was happy to have dropped off the luggage before they went there.

They were shown into Eric Sinclair's office and he shook hands with them both. "Welsh I hear, south Welsh if I am not mistaken, right, DC Sayer?" he said to Catrin.

"Yes sir, from Pontypridd. And I don't think that is a Glaswegian accent either." She had taken in that he was a thin, medium height man in his late fifties, with short, bristle length hair and a face which had been through the mill. He had a boozer's nose, but the eyes were sharp, missing nothing.

He laughed. "You are right, too. I am from near Inverness originally."

Worsley asked, "So can you two speak Gaelic together? I know Catrin speaks Welsh."

Sinclair smiled, "Only if we were both about eight hundred years old, Jane; that was about the last time the two were a common language, I think. It may apply to me, but not this young constable."

They got down to serious business.

"My superintendent talked to yours, so here we are. I

have asked Detective Sergeant Peter McPherson to be available and for two other colleagues to join us. Let's go into the meeting room."

A man Catrin judged to be in his forties with sandy-coloured hair was already there, checking through materials. He was introduced as DS McPherson. A young uniformed constable and a scruffily-dressed detective came in just after them, obviously alerted to their arrival. They did the round of introductions and helped themselves to refreshments; someone had laid on coffee, some sandwiches and soft drinks.

"Peter, take us through it," Sinclair said, without preamble.

Catrin looked at her watch. They arrived at Glasgow Central around noon. It was now 1.45 p.m. It was going to be a long afternoon for them, she predicted. McPherson stood by the incident board and began.

"At 11.03 last Wednesday the call came in that a man had collapsed at the Kelvingrove Museum. An ambulance was dispatched at 11.05 and arrived at 11.09. They found museum staff trained in first aid doing CPR and they took over."

His hand was moving down the timeline checklist on the side of the whiteboard.

"The first police vehicle arrived as the ambulance crew were taking the man to their vehicle at 11.20. They had used the defibrillator on him without success. According to protocol he was taken to the Western Infirmary, a hospital literally next door, where he arrived at 11.24 a.m. He was taken into ER and subsequently pronounced dead after two further attempts to resuscitate him. The man was identified as Reverend Alexander Gault from documentation on his person. His body was then taken to the morgue.

"A second police unit arrived at the hospital at 11.45, talked to the attending doctor who said that the preliminary indications, given the heart medication Nitro XLA10 found in his pocket, were that he had suffered a massive heart attack. A post-mortem was to follow."

He paused, looking around the faces in the room.

"As you can see, so far, pretty routine," he said.

"The next of kin is his wife, now widow, Mary Gault, who lives in Oban. That's about a two-three hour drive from here. We contacted the local station to have them break the news in person. Mrs. Gault is elderly also and she had the officer call her daughter, Elizabeth, who came over to look after her.

"A little after noon, 12.07 to be precise, PC Shortt – he nodded to the young uniformed officer – had a call from a Mrs. Susan Hetherington, the security director of the Kelvingrove Museum, who had naturally been informed of the incident. She had not attended the scene, being on a conference call. Shortt is the liaison with the Museum and has met her from time to time.

"Hetherington had gone down after the conference call finished to check on the incident. It was then she realized that the person taken in the ambulance was her 11.30 appointment, Reverend Gault. In talking to the security guard who had first seen Gault in trouble she was told that a letter had been found on the floor after the ER Team had left. It was addressed to her so had been handed to reception. The guard thought it might be either from the man who collapsed or one of the other visitors who came over to help, but she wasn't sure.

"Hetherington asked Shortt about the status of Gault and mentioned that she had an appointment with him. She then told him about the letter she had received a few minutes earlier. Shortt said he was not aware of the incident, but if the letter was sealed and addressed to her, she should open it, which she did. Kevin?"

PC Kevin Shortt was obviously happy to be in a meeting of detectives in an investigation. Catrin recalled her own first experiences of this sort.

"Mrs. Hetherington opened the letter and I waited for her to close the call. I was just about to do so myself when she said, 'I think I need to speak with a detective, Kevin. This letter, and I assume his reason for meeting me, may relate to a crime'."

"I said I would call her right back. I then came and reported the discussion to Sergeant McPherson."

Wolsey had been looking at the notes during all this and seemed about to ask a question then simply said, "Please continue."

McPherson said, "I told Kevin to call her back and say we would come round first thing in the morning, which we did, on Thursday."

Catrin wondered why they hadn't gone around straight away, or at least have Shortt go round to talk to Hetherington. She didn't ask.

McPherson continued, "We met with her at 9.30 a.m. in her office. I saw clearly that she was concerned and based on the information she gave us I phoned DCI Sinclair."

"And I, in turn," said Sinclair, "immediately informed the superintendent of the matter and we agreed that the death of Reverend Gault would be treated as suspicious. We collected the possessions bag of Reverend Gault's clothes and belongings from the hospital. The Procurator Fiscal's office stopped the planned general autopsy going ahead. A forensic autopsy was completed the same afternoon and the pathologist sent blood and other biological samples for analysis. His conclusion was confirmation of the initial finding, that Gault had a massive heart attack.

"Sergeant McPherson contacted the Gault home and talked with the daughter, Elizabeth. She was in discussion with a funeral home about the transfer of the father back to Oban. He told her that we were still pursuing enquiries given the unfortunate demise of her father in a public place, and he would inform her when the body was released. The possessions were sent to the forensics lab here."

Now Catrin understood the reason for the formality of the meeting. The witness statements were only by the museum staff. None were by the people in the immediate vicinity at the time of Gault's collapse. A possible crime scene was not sealed off before a day's worth of visitor and night cleaners had passed through it. They were drawing in the barricades.

"CCTV in the museum?" asked Worsley.

"We will come to that, Jane," said Sinclair. "Let's just finish the sequence. Peter?"

Sergeant McPherson continued his report. "The envelope contained a handwritten list of fourteen paintings from the early part of the last century by Scottish artists, part of a group known as the Scottish Colourists. You probably know more about them than I do, DCI Worsley - but then I know more about Glasgow Rangers than you do, I bet."

Catrin smiled to herself. Jane Worsley's knowledge of the Colourists was probably on or below par with her knowledge of the football team.

Catrin's own memory of the Colourists from her courses at university in Aberystwyth was of some names;

Fergusson, Peploe and Cadell came to mind; there was a fourth name lingering just out of reach. Some of the artists had lived in France and worked with the post-Impressionist painters there.

Their approach to painting involved bold colours with an emphasis on form, whether of still-life, people or landscapes. These paintings were a far cry from the art in vogue in Glasgow and Edinburgh at the time, paintings with classic images; the lords and gentry, the landscapes of moors and heather, balancing colours, textures and tones; the 'stag and hounds' paintings, as she heard someone once refer to them.

Shortt stepped in, "The paintings by the Colourists at the Museum are valuable, in part, because they represent some of the best from this group of artists, we gather. The significance of the list is not known, but as Gault is the son of the curator who had some responsibilities for many of them during the war, it concerned Susan Hetherington a lot. They are looking into the matter now."

McPherson continued, "On that basis we took the steps mentioned earlier. The forensics officer assigned called me early Friday morning saying that the medication in Reverend Gault's possession at the museum were sublingual nitroglycerine tablets, a generic brand by the label on the little bottle. They had been sent for analysis also. He had the results back both on Gault's blood and the pills. The pills were not nitroglycerine; they were a placebo, inert. They weren't just similar size blank pills; they were exact copies, with the right stamp on them but without any medical effect whatsoever.

"Gault died of a massive heart attack. Whether or not the pill he took would have helped if it was the genuine article is unclear and is a matter for the pathologist and the Procurator Fiscal. We are treating this now as a suspicious death for that reason."

Sinclair said, "Let's move on to the envelope and the list."

5 GAULT

Sergeant McPherson took over again.

"The envelope contained a list of fourteen paintings, as I said. We now want to see the files concerning the history and handling of those paintings that are in the museum's possession. We wonder if there is a basis for someone trying to kill Gault, perhaps to prevent him from talking about them.

"Kelvingrove staff said that they first wanted to check with their own legal advisor but clearly want to co-operate so we haven't asked for a search warrant at this stage. There is an appointment scheduled for us," - he looked at his watch - "at 16.30, in an hour and a half. So I am only going to give a brief outline.

"During World War II, the collections at the museum were stored in various locations away from Glasgow, which was just as well as the museum was damaged in one of the bombing raids. There has been a rumour that resurfaces from time to time, Hetherington says, of artefacts being lost or damaged or missing during that period, but there is no substance to the rumour.

"The last time it came up before the contact by Reverend Gault was twenty months ago. It concerned again the Colourist paintings; an allegation that someone had seen a Fergusson landscape that had been copied or forged by Alistair Gault. The Security Director for the Museum then was a Malcolm Drummond and he decided to follow up himself.

"He went to see several people including Reverend Gault and his wife, we understand. He then went on to Fort William for another meeting with the daughter of another conservator, now dead, who apparently has several of Alistair Gault's paintings, as he had been a close friend.

"On his return journey to Glasgow he was in a single-vehicle accident. Drummond's car went off the road and he was killed; the vehicle caught fire. There was some talk noted in the investigation file that he had a drinking problem and his car had been seen parked near a pub earlier. It was declared an accident and the forgery rumour was dropped.

"The letter possibly opens that case up again also, we think."

Catrin was looking at the photocopies of the list and the envelope in her folder.

McPherson continued, "We are assuming the writing on the envelope is Reverend Gault's, but still need to verify that. The writing on the list is in a different hand. Of the fourteen Colourist paintings listed, eight belong to the Kelvingrove. Two are in the Portland Gallery in London. The others, at this point, I don't know where they are. We have only been on this just over a day, given the weekend."

DCI Sinclair interjected, "The Kelvingrove are keeping

tight wraps on this and want us to do the same at present. Their director has spoken to the Chief Constable and those are our orders, at least within Police Scotland."

He looked at his watch. "I need a smoke and we all need a break. Let's take ten and then wrap up."

Catrin came back from the washrooms and found the only person in the meeting room was the detective who had not spoken yet, called Coleman. He had just finished talking on his mobile.

"So what's your part in this?" asked Catrin.

"Drug Enforcement Agency as was; now we are all Police Scotland. I guess my pirouette will be after the discussion of the CCTV, according to Sinclair's game plan."

Catrin nodded, "I worked in Narcotics with the Met before this assignment."

He brightened up. "Where?"

"Brixton, uniform PC."

"Same issues there I suspect that we face in Glasgow; big city drugs and a lot of heartbreak. But how long have you been in the Art Crime Unit?"

"I am in my first year here."

The others had re-entered, Sinclair last, taking a deep breath and filling the meeting room with second-hand smoke.

"Right, McPherson, the CCTV analysis."

Peter McPherson started again. "We are in the process of working through this now, so at this stage we have only the footage from cameras by the painting to show you. The Kelvingrove is big, a lot of cameras, so we are working through others in time sequences before and after Gault collapses. It is a more complex job than it sounds."

He switched on the computer video sequence.

Catrin saw the man McPherson then identified as Reverend Gault in a small group of people walking into the area with the Dali painting. He was dressed in a sports jacket, collar and tie. As he stood looking at the scene of 'Christ of St. John of the Cross', his back arched a little and he stepped away. He came out the other side of the 'L'-shaped entrance and stopped, reaching into his jacket and pulling out a small bottle. His hand was seen to open the cap and place something in his mouth but it was indistinct; the image would need some work to be sure whether or not he inserted a pill.

Two people near him were looking in his direction now, so obviously he was in some distress or otherwise attracting their attention. One of them called to someone out of frame. A female guard appeared and led Gault out of frame, presumably to give assistance.

"We can cover more on that tomorrow," said Sinclair. "Let's talk about the pills. DC Coleman?"

The drug squad detective spoke. "The alert about the pill came to us and I saw it only this morning. It is routine procedure to flag to us anything in another incident that relates to drugs. I recalled a report of chemist shop break-in that had that brand name, Nitro XLA10, as part of the list of stolen pharmaceuticals, so re-checked the file. A negative. However the database also listed a report from the generic drug formulator in Edinburgh that there had been a theft of placebo tablets during a market research trial about a year ago.

"They had been testing different pill shapes and coating finishes for customer acceptability and preference. The report was simply that the small stock of these blank pills, which should have been destroyed at the end of the trial, had disappeared. They were concerned that the pills could be sold and have consequences of the sort that happened at the museum.

"We were up to our eyes with some major cases. Someone called them to follow up about their security arrangements, but otherwise we took it no further. But there may be placebo pills of Nitro XLA10 out there somewhere; we think it is possible."

He sat back, waiting to see if there were any questions.

Catrin found her mind wandering back into her former role in Brixton; there was always too much immediate work to do in policing the world of illegal drug use to follow up on this sort of report, she knew.

"Jane," said Sinclair, "Peter is going to take you and DC Sayer over to the Kelvingrove Museum to meet Mrs. Hetherington and let you take a look at the scene. I have a meeting here now that I can't miss and one downtown this evening. So can we meet up for a pre-dinner drink at the bar in your hotel before my meeting – we can catch up then?"

Jane nodded.

"Thank you everyone. Let's keep at it," said Sinclair.

6 FRONTS AND BACKS

John Dalton had told Niall Irvin that he needed one of the paintings by Gault, smaller rather than larger. Niall had wrapped it in tissue paper and then Bubble Wrap and it just fitted nicely into a canvas, soft-sided briefcase he had available. He passed it over to Dalton at the table in the restaurant.

The two men spoke complimentary remarks about how the other had changed and then Niall laughed, "John, we are just getting older, that's the truth."

"For me it is, but you are still young, Niall. And not married yet, Dominic tells me. No-one trapped you yet?"

Niall smiled but said nothing. A long-standing affair with a married doctor was not for discussion with anyone.

"So where do we go on this next, John?"

The waiter appeared and they ordered.

"Dominic tells me that you don't want help choosing the works, is that correct?"

Niall nodded.

"So my job is simply the fronts and backs. The work on the fronts will be no problem. I need to acquire some paints of the period but I have a source; it is only last century. The backs though and the other documentation needed; I can only do that when I know the story you want to tell. So tell me - and be prepared to accept that for practical purposes you may need to make some adjustments."

Niall took him through his plan, in as much detail as he could.

John sat silently taking it in. "Now tell me about the 'mark'; the customer. I don't want the name; best not, to be honest, but what level of art knowledge, access to testing do they have? You know."

Niall told him that the customer was art school educated but was no professional expert, with no ready access to forensics and, he was sure, no willingness to create any visibility for the work. "It will be clear that the paintings can't see the light of day for years and I think she will be quite happy with that."

A woman, John noted.

"Is she in Dominic's business circle then?"

"More or less; at least she is someone who doesn't want the law poking about."

John Dalton was thinking of his own health, his own plans. "So we are aiming for this educated art student, probably a self-appointed connoisseur, to be convinced by what she sees? She will not seek any separate forensic appraisal or authentication by others? You are sure about this; it is important."

Irvin nodded, "That's the way I see it."

John Dalton said, "Then the first painting should have a French provenance. It will make the later ones from Scotland much easier; she will then just cross-reference the signatures, as there won't be any of the same dealer documentation available then."

They talked of other things until the coffee came and John Dalton said, "Can you get the one you need completed first to my flat in Berwick within a week? And the precise dimensions of it to me as a text by tomorrow, both in its current frame and also the unframed size?"

Irvin agreed.

"Finally, the canvas, you said, for all the paintings is the same as this one – he pointed at the bag."

Niall said, "For the first three, it seems so. I don't know about the others yet."

Dalton said, "Two weeks, then. You can have the first in two weeks."

As they came out of the restaurant John Dalton collected an overnight pull-along bag he had asked them to store on arrival. "Can I give you a ride, John?" said Niall. The valet had gone to collect his car.

"If you could. I was going to take a taxi to the railway station. I am going down to London then on the Eurostar."

Dalton thought about the task ahead as the train whisked him south. He felt alive again, so whatever happened, he was glad he got into it. But, he realised, so much of this would depend on Niall Irvin's skill at lying. As a lawyer, he thought, that should come easy; it is all word skills.

Then he thought back to Niall as a boy and realised that he had been the most fluent liar among the gang of kids that had hung around with Dominic.

7 KELVINGROVE

Catrin watched the city as they drove from Govan across the Kingston Bridge over the River Clyde. A little later the impressive building and park that made up the Kelvingrove complex came into view.

A man and woman were waiting just inside the arched entrance for them as they drove up. Sergeant McPherson had called as they drove to let them know they were on their way and almost there. When they met up in the impressive lobby they found they were with Susan Hetherington and the Museum Director, Dr. Edward Bryant.

Catrin recognized Bryant's face from a news article following his appointment a year or so ago; young, vibrant, loud. Someone to shake things up came to mind. Hetherington was middle-aged, in business attire, with a friendly smile.

The Museum was fairly busy. Susan Hetherington led them through the sequence she thought was the probable path of Reverend Gault from arrival until his collapse. As she finished, Catrin's eyes lingered on the crucifixion painting by Dali. Other museum visitors were in front of them. Bryant began, "You haven't seen it before? It's by Salvador…"

Worsley said, "DC Sayer is an artist and has a degree in art history."

'Ah," said Bryant, "Sorry. I was going to give you the vanilla introduction. Let's go to my office."

He looked at his watch. "We will be closed by the time we finish, so I can bring you back to see it properly."

When they were all settled, DS McPherson kicked off, but in a way which immediately set DCI Jane Worsley as the lead. They hadn't discussed this in the car, Catrin realized, and based on her experience in the Yeung case in Wales where DI Dafydd Powys or his staff had led each external meeting, she had assumed it would be a similar approach here.

Jane began by explaining the role of the ACU briefly. They knew that the museum staff would still think Reverend Gault's death was accidental.

"It could have been stress," said Bryant, "having a heart condition and bringing us such news."

Jane asked him about the status of the review of the paintings listed.

"We have made a quick check yesterday evening, just Susan and I. We didn't think it was appropriate to take it further at present."

"Very wise," said Jane, "and?"

"We still don't think that there is any substance in the matter. And, I should add, in the original preliminary investigation by Drummond nothing had come to light that worried people here at the time; at lease from what is on file."

Bryant continued. "Our legal advisor has confirmed that we should pass over the files and help in any way.

Our only request is that we keep this very confidential if at all possible until we know the extent of the problem."

Sergeant McPherson said, "Can we ask how much these paintings are worth?"

"Well, it is hard to say, at auction, but between £250,000 to half a million or higher, each. Our collection contains the best examples…."

McPherson nodded. "Quite a sum, given there are fourteen on the list and you own a good number of them."

Jane said, "There is more at stake than that, sergeant, relating to the museum reputation. If word gets out and it isn't quashed, it places a question mark that could affect the status for future exchanges of exhibits."

Edward Bryant looked at her appreciatively. "Correct, Chief Inspector; if a painting is stolen and recovered, it can actually bring people into the Museum; add to value in a sense. If a fraud or theft is revealed and all we have is uncertainty it can devalue the museum's standing."

"Anyway, Susan will give you the files. You will probably find it more useful to go through them and then we can try to fill in any blanks. Probably the area to focus on, I expect, is Alistair Gault, Reverend Gault's father. Other than the information in the file, though, we know nothing. He wasn't a senior member of staff and, given his retirement date, I doubt anyone employed here now knew him. I actually checked the personnel database and no-one here was even around at the time.

"Do you have a list of retirees still living, perhaps still interested in the museum?" asked Catrin.

Bryant blushed. "I should have thought of that… but I didn't."

Hetherington smiled, "I am actually preparing exactly that list now. We have a few who may have overlapped but you may have to track them down if their addresses have changed. I expect some will be in retirement homes now, or living with relatives."

They spent the next fifteen minutes going through the file system structure and some of the items in files on specific painting. As they started Bryant went out of his office to make some calls using his mobile.

When Catrin and Jane had an understanding of the system Susan put them in a file box and McPherson came forward to carry it out. Bryant saw the discussion was over and closed his phone.

On the way out the director was good at his word and Catrin and Jane were shown the Colourists on display and then the Dali and the Spitfire in peace. Catrin would have lingered more over the Crucifixion painting but Peter McPherson was anxious to leave; he had to drop the visitors off at the hotel and he had a family commitment he needed to get to, he said.

8 IAIN

After McPherson left them at the hotel, Catrin went to her room and took the box with Melanie's package of pottery back to the hotel lobby, waiting for a person called Iain Simmons. She had phoned the number of the Glasgow pottery shop from the train later that morning and the woman who answered, Marjorie Simmons, had said that her son could collect it this evening as he lived downtown. They talked briefly about Jean and Melanie and Marjorie complimented Catrin on her ceramic decoration.

"You have seen it?"

"Yes, at the Cwmbran Kiln when I was last in London. And I saw a piece she was sending over to 'Liz's Place' that she had just taken off display. I hope we can meet some time during your visit."

"Well, I am here for my other work, Marjorie," said Catrin, "but if I get the chance I would really like to come out and see your shop." She was trying to sound a little more sincere than she really felt.

Jane had said that she wanted time with Sinclair alone

and would meet him in the bar, but she would have dinner with Catrin afterwards. Catrin had called Iain Simmons to check if the timing worked. It did nicely.

For some reason Catrin had expected Marjorie's son to arrive dressed casually, in jeans, looking artsy. So when the man in the grey formal suit came up to her and said, "Catrin Sayer?" she was a little surprised.

"I see a box that I suspect is the one my mother was talking about. I am Iain."

They shook hands. Iain was about her height, dark hair neatly trimmed, good looking.

"My mother has talked about the girls at the Kiln, so you must be one of them… but very neatly turned out, I might say, for a potter."

Catrin laughed, "I am a ceramic decorator, not a potter and I'm in Glasgow for my day job. I could say the same about you!"

"Oh, I don't work in the shop full-time, that's my mum's pride and joy. I just help out there. I work at a bank in town. Look, would you like a drink before I take these away from you?"

Catrin looked at her watch. "Sure," she said, "I have time. I am having dinner with my boss. Let's go in the bar and find somewhere away from her and her colleague. They are in there already."

He picked up the box and followed her in.

The bar was busy but they found a table which Catrin guarded with the box while Iain got the drinks. She had asked for a soda water with a slice of lime. She found herself sitting in a line of sight where she could see Worsley's back and Sinclair's face. He was drinking tomato juice, she saw, and Worsley had, as usual, a glass of red wine.

"So you work in a bank," said Catrin, after Simmons had sat down.

"Yes, for my sins. I was a good cricketer at school." He had an impish expression on his face.

"And?" said Catrin, wondering where he was going.

"I impressed one of the umpires at a junior county trial and he was the head honcho for the Bank's cricket team and it needed help. So, he inveigled me to join. I never went to university, just straight into the bank from school where... I played cricket a lot."

She laughed. "You need more skills than that to work in a bank, Iain, so..."

He smiled. "I am pretty good at numbers too, at investment rates and talking to clients and dealing with staff issues. And I wear nice suits. That always helps in the banking profession. But you wear a nice suit for a ceramic artist."

He was amusing, she found.

"I am a police officer," she said and waited. Over the last few years this had always been a testing point with guys she met. Some left as quickly as they could, some others made inane jokes, generally about handcuffs.

"So, as a police officer, can I ask what brings you to Scotland?" Iain said.

"A case, that's about all I can say. I work on art-related crime at Scotland Yard."

He just nodded. "It must be interesting."

"At times it is, probably just like your job, it has its ups and downs."

He changed the subject, "Marjorie is hoping you can come out to the shop some time, if it works. And if it does, let me know, I would be happy to collect you and drive you there."

Worsley left the bar, noticing Catrin and smiled. She didn't come over, just mouthed "dinner in ..." and held up all her fingers. Catrin nodded and wrapped up with Iain, walking out the front entrance with him to say goodbye. Sinclair had left a minute or two earlier. In the distance she saw him going down some steps at the side of a church across the road.

Later, in a different pub bistro while they were eating, Worsley, said, "He looked nice."

Catrin explained the reason for their meeting and the parcel on the train.

"Well," said Worsley, "it was nice to see you relaxed and laughing with a man who isn't inside a police station."

Catrin realized that she had really enjoyed the half-hour discussion with Iain. He hadn't made any remark about her not drinking alcohol and wasn't nosey after she had answered his question about the work she did. And he had a sense of humour she really liked.

Worsley mentioned that during the discussion with Sinclair they had agreed that Catrin would go with him to interview Mary Gault in Oban tomorrow; she herself would have a number of other things to do but they would regroup later with the others.

Worsley said, "Sinclair was on tomato juice. I always knew him for a whisky man in the past, but he must be on the wagon."

Catrin had never mentioned to people that her own reason for not drinking was that her mother was a recovered alcoholic. The experiences in her teens with her mother drinking had made her realise she may be too much like her, so she didn't drink alcohol at all. She didn't want the pain of it all if her fear proved to be grounded. She had heard that alcoholism ran in families but whether it was genetic or not was disputed. But she knew how hard it had been for her mother to stop drinking and didn't want to go through that herself.

After dinner she returned to her hotel room and started to look up information on the Colourist painters on the internet, bringing back some of the detail she recalled from her college days.

She was about to finish for the night when, on impulse, she pulled up the Glasgow Alcoholics Anonymous meeting list. There was a regular meeting twice a week at the church across the road, one about the time Sinclair was going down the steps. Good for him, she thought.

She sent an email to Jean and Melanie saying she had passed the pottery on to Iain. She was about to go to sleep when her tablet beeped, reminding her she had not switched off the sound. It was Melanie, with a link and a picture of Iain from the shop web site where there were head shots of both Iain and Marjorie, described as co-owners. Melanie's comment was, "Good looking, isn't he?" with a smiley face.

Catrin didn't email back. She didn't want Jean and Melanie giving her the job of carting back a box of someone else's pottery to the Kiln.

9 OBAN

Catrin was in Govan Road Police Station reading the files from the Kelvingrove Museum that McPherson had brought in. Worsley was joining a conference call on another matter from the hotel room and would be in later.

Alistair Gault had started at the Kelvingrove Museum in 1934 in an apprenticeship as a junior trainee conservator. By the start of World War II he had been promoted to junior conservator and, Catrin wondered, given that his post wouldn't have been declared a reserved occupation, why he wasn't called up for military service. Probably they would never know.

In 1941 during a bombing raid a bomb fell on Kelvin Way outside the museum causing a lot of damage and great quantities of flying glass. By then the museum exhibits were largely dispersed to a number of secret locations in the country, so they were unharmed.

After the war Gault, now a senior conservator, assisted in the growth and development of the Kelvingrove. In 1954 he started a part-time assignment with the newly-established college at Lewis Castle, in Stornoway in the Hebrides, teaching art conservation. It clearly blossomed as a relationship. From then until his retirement in 1978 he would spend some time on the Isle of Lewis each year but remained throughout an employee of the museum.

His personnel file noted him to be diligent, reliable, exacting in work habits but a little uneasy socially with other staff. The greatest criticism came from his department manager in the late-fifties who noted that Alistair had intrinsic skills to enable him to seek higher qualifications and further promotion, but he seemed positively adamant about not doing so. A man happy with his lot in life, it seemed to Catrin.

She pulled up details of Gault from the government databases. No criminal convictions, born in 1916, died in 1994 and buried in Glasgow. Nothing struck any bells of past problems.

DCI Sinclair came up to her desk. "Ready in five, Sayer," he said.

"Yes sir." She closed the file and headed to the wash-rooms.

They had cleared the outskirts of northern Glasgow and were on the A82 to Crianlarich. There they would turn west to Oban. Sinclair had said the trip would be a little over two hours once they cleared the city.

They had been talking about the preparation for the interview of the widow, Mrs. Gault. Sinclair had called ahead to set up the meeting and said he had spoken to the daughter, Elizabeth. She had enquired when the body would be released so they could plan the burial. That was one of the items they would cover with them.

Sinclair had moved on to probing a little more about Catrin. How did she like working in a specialist unit after

Brixton?

Catrin told him in general about the Yeung case and how it brought her into the ACU in the first place.

"I know Jack Taylor, worked with him on one case," said Sinclair, referring to Jane's boss, Superintendent Taylor.

He talked a little of his own career, all with the former Strathclyde Police.

"And now we have the new structure," he said, "I am not that bothered, really, being so close to retirement. It is different, but I can live with it for the next year and half."

They passed a pub on the highway and Sinclair suddenly remarked, "You have to watch the drink in this job, Catrin. The work and the worst part of it, the misery, will get to you. It's easy to get into the bottle, so watch it."

Catrin said nothing.

"That pub back there. I was there one night shortly after being made inspector. I was full of myself and had too much to drink. Came out and an older uniform constable I knew was sitting in his car parked right across the back of mine, blocking me in. I told him to get the hell out of the way and he wouldn't budge, just said, "Get in the car, Eric, I am driving you home."

"I was so pissed. He didn't even call me 'sir', I thought. He just ignored it all and drove me home. I apologised to him in the morning."

Catrin said suddenly, "I don't drink, sir. My mum is an alcoholic and I am too much like her. I think if I started I would be in trouble, so I don't."

He nodded. "Is she still drinking then?"

"No, she's been sober nearly four years now. She had relapsed after seven years of being sober earlier. She doesn't miss her AA meetings now."

"Good for her. So you know if you ever get... that's the place to be."

"Yes sir." she said, thinking, I don't think you miss too many of your own meetings either.

Catrin was enjoying the drive, seeing Loch Lomond and the Trossachs. It seemed beautiful, reminding her of some of the more remote parts of Wales. As much as she was enjoying it, she started to think that not much would get done this week on her other cases or Keith Marshall's files.

The address for the Gaults in Oban turned out to be the old rectory of St. Andrew's church. Mary Gault's daughter greeted them and settled them into the living room with her mother, and then went off to make tea. It was obvious that preparations had been made; she arrived back fairly quickly with a large tray with a plate of homemade scones, nice china cups and saucers and a matching teapot. Catrin thought about the different receptions that police officers encounter during enquiries, from verbal abuse and doors slammed in their faces at one end to tea and scones at the other.

DCI Sinclair, she saw, as hard as he came over in the context of his role at Govan, had a softer side. He had started out expressing his condolences and soon had the two women settled, talking easily. Clearly he was well-versed in the terminology of the Episcopal Church, Alexander Gault's denomination.

He had told Catrin on the drive that they were to make no mention of the placebo issue.

It turned out that Reverend Gault and his wife had been offered in retirement the use of the rectory until they no longer needed it. They had been talking only recently, though, about the move into sheltered, smaller accommodation before her husband's trip to Glasgow. Now they were not sure when, Elizabeth said, it would probably be soon. Mary Gault would move to a smaller place; the large house was a lot to handle for her mother, even with help.

Catrin had noticed a painting in the hall on entry and another, larger one in the living room. She asked about it during a pause in the discussion.

Elizabeth said, "It's by my grandfather, Alistair Gault, my father's dad."

Catrin said "May I?" She got up and looked at it closely. It was certainly consistent with the style of Francis Cadell, she thought, one of the Iona landscapes she had seen in her researches. That had been painted on a panel, this painting was on canvas. For some reason the rock formation in the lower left caught her attention; she knew she would have to go back and look up the painting it brought to mind. She knew it wasn't one of the Cadell paintings in the Kelvingrove, though, she must have seen something similar in her review of Colourist paintings on-line. In the lower corner was the signature, two initials, AG.

"When was this painted, can I ask?" she said.

"I'm not sure. Mum?" Elizabeth asked.

"Do you like art?" was Mary Gault's indirect response.

"Yes," said Catrin, "I decorate ceramics myself."

"It is Iona, painted around 1943, I believe. My father-in-law worked at the museum in Glasgow."

"Was he able to visit Iona in 1943 then?" Catrin asked. Travel restrictions were in place, she knew.

"You know," said Mary Gault," That is a good question; I really don't know. It may have been from a sketch made on an earlier visit."

Catrin glanced at Sinclair and saw that they had both

picked up a slight change in tone, the wariness, perhaps, in Mary Gault's responses.

"It is part of the reason why we are here, Mrs. Gault," said Sinclair, "I am not sure if you are aware but your husband had a letter on him that was delivered to the museum about the reason for his visit."

Elizabeth was looking a little lost. She doesn't know, thought Catrin, but clearly Mary does.

'I wasn't sure, given the circumstances," said Mary Gault. "I thought it might just die away, be forgotten, be returned with his things and we could just move on."

She looked at her daughter, then at Sinclair, who just waited.

"Elizabeth, your father was convinced that his own father had forged or stolen a painting, perhaps more than one, I don't know. I am thinking the worry of it all killed him more than his heart condition, to be honest."

Elizabeth looked shocked and was about to say something when Sinclair said gently, "Please go on Mrs. Gault."

"Alistair died in 1994 and Alexander was the executor of the estate. Like me now, it was time for adjustment, for my mother-in-law to move from their home in Glasgow. Her health was not good and it had been Alistair who had been looking after her. So as well as a busy parish life, we had to deal with the sale of their house, deal with the possessions, you know.

"My brother's son is a lawyer, Niall Irvin. He had just started in legal practice so he obtained the help of someone in his firm with the conveyancing and legal aspects 'pro bono', they said. But I think Niall actually paid the bill although he can't have been earning a lot at the time, not like now."

"During the clear-up Alexander found something, a

notebook, I think. He believed it showed that Alistair had a painting from the museum. We looked high and low for something which fitted but all the paintings Alistair left had his signature on – like the one you are looking at now. Alexander did some research into it all but then he dropped it, I thought.

"His mother lingered; that is probably the best description, not an end I would want for myself, I must say. I didn't think of the painting thing again.

"A couple of years ago we had a brief visit from a man at the museum, the Kelvingrove museum. He and Andrew talked and he looked at the painting, I think. I was busy with a church function that day; I wasn't here. Andrew mentioned it briefly, but I thought no more about it.

"It was recently, as we started to work out what to take with us if we moved from here, that Alexander's concern re-surfaced. He had a list of paintings by famous Scottish artists, one he had found in Alistair's documents. He said he was thinking of going to visit the museum and discuss the problem as he had talked to Niall and had a legal opinion.

"I hadn't realized he was still occupied with the issue and told him it was not worth the stress it was causing him. Next thing I know he went to the museum and... you know the rest."

She sighed. "Now I am just waiting to bury him."

"The stress you mentioned, did he have any deterioration in his health, other health conditions?" asked Sinclair.

"He had suffered from angina for years. The incidence of minor pain had increased, that was a worry for me and for our GP, Dr. Hartley. He always carried his heart tablets, though. But they didn't work this time, I gather, from what we heard from the police sergeant who came round."

"That's correct, I am sad to say, Mrs. Gault. I think Reverend Gault's body will be released in the next couple of days and the death certificate issued to let you make arrangements. It was a massive heart attack, I gather. Given it occurred in the museum, we have to look into it from all angles. The letter he had taken to the museum was part of that, you understand. Again, you have our deepest sympathies."

He looked at Catrin, clearly wanting to close out. She said, "Do you mind if I just take a photo of this painting? It is very nice." She had pulled out her iPhone.

Mary Gault looked amused. "No, go ahead, dear, if you wish."

She turned to Sinclair who had stood up and placed both his and Catrin's teacups on the tray. "Young people photograph everything these days with those cameras on their phones."

"Yes they do," said Sinclair, moving towards the hall. "Thank you again."

Elizabeth showed them to the door where Sinclair said, "Mr. Irvin, your cousin, I think, is he a solicitor in Glasgow? I know an Irvin who is a lawyer there; it's an occupational hazard," he smiled.

"Yes, Niall works in Glasgow. He still lives there, I know, as he called from there after the news of my dad. He has offered to help with any legal matters. I am the executor now, being the only child. But to be honest, I hardly know him and a local solicitor, a member of the church, has offered to do the same thing and he is someone I know well."

"Yes," said Sinclair, "a local person is probably more appropriate for everything that has to be done, I expect."

10 NIALL IRVIN

When they were back in the car heading away from the Gault household Catrin said, "I was hoping to see other paintings, sir. The work in the living room had Gault's signature and is certainly consistent with the Colourist style; it looks similar to a Francis Cadell work or a good copy."

DCI Sinclair said, "We need a lot more detail from them, but not now, Catrin. I wanted to keep it low-key once I heard the name Niall Irvin. He is on our radar. Niall is the legal counsel for Dominic Connolly and has been associated with him for a long time. And Connolly runs most of the drug business in eastern Scotland south of the highlands. Hard, soft and, would you believe, illegal prescription drugs are his business."

"So he could have had access to the placebo nitro pill, perhaps?"

"Exactly."

Then he added, "I will call the team together this afternoon. Once the name Irvin comes up, so does Connolly. And we are getting into very sensitive and dangerous territory, believe me. We will be doing a lot more checks before we talk to the Gaults again."

As they passed the village of Lochawe, Catrin asked Sinclair if he could say any more about the nephew of Alistair Gault, the lawyer Irvin.

"Niall Irvin and Dominic Connolly were born in the same street in the Gorbals, which has all changed these days. There are fancy-looking terraces or town houses there now where there used to be rows of old two and three story houses and later high-rises, all packed with poverty and problems. It was a hard area to police.

"The two men were friends from childhood. Irvin's academic bent got him into university, with a local education grant and some help from his grandparents. Connolly's dad was in the ice cream vans - you know about those?

Catrin knew what he was getting at. "A little, from my Brixton days. They were a drug distribution route, right?"

"Exactly. They called the turf battles between the gangs selling from different vans, 'The ice cream wars'."

"There is a an American video game which features the ice cream vans selling drugs these days, evading police," said Catrin.

"My God," said Sinclair, "is there really? I tell you, Catrin, those vans didn't drive that fast." He was chuckling at the concept.

He continued. "Dominic Connolly got into the drug business through his dad. Niall went off to Lancaster University - away from home, but not too far. That's where he picked up his accent. A tutor said that they couldn't understand a word he said, with his heavy 'Glasgow Patter', so he did something about it. Got to sound like a BBC Scotland announcer as a result - useful in court.

"He is one of those defense counsels that went down the road of no return, as I call it. Started out clean and idealistic, defending street villains against the law of the upper classes, as he saw it. Over time he focused more and more on Connolly and his associates, who were always in trouble one way or another, as much for violence as for drugs.

"Then, I think, he crossed the line. And I actually blame a policeman called McIntyre, now long gone. Anyway it's all water under the bridge. Word had it McIntyre stitched up one of Connolly's people for a long prison term. He was due to go in, I have no doubt, but evidence came to light which others say was planted. I don't know, but I wouldn't be surprised. The man went down and most of us were just happy he was out of circulation. God knows he had enough free rides for things he had done in the past due to lack of evidence.

"But Irvin took it as a failure of the legal system and a failure personally. Sometime thereafter we know he moved into helping plan things with Connolly. Never proven, of course. But to me he is now a villain masquerading as a lawyer, despite the fact he is damn effective in his professional capacity.

"He needed none of this, really, to be successful, but the relationship with Connolly is that strong. Like brothers, really."

Catrin nodded. "I can see how this would send some alarm bells into the drug squad's area."

"At present Catrin, more than you could imagine. I expect DCI Strachan, Coleman's boss, will be joining us when we next meet." He went quiet.

~~

It was late-afternoon. Sinclair had called ahead and the same team got together soon as they got back. Now it included an older woman from the Drug Squad, making the third DCI in the room. Sinclair summarized the news from the Oban visit then invited Catrin to comment.

"I would just add, sir, one of the paintings I saw looked a lot like a painting by Francis Cadell, one of the Colourists, but it had Gault's initials. If it is just a copy that, of course, is fine. It is quite legal. But it does also show a possible link between Gault and the Colourist art."

He nodded.

"DCI's Worsley, Strachan – nodding to the new person – and myself have had a quick de-brief, so here is where it sits and where we are going. First, we have a line of enquiry into the alleged art, missing or substituted at the Kelvingrove. Jane and Sayer will handle that."

Catrin had just been told by Worsley before entering the meeting room that she needed to plan on being back in Glasgow next week.

"Second, we have a line of enquiry into the Nitro XLA10 placebo found on Gault that may or may not have contributed to his demise. DCI Strachan will be in charge of that and all information that may surface relevant to that goes to her. No-one outside her team pursues that line of enquiry. Let me repeat that. No-one asks questions about the placebo, right? There are aspects of enquiries around the activities of the Connolly gang that are very delicate at present.

"Finally, there is the suspicion that Drummond's death nearly two years ago may not have been an accident. Shortt and I will re-open the files and look into it."

Several questions arose from team members and

Sinclair dealt with them expeditiously. Then he said, "Let's gather the facts and get together next week on this. Jane, I have a car to take you and Catrin to the hotel to collect your things, then it will take you on to the train station. PC Hammond will call through your reservation changes and contact you with the details."

Thank you, everyone."

He was out the door heading to some other meeting before most of them had stood up.

Catrin called Iain while they waited for the train and said that she was leaving now, but would be back probably next week and perhaps she could take up the offer one evening to see the pottery shop? He sounded happy with her call and said he and his mother would look forward to it.

On the train south Worsley and Sayer were absorbed in their laptop and iPad, respectively. Worsley had joined a conference call on a case that Catrin had heard of but had no involvement in as soon as they settled on board. Catrin had her own cases to be following up on, much of it routine 'grind', so she worked away on emails.

After Worsley finished her call she sighed and asked, "What's your take as an artist on these Colourists; I was reading up about them and their paintings on Google."

Catrin smiled. "So was I, ma'am."

She continued, "As you have read, there were four 'Colourist' artists, John Fergusson, who spent a lot of time in Paris before the First World War, Francis Cadell, Samuel Peploe and Leslie Hunter, but I think that belies the nature of artistic communities, which are more complex.

"They were all influenced by French impressionism, which was still a controversial subject at the time. They brought their thinking and experimentation back to Scotland. So they have paintings in France, set in France, paintings in Scotland, including landscapes in the Hebrides and the Highlands and they challenged not just the painting style but the choice of subject. They covered the gamut; still-life, portraits, figures, landscapes.

"From a theft or copyist perspective, which seems to be the issues we may have here, Alistair Gault must have been captivated by them. Probably some others in the Kelvingrove Museum were also excited by the style and but there would be many who thought they were unimportant or strange."

Worsley replied, "I see that a painting by Francis Cadell sold for nearly half a million pounds, yet he died in poverty in 1937."

Catrin nodded. "That's the way with art. Sometimes it leaps to public prominence straight away, a lot of the time it is only valued long after the artist can benefit. And it's 'Cadell, like 'paddle' I think, ma'am, not like 'dell'. I think it was originally a Welsh name."

Jane Worsley smiled. "Then I guess you would know."

Later, Catrin remembered that Worsley had some meeting in London on Thursday and had suggested that Catrin accompany her to it in Keith's absence; it was a meeting he normally would attend. She asked her about it.

Worsley said, "Yes, I am glad you reminded me and yes, you should. Let's see how the work tomorrow goes on this file and others you are handling, but it would be good experience for you to attend. It is a quarterly art crime coordination meeting with various museum people that DCI Coltrane organizes."

She added, "And please, we need to be very delicate on this Glasgow thing at present, particularly around the drug aspect."

Catrin responded, "Yes ma'am, I did get the message. And I did spend over two years in a narcotics unit when I saw similar strain on faces."

Worsley looked at her. "And…?"

"It was generally when a major operation was in place. And sometimes when there was someone on the inside of it that was at risk."

"Catrin, I suggest that you don't speculate further. Just act as if that is good enough reason for you to be treading very carefully."

11 THE COORDINATION MEETING

Wednesday was busy for Catrin as she researched further into the background on the Colourist artists, their paintings and any associated files on thefts or criminal activities. She also followed up on other files she was working on, as well as two time-critical items that DI Marshall had requested. As the day progressed it made her feel better to catch up on the other cases, as they had been nagging a little.

There wasn't a lot on the crime database regarding Colourist art cases. A dispute between two Scottish brothers, one now resident in Nova Scotia, Canada had garnered some coverage and an 'utterance of threats' charge – and showed how the value could escalate as Dr. Bryant had said. A relatively minor work by Leslie Hunter initially valued at around £18,000 had risen to an offer of a transfer price of £120,000 from one brother to the other. It has been rejected.

On Thursday Catrin took the Tube to Trafalgar Square and met Chief Inspector Worsley at the National Gallery for the coordination meeting. All she knew was DCI Neville Coltrane chaired it, that it had been running for years and had a number of other groups involved in art crime issues attend.

"We are still very much outsiders on this. DI Marshall used to attend when he was in A&A so he and I now go," Worsley said.

"Does Hetherington attend this meeting, representing the Kelvingrove Museum?" asked Catrin.

Worsley chuckled, "I haven't seen her here in the time I have been attending. I get the impression it is a 'by invitation' network, not a formal representation by art institution. In fact, if Keith hadn't been attending already, I wonder if I would have heard about it at all."

Once inside, they went to a large conference room with a side table with coffee and tea set up on one side of the room. A u-shaped meeting table occupied the centre, some chairs claimed already, Catrin saw, with bags and brief-cases on them. A number of people were there and Jane introduced her to several of them before herself being hauled into a private pre-meeting chat.

Catrin got herself coffee and moved to one side to drink it. She found that she was standing next to an older man doing the same, watching the noise of the growing gathering. He was dressed in a rather worn but well-made suit, not quite the smart set she had met on entry. She introduced herself.

"Ah," he said, "You work with Keith Marshall, I gather; he mentioned you, the new member of the team." He nodded at Worsley in the distance.

"Well, nearly nine months now," she said.

"Keith said you are an artist, ceramics, I recall, and that Liz thinks highly of you."

So he knew Keith's sister, then, she thought.

"Yes, I paint and decorate ceramics; a friend of mine is the potter."

He nodded, "What techniques do you prefer?" He was looking at her intently.

This is getting heavily into detail quickly for this early in the morning, thought Catrin; he hasn't even said who he is yet.

"I do overglaze enamelwork mainly, but not exclusively. I mix these with majolica underglaze work at times. It is constant experimentation…"

"Thank God for that," he said quite passionately, interrupting her. "Don't stop. It's what art is about."

She laughed. "I was talked once into doing a dinner set for a bistro by my potter. Repetition of good work can pay bills for a pottery business, but I like the sense of a new start with each piece."

"Exactly! That's what I always felt," he said with enthusiasm, and started talking about sculpture. Catrin suddenly realized who he was; Sir John Vale, one of the leading names in British sculpture. Vale was looking quite a bit older than the photo images she recalled. She blushed at her oversight.

Her focus on the man's mini-lecture was interrupted by the appearance of DCI Coltrane at her shoulder. He said, "Good morning, Sir John… and DC Sayer. I see you two have met, but I would like to get started and, Sir John, if you would sit next to me."

Catrin found herself being signalled by Jane Worsley to a seat next to her near the bottom end of one arm of the meeting table.

Coltrane called the meeting to order and welcomed everyone. The round of self-introductions started, during which Jane passed a copy of the agenda over to Catrin, whispering to her, "I only printed this out late last night; I should have emailed it to you."

She saw on the agenda that the first item was 'Guest opening speaker: Sir John Vale, OBE' and the title of his speech was 'Trends in the theft of larger sculptures.' Then she recalled that one of his own works had been stolen from outside a museum in Barcelona a decade ago, a two-element exhibit. Half of it was recovered; the other had been melted down for the value of the bronze.

The other items were apparently standard agenda elements - reports by members of incidents and progress or lack thereof in solving the cases.

She was reminded again how well-connected Keith Marshall was, if he was on first-name terms with Sir John Vale.

As they left the building later Jane said, "Well that's over for another three months. While I think of it, on Monday you will be going up to Glasgow after the morning meeting. Aina was fixing the details today."

On Saturday when she entered the Cwmbran Kiln Melanie was serving a customer. The Art Market was active; there were a lot of people about. Catrin had just one piece she wanted to do, an idea for a wall plate that had come to her while in the Kelvingrove. She had asked Jean by email to prepare one of their platter-size bisques, the fired pottery 'blanks' ready for decoration.

Jean said, "Marjorie liked the stuff we sent up, we already have an order for a dinner set in the blue finish. She said you were going back and would see her and Iain next week."

"No, I am not carting …"

"Relax," said Jean, "No need. Shipping costs are to the client direct. And we have some of Marjorie's items by parcel post. They are still in the storeroom. Go look."

Melanie finished with the customer as Catrin examined the Scottish pieces. They were good pottery but nothing stood out for her as a 'wow - I'd like that'.

Melanie came into the back after the customer had been served. She said, "Do you want dinner with us tonight? We have a gift voucher from a supplier for use at a restaurant in Knightsbridge."

Catrin thought. She had been thinking about work then thought it was best to drop all that until next Monday, so she said, "Yes I would, if I can buy you two a nice bottle of wine there."

"Sounds like a plan," said Jean.

Catrin pulled out the sketch she had made at one point on the train back from Glasgow, sounding out the platter design. She headed to the bench in the back that she used. "Down to some different work," she said to herself.

Later at dinner, Melanie asked about Iain.

Catrin responded, "He seems nice, but I only spoke to him for half an hour."

"But you like him," said Jean, "We can see that."

"I am a police officer; no-one can read me. I am a trained professional."

They laughed. "We have known you since... well Jean has since you were four," said Melanie. "When I sent the email last week with his photo Jean asked 'did she respond.' I said no. 'She likes him,' she said."

Catrin said, "You know, it was the easiest half-hour discussion with a stranger I can recall; we hit it off well. But he could be married with two kids for all I know."

"No he isn't," said Melanie, "I asked Marjorie. He was engaged, but they broke it off about a year ago; her name was Laura and Iain really liked her. And he is not gay, either. We asked that, too."

Catrin looked amazed. "What are you two doing, asking such stuff?"

"Matchmaking," said Jean, "it's years since university and you broke up with David. You have had two short-term relationships in the time up until now. You are lost in all the work - your police work and our pottery."

"Ask Li," said Melanie, "Chinese parents do it. Find partners for their sons. We are feeling parental." Jean just burst out with laughter at Melanie's deadpan humour.

Jian Li Yeung was a new friend of Catrin's that had been involved in her first case with the ACU. She was from Hong Kong, now studying at Bangor University. Li had visited London to see Catrin last month and had got along well with Jean and Melanie.

Catrin sat back. "Well, I never..."

Melanie added, "And Catrin, Iain is really looking forward to meeting you next week."

Catrin looked at her friends. For quiet potters, she thought, they occasionally could amaze her. Having the guts to set up a pottery business in London was one of those times. Acting as Cupid was another.

12 THE CASTLE

It had been Dominic Connolly's idea to rent the best suites available at the exclusive Fonab Castle Hotel near Pitlochry for the weekend meeting with the Milnes. It was the third 'alignment' session between the Edinburgh and Glasgow drug gangs. Until recently they had been in conflict over territory and street pricing. A call between Dominic Connolly and Steve Milne had been the start of the discussion.

The first meeting had been just Dominic Connolly with Francis and Steve Milne, the two brothers from Edinburgh, with a few heavies from each side. They met in the rented back room of a pub in Armadale, a town about half-way between the two cities. Armadale didn't know it had been declared no-man's land in the south Scotland drug war; it just went about its business.

By the third meeting the thawing out had progressed sufficiently that Dominic decided that the Fonab Castle was the venue to provide the right atmosphere for the progress of negotiations. His wife Joan was less enthusiastic.

She said, "It will be me looking after all the kids with Steve's wife. You will be out swinging clubs with Steve and Francis; 'doing business' I think you call it. Madame Muck will be off by herself."

Joan was not too impressed with Daniella Milne, Francis's wife.

"Not quite," smiled Dominic, "Niall's coming. He is coming to the hotel to talk with Madame Muck about art. She will like that."

Joan just burst out laughing. "He will have to join her in the spa, then."

In fact, Niall invited Daniella Milne to go riding on Saturday afternoon and took along Dominic Connolly's older child, Jason, whom he knew had taken riding lessons. The three turned out to have a pleasant time, keeping a good pace and enjoying the horses and the countryside.

Jason's enthusiasm was infectious. He was totally unaware that on a neighbouring golf course his father and two other men were carving up more misery and premature death across southern Scotland in the guise of 'business efficiency and good relationships'. He just thought they were off playing golf and he was enjoying the time with 'Uncle Niall' and this friend.

On their return Jason asked if he could be excused so he could catch some of the football on the television in the children's room in the Connolly suite. Niall let Joan know and then invited Daniella to have a drink or tea outside. "Twenty minutes; a shower and change?" she said. "Then a drink?"

She had a champagne and orange juice cocktail, a large one in a glass to match his lager.

"So you bought a painting by Cadell recently, I saw,"

said Niall without preamble. "Why do you like him?"

"We have three now, the Cadell, a Peploe and a Fergusson. All are Scottish scenes. Francis likes Scotland and I like art that reaches out at me. Post-impressionism is one of my interests."

Niall looked at her. "So a still-life Colourist painted in France would not really appeal then?" His expression was slightly mocking.

"You know of one? For sale?" she said.

He said nothing.

"You have one, Niall, is that it? Do you collect also?"

"Let me tell you a story, Daniella. It's a hypothetical story, of course."

Half-an-hour later 'The Boys' came in from the golf course. Niall and Daniella were in intense discussion, Dominic Connolly saw. The choice of the Fonab Castle had been a good one.

13 GOVAN

In the usual briefing session in the ACU on Monday morning, now with DI Marshall present looking tanned but far from relaxed, DCI Worsley went through the status of the current case load and the expected activities of the week.

Keith would be catching up on a case that he had hoped Catrin would work on last week, not knowing about the new issue in Glasgow. She would report directly to Worsley on the Gault case until further notice, she was told, unless this was devolved to Keith due to Worsley's own caseload. Worsley herself would be out of the office for two days, but responsive by email.

"Look after yourself with the villains up there," he said as Catrin prepared to close down her desktop and lock up.

"I expect I will mainly be in the Govan station."

"That's what concerns me – a bunch of Scotsmen." He smiled.

"And enjoy Bournemouth," Catrin parried back.

Marshall was involved in a case arising from an expert

numismatist who appeared to get in the way of a precious coins robbery. He had been badly injured. There had been three similar coin robberies in eight months across southern England and the enquiry had gone cold. Marshall was re-interviewing the witnesses at the two robberies which had not turned violent; he hoped to see if any commonalities emerged that could reactivate the investigation.

The game plan Catrin and Worsley had discussed was for her to attend the briefing Tuesday morning in Govan and see what leeway she had for additional interviews based on her researches. In any event she had already scheduled a meeting with Hetherington at the Kelvingrove to delve more into items thrown up from Alistair Gault's employment record. She had also been put in contact with an expert on the Colourists at the University of Glasgow.

Travelling up by train she had time after arrival and the evening free, so she had texted Iain to see if he and his mother were around. If Marjorie wasn't, she was going to go back and ask whether he was available to meet for a drink, anyway.

In fact, it worked out that Marjorie Simmons was delighted to have the chance to meet her and Iain would meet the train and take her out to Greenock.

Catrin had never ridden in an electric car before, so she was surprised both by the vehicle's performance and the owner's selection of it. The Peugeot iOn was new and still had the new car smell. Iain said, "I had a small Audi but realised that most of my driving was around Glasgow so I decided to change to this car. Favorable loan rates for bank employees helps."

They were moving rapidly through traffic towards

Greenock. He had shaken her hand and grabbed her bag as she came through from the platform, all businesslike. On the train she had wondered what to expect, particularly if his mother had been having the same conversation with him that she had experienced on Saturday with the pair of Cupids.

"How busy will you be this week, do you know?" he asked.

"To be honest, I don't. It all depends on decisions made by more senior officers. It's part of the job, not knowing exactly the working hours or what I will do next."

"Well, perhaps if it works out, we could go to dinner or have a drink, if you like. Short notice is fine. I will leave it to you, but if you do get the chance, I would like that."

"So would I," said Catrin.

Marjorie Simmons was surprisingly young-looking yet her hair was mainly grey. It was hard to place her age accurately, Catrin thought. Trim, well-dressed but wearing an apron bearing the logo of her pottery shop as she prepared dinner in her kitchen, she welcomed Catrin to the small home on Fox Street. Catrin could smell the dinner cooking; beef in red wine she thought.

Marjorie read her thoughts. "It's French cooking tonight. Start with a salad, then boeuf bourguignon and new potatoes. Sound good?"

Catrin smiled. "It does to me."

They talked about pottery, about Catrin's art and Marjorie's experiences in running a pottery shop. Catrin knew that Melanie had first met Marjorie on a weekend seminar on small business management. Realizing that the talk was all about the two women, she asked about Iain's work.

"I went straight into the bank from school, as I said," he answered. "All my additional training in accounting and management came through their support."

"He probably lied that it was his cricket that got him in, I expect; he does that," said Marjorie.

Catrin laughed.

"He did, but I took him to task about it; he admitted that he can actually count as well."

He talked a little about his role at the branch. "It's largely a front-line role in branch banking at present, managing staff, dealing with the major customers. It's what I like doing, at least for now."

Marjorie said, "Iain looks after the shop here sometimes, mainly when I go to teach courses."

"There you go," said Iain, smiling, "more customer relations work."

"When do you teach?" Catrin asked.

Marjorie said, "In March and April, generally; I teach a course in setting up an arts and crafts business using my pottery experience as the example. There is a lot of training for young people in the arts themselves but little practical experience-based training on how to start their own small business. I do two one-week courses at the local campus of the University of the Highlands, Argyll College."

"And when do you get holidays, both of you?"

"Mum never takes holidays," said Iain, "unless you call teaching a holiday."

His mother started protesting about the days and long weekends she took for this and that. Iain waited and then said, "I used to take in Wimbledon - the second week - with my former fiancée. She and I both played locally in a club and we enjoyed the big competition live. And we had some overseas package holidays together. But I didn't take any holidays last year. And you?"

Catrin talked about her life balance – busy between the two worlds she occupied and also not having a holiday in over a year. "I have plans to go to Hong Kong, though, to visit a friend, a Chinese woman who will be returning there shortly. First I need to sell some more pots and pay the way…"

Jian Li Yeung had organized it. Through a family friend in Hong Kong it was arranged that if Catrin bought a discount economy ticket, she would be upgraded to First Class. She was looking forward to the trip. Both women were a little sensitive about no-one but Catrin buying the ticket, though, given that they had met through police work.

Catrin had picked up the keys to the rental car at Glasgow Central station before setting off with Iain, knowing she needed to get around under her own steam this week. When he dropped her off back at the rental car park rather than at the hotel she thanked him again and he leaned forward and kissed her on the cheek. She looked at him and then kissed him gently on the lips.

She said, as she moved away, "I will give you a call."

~~

On Tuesday morning at Govan Police Station DCI Sinclair reviewed the cases with the assembled team. No-one had made much progress. Shortt was heading up to Fort William this week, to see Marilyn Thompson, the daughter of the former colleague of Alistair Gault. She was the last person known to have talked with Drummond, according to the file.

Steve Coleman from the Drug Squad said he had nothing to report. Catrin wondered if they were doing anything at all on the placebo drug enquiry.

Catrin said she was planning to meet with Hetherington at the Museum and then separately with Professor Pauline Cantrell, an expert on the Colourists who was on the faculty of the University of Glasgow. Neville Coltrane had recommended her and said that she could be relied on for confidentiality, so nothing would get back to the Museum staff even thought they were located just across the road from each other.

Susan Hetherington had not produced any new material other than the name of a retiree who knew Alistair Gault. When she had reviewed the list of retirees again she had recognized one name, Victor McGill, as being the same as a current employee. She talked to him and found out that they were father and son; one was a current security guard and the father had served in the same role at the Museum.

She took Catrin to meet the son. He was on duty, a man in his thirties. She explained that the detective wanted to talk with his father about a former conservator at the museum.

McGill said, "Strangely enough, he may be able to talk about that, but whatever credence you give to it is another matter. He has Alzheimer's but talks more about that period than anything else. He is not far from here, in long-term care. Not a bad place he's in. Probably it would be best with me there and early afternoon is his brightest time."

He looked at Hetherington, "But my shift doesn't finish until closing."

Susan said, "Vic, you go with the the police officer

after lunch and I will sort it out."

Catrin agreed to collect him at 1.00 p.m. and drive him, if he gave the directions.

Catrin arrived at the University of Glasgow in the Hertz rental car, finding herself on the campus just behind the Kelvingrove Museum. She found her way to the room of Professor Cantrell, a short, very buxom woman in her forties with heavy, studious glasses. The glasses make her look the epitome of an academic, thought Catrin.

She reconfirmed the issue of confidentiality and explained their issue with the Scottish Colourists.

"We are in a very different league than the Picasso's and Goya's that Neville likes to chase," said Cantrell.

DCI Coltrane's office had phoned ahead to introduce Catrin and confirm that Cantrell was free after a lecture that morning. Catrin wasn't sure whether she was speaking about Picasso and Goya in general or whether Neville Coltrane had mentioned any investigations to her.

"I gather you have an art history background so I'm not going to go into the big picture, you will have read that. I'll just say that you probably know that the influence of the four Colourist painters was only recognized well after their time. The same can be said of the commercial value of their work today. In the last decade or so prices have gone up significantly, in general. The figure of £200,000 to £300,000 is reasonable for most of the top works but will be low for some of them. Other paintings by them will be selling in the £10,000 to £50,000 range; good paintings, just less well-known, or less interesting. But the names are selling and prices are increasing; there is only a limited amount of work by the Colourists out there and much has been secured already for major collections.

"An element of pricing for them is the current 'Scots' Pride' wave rolling through, tied to the political changes in Scotland and a sense of valuing more highly our own art these days. That, of course, includes all those American Scots with money who want to take works back to the USA. And you are always going to get one obstinate wealthy Scot bidding against another – the price will keep going up until the financial blood flows."

"What about fraud and stolen works?" asked Catrin.

"Reports of theft are increasing from private owners but I am not aware of any frauds reported. This is all probably in police databases, if there are any. As to thefts specifically from museums, there was a theft of a Peploe from the Kelvingrove in the 1990's, part of a broader series of thefts, including one painting by John Constable. I am not aware of other museum losses."

Catrin nodded, she had read about the Kelvingrove theft; a curator at the museum had spotted one of the missing paintings sometime later, advertised in a catalogue.

Cantrell continued, "Interestingly enough though, both Keith Murray - he is another faculty member with a research interest in the Colourists - and myself have had separate enquiries about the potential value of a Colourist work if it was previously unknown, which was quite interesting. The enquirer was a man, he wanted a rough value. Neither of us said we could speculate without seeing it and were cut off with a brief 'thanks'. Clearly he wasn't someone we regularly talk to, or was familiar with art appraisal, but he was a Scot, a local man, I think.

"You suspect something less than legal, perhaps?"

"It could be, but it could be a red herring. You know, it could be someone without any knowledge at all, bragging about a work they came across in an attic. They think it is a Colourist, perhaps. However, people who have paintings they are trying to validate are generally open and... persistent. I have trouble with some of them, frankly, so have to be careful when I get these phone calls. But this man was not like that, he just wanted a dollar or sterling number."

"And when was this, as precisely as you can?"

She sighed. "It was six weeks ago on the day I met... I had a meeting with a visitor, at the time."

Cantrell looked at her computer calendar.

"Yes, six weeks ago, to the day."

"And do you know when the call to Professor Murray was?"

"Not sure, but around the same time, within a week. His extension is 3439. I expect if you are pursuing this you will be looking into phone records. I know, you can't tell me anything." She smiled.

Catrin wound it up and headed back to the car. She had called the extension for Professor Keith Murray on the way out of the building and left a message.

Catrin thought back to the interview with Mary Gault. Her husband had spoken to the lawyer, Irvin. Presumably he also informed him of the concerns about the paintings. Now we hear there is recent interest by someone, probably outside the art interest sector, enquiring about the value of Colourists. Was there a link and if so, what was it?

Her phone rang. It was the number she had just called. Dr. Murray identified himself and Catrin explained briefly her reason for calling. He was working at home today, he said, but would be happy to see her – but he would be collecting his daughters after school and would have little time then.

She checked the timing. She could fit it in, just, if she grabbed a quick snack for lunch. She put his address in the satnav; it was about fifteen minutes' drive away.

Once inside his home she was offered coffee. The front room of the semi-detached house had been converted to a double office, fairly messy, with two desks, one with his laptop on it. A photo of two girls around twelve years old was on his desk, a family photo on the other.

"My wife teaches at the university, also."

She went through again the reason for her interest, her notebook open. Much of what he had to say overlapped that of Professor Cantrell.

Then he added, "There is interest in Colourists. Two were recently put up for auction in Edinburgh. I had gone over to see them; not to consider buying, of course, but I have the idea that the university should be looking at acquiring a painting through donor support and it would be interesting to see the market interest first hand.

"They were nice works, one by John Fergusson, the other by Samuel Peploe. The man who got the Peploe was set on it. He wouldn't have stopped, I think, and the others present, including two telephone bids, just folded. I don't know who he was, but he was nicely dressed. He had a woman with him, looked Latin, Spanish perhaps. She was the one really interested in the works, I think."

"He bid on the Fergusson too, but was not in at the end. I think the woman with him realised that they were attracting attention and said something to him, so he dropped out. Or perhaps they had hit their price ceiling, I am not sure."

Catrin got the details of the auction and date and thanked Murray, then headed back to the Kelvingrove

Museum to collect Victor McGill.

The older McGill seemed pleasant, amiable. He had a nice little room in the retirement home. It was clean, with less memorabilia around than she would have anticipated. She waited until her son had settled him down with the presence of a visitor.

Susan had told her that Victor McGill Senior was 92 and he had started at the museum after World War II, so he wouldn't have known Gault during the war period.

When she talked to him and asked him about his memory of Mr. Gault his first comment took her by surprise.

"Are you going to arrest him; Mr. Gault?"

Catrin said, "Why should I do that, Mr. McGill?"

"My son says you are a policewoman, so I had to ask, but you seem too young to be a policewoman, to be honest."

"No Mr. McGill. I just want to know more about Mr. Gault, that's all."

He looked at her. "He was a nice man. Quiet. Very involved in his church I recall. So I don't think you would have any reason to arrest him. Not like Mr. Waring, he was always after the girls in the place, married or single."

Catrin cut across. "No, Mr. McGill, I am not going to arrest him. Which church did he go to?"

The old man shot straight back with the answer, "Kinnington Church, the Episcopal church. He went every Sunday except when he was away in the Hebrides teaching, regular as clockwork."

"What did you think of Mr. Gault, was he friendly?"

His face clouded a bit, "No, not friendly. He was polite, courteous, but not friendly with people. He kept his distance, a bit shy. He loved his work and the exhibits.

I could catch him at any of them and he would tell me about it if he had time. He was a very knowledgeable man and a good painter, too. I watched him fixing up damaged paintings at times. He was very good at it."

Catrin looked the son, who was nodding at him encouragingly, pleased his father was responding so actively.

The old man suddenly closed his eyes. When he opened them again he was staring into the distance.

"Hello, who are you?" he said. Then he saw his son. "Vic, when are we going home?"

Catrin looked at the son, unsure how to proceed. Victor said, "Dad, this is your home now. This is a police officer, asking questions about Mr. Gault."

The father seemed to clue back in a little. "Yes, he was a nice man, quiet, didn't know him well, though. Don't think anyone did."

"Thank you, Mr. Gault, you have been very helpful. But I must be going in now. I may come back and ask you more if you will let me."

He smiled. "Of course you can, a pretty young lady like you. Come any time. Do you work with Victor at the museum?"

The son cut in and said, "We have to be going now, Dad. I will be back to see you."

In the car, he apologised for the pointless drive over.

Catrin said, "Mr. McGill, it wasn't pointless. In fact, if I get specific things I want to check I will ask to come and see your father again. His recall of that period seems good. The problem was mine; that I had no specific questions that would fit the sort of knowledge that your father might have had of a curator.

"But I do appreciate your cooperation and it did give

me another lead; to talk to people at Kinnington Church.

"Now, can I take you back to the museum or drop you somewhere else?"

She dropped him at a bus stop, one he said that would take him home easily. If she was going back into the city it would be the best solution for both of them given the rush hour traffic. She decided it was not worth going back to Govan Police Station either. On impulse she called Iain.

"You said call, so I am. I wonder about dinner this evening. It will be my shout, if you are free."

"I'd love to," he said, and sounded like he meant it.

Catrin said, "I don't know too many places, though."

"That's dangerous, offering to pay and leaving the choice to me."

She laughed, "I'll trust your judgment."

He said he would make a reservation and text her. She wondered what he would choose. She was in a Novotel just south of Sauchiehall St., she had told him.

His text a few minutes later was a reservation for 7.00 p.m. at the Loon Fung Chinese Restaurant, not too far from the hotel. She checked it out on her phone. It had a good reputation, was long-established with a big menu and, she noticed, sensible prices.

She headed back to the hotel, had some tea while she thought about the day's interviews and called the Auction House in Edinburgh. Then she went for a workout and showered, choosing from her limited travel wardrobe what she would wear for the evening. A little more attention on the make-up, the diamond studs her parents had bought for her twenty-first birthday she had brought with her, just in case. She looked good, she thought.

She met Iain at the restaurant. He was waiting outside

and took her arm as she came up, giving her a little kiss on the cheek. Again he was nicely dressed, casually this time. They went in and were led to their table.

Catrin's knowledge of Chinese food had expanded a lot with her friendship with Jian Li, including her ability to eat with chopsticks, so she was very comfortable with the menu and the style of eating. She found that Iain ate Asian food a lot, was knowledgeable and preferred Thai cuisine. The Loon Fung was a good choice, she felt. He had been once to Thailand on holiday with his former fiancée. He drank a light beer, Catrin stuck to jasmine tea and water.

As in their first meeting, conversation flowed naturally and Catrin found she was having a good time. He could be funny, but behind it she sensed seriousness of attitude and intent. And he was clearly interested in her. She hoped he was picking up similar signals.

Afterwards, he walked back to her hotel and she wondered what to do next. She leaned in to kiss him goodnight properly and felt him move his hips back slightly. She remembered her first boyfriend doing that to hide his arousal; he had thought it might be off-putting. In fact, she found it a charming touch.

"Can I see you tomorrow, or am I becoming a pest?" he asked lightly, but she was watching his eyes.

"Yes, I would love that, at least if I don't get hi-jacked somewhere by my Chief Inspector. Police work you know… but I would love to. I like you, Iain."

He smiled and moved back a little further. "I'll see you tomorrow then, officer."

She watched him walk away then she turned into the hotel.

14 THE COLOURIST CONUNDRUM

DCI Strachan again attended the Wednesday morning briefing. This time she talked about a complex operation involving a number of other forces that was targeting illegal drug import by the Connolly gang.

"We are being very cautious. Potentially what is going down is a trade flow change, including supply routes with new alliances between Connolly and a major supplier in the Edinburgh area; two gangs that were, until recently, at each other's throats. So we are still treading carefully on this - what you have to admit - is a smaller issue of the placebo pills."

Meaning they have done nothing on it, thought Catrin.

Shortt reported on his work on the Drummond case.

"I went to see Marilyn Thompson in Fort William. She is the daughter of Archie Thompson and now has the house. Her father is long dead and died of natural causes, she said. She had no recollection other than the man Drummond had called to see her, had a discussion and looked at the paintings. She has three paintings by Alistair Gault and showed them to me.

"Catrin, I took photos of the paintings - I will send them to you.

"I also went to the pub he supposedly stopped at or where his car was spotted before the accident. No one recalled him, although the same landlord was working that week. Across the road was a petrol station and café, so I tried there also. The woman supervisor recognized him. His photo had also been in the obituary and the young woman who served him had seen it and talked with her at the time.

"Neither the server or this woman was interviewed then. Drummond had wanted a steel thermos washed and filled with coffee, she recalled. He put the Thermos on a table and went to the toilets, then collected it as he set out; someone had handed it in, finding it on the table, the server had told her. Then they read about his accident. That's why she remembered the conversation.

Sinclair said, "Kevin has done some good work here. There is a possibility - remote as it may be - that someone interfered with the flask, perhaps adding something."

DC Coleman asked, "What about re-examination of the retained tissue samples?"

"There aren't any," said Shortt. "The fire in the vehicle was intense and it wasn't seen as a crime anyway."

"Our next step is to try and track down the server from the café. She was seasonal, and left the area. If we find her, then we can see if she can remember what the man who handed in the flask looked like."

They turned to Catrin. "Constable Sayer?"

Catrin recounted her progress. "Sir, so far I have made an estimate of the possible value of the fourteen Colourist paintings listed. It ranges at the high side of the two to three million pound range but could be a lot less. It is going to be very variable and unpredictable.

"But the list is not of stolen works; the paintings on Gault's list are largely in the possession of museums. So I am looking first at the potential for fraud and copies.

"I did discover that there have been enquiries about the value of an 'undiscovered' Colourist painting by someone unfamiliar with the art market and that a Francis Milne and his wife are buying Colourists that come onto the market as if price is no object. They are from Edinburgh. They bought a Peploe there recently and bid unsuccessfully on a Fergusson, both Colourist artists.

"I would like to get Professor Cantrell to visit Mary Gault's home and look at Alistair Gault's own paintings. It could give a lead on his capabilities to reproduce these artists. As a conservator, it is clear he could repair such works."

Sinclair nodded, it seemed reasonable to him.

"I would also like to pursue enquiries in Edinburgh and find out more about the interest the Milne couple have in the Colourists."

Strachan said, "Not now. No-one goes near anything to do with Irvin at present. That includes the Milne couple in Edinburgh."

Everyone looked at her.

"The Milne family are leads in the Edinburgh drug world. I want no noises back their way."

Sergeant McPherson said, "But then the link is more than coincidental, surely?"

Catrin said, "We know art is used for drug business trade, as a security. What we could have here is something similar, given links to two Scottish drug gangs."

"Still," said Strachan, "I don't want any action with either the Gault family, with their link to Neil Irvin, or the Milnes until I say so. Eric, that will come down from the top if needed, you know that."

Catrin looked at Sinclair and could see his frustration starting to build.

"What about this idea, as an alternative?" Catrin said, outlining a proposal.

~~

On Thursday afternoon Susan Hetherington and Catrin sat in the same front room of Mary Gault's house. Elizabeth, the daughter, was seated by her mother.

Hetherington said, "I wanted to put your mind at rest, Mrs. Gault. Constable Sayer mentioned to me the concern you have, given the visit of your late husband to the museum. I can understand how upsetting it could be for him, living with this worry. I am sorry I did not get the chance to meet him."

"Your father-in-law was a very valued employee of the museum. His work for us, according to his records and some of the people I have talked to, was exemplary. He was very active in managing the safety of our collections during the war period and gave long service to the museum afterwards.

"I hate to see this linger with you, as a concern. Let me say that the Kelvingrove Museum has no suspicions of any malpractice by Alistair Gault and he was regarded as a staff member who was highly trustworthy. I didn't get the chance to meet Reverend Gault, but that is what I would have told him, if I had."

"The old lady's eyes were filling with tears. "Thank you. It was such a worry for Alexander. I am glad you came and told me."

"Constable Sayer also said she saw a painting of Alistair Gault's here during her visit with Inspector Sinclair. She thought it was very good. I am wondering if you would let us see it or others by him. He was very talented as a conservator and restorer, I understand, and we are a museum of Scottish heritage. I am not saying anything, making any promises, but if we ended up exhibiting a work by a former staff member as a result, it would be quite a special find for us."

"We have the funeral this coming week," said Elizabeth.

Susan Hetherington responded, "I know. Dr. Bryant, the Museum Director and I plan to attend, under the circumstances. I was thinking perhaps I could see them later on."

Mary Gault looked at her daughter. "Let's be practical, Elizabeth. Mrs. Hetherington, it would be a privilege to let you do as you propose. Why not take one or two now for a preliminary evaluation? You can choose. I would like back as soon as possible the painting that Detective Sayer saw, if you want to evaluate that one, as it is my favorite. And we have more that you can come back for after the funeral. I am moving into a smaller accommodation in Oban for seniors the week following the funeral and frankly I would welcome some of the paintings going somewhere other than into storage or to over to my nephew Niall's place."

Catrin said, "Do you have a lot, then?"

"We have quite a few, most of the ones he didn't give away. Alistair was more prolific in retirement, moreso than during his employment period."

"He didn't sell any?" asked Catrin.

Mary smiled, "I think his wife would have dearly liked him to but he never did, Alexander said. He wasn't interested in the commercial side of it, I suspect. He was a very reserved, shy man. Selling would not have come easy to him."

She paused.

"There are other paintings, too." she added.

Hetherington, picking up Catrin's line, asked "Do you know where those are?"

"Well, some are over at Stornoway. Alistair did some work there at the college, the university as it is now called. I am not sure where. And he gave some to a couple of his former colleagues; he seemed to have no real friends outside his work, as I recall. And he gave several to the church, the one in Kinnington he attended."

She was clearly thinking her way through past memories.

"I think Niall has a few. too. I know Alistair gave him paintings from time to time.

"Perhaps Archie Thompson's daughter has some, in Fort William. Archie and Alistair worked closely together at the museum. But he is dead now too."

Catrin just nodded. Archie Thompson was the late father of the woman that Kevin Shortt had interviewed.

When they left with three of Gault's paintings on the back seat carefully placed in storage cases brought with her, Susan Hetherington promised to be back after the funeral with staff from the museum and a small van.

~~

It was late afternoon. Catrin, McPherson and Sinclair were in his office at Govan, linking by speaker phone with Worsley.

"So could this man Irvin could be involved in both the matter of the death of Andrew Gault and the theft or forgery of paintings?" Worsley said.

"It is a possibility, ma'am. He already owns some of them," said Catrin.

Worsley continued, "And Eric, I know we can do nothing directly about that at present. So we will need to wait on the evaluation of the works by the Kelvingrove; what they have now, what they find next week."

Catrin added, "I can check the church mentioned by Mary Gault, see if they have any paintings. The security guard McGill also recalled Alistair Gault being a regular member of the Kinnington Church over a long period. I could also visit the University of the Highlands in Stornoway. It's one of their campuses, Lewis Castle."

"One moment," said Peter McPherson. He opened the door and yelled for Kevin Shortt, who came running. "Wasn't there a report of something at the university campus at Stornoway last week?"

"Yes," said Kevin stepping inside and pointing for permission to use the desktop computer that Sinclair hardly used. He nodded.

A moment or two later Shortt read, "There was a break-in at the main building of Lewis Castle College, apparently. It was interrupted by a security guard who was fortunate, in a sense. The intruder hit him with something and broke his wrist. It could have been worse, I guess. Nothing taken, they believe, but some paintings were found off the walls."

"Yes, Catrin," said Worsley, "I think it is worth a trip to Stornoway, after all."

15 CHENEY

Niall had been quite reasonable with him, Colin Cheney thought, even though he had screwed up in Stornoway. Dominic would have been quite different in his response, he knew. Clearly Niall was disappointed but all he said was, "I should probably have come with you, gone through the place with you earlier when it was open and pointed them out exactly."

Cheney had travelled to and from Stornoway by ferry. He enjoyed the trip, the first time he had been to the Hebrides despite living in Glasgow all his life. His rental car was waiting and he drove around town, went to the café to meet the person he needed to talk to and then drove around the island a bit, acting the proverbial tourist. He eventually worked his way back to the college campus and found the building he wanted with no trouble. Colin walked around it in daylight and worked out his entry to the paintings. In the day it was absolutely clear to him which ones he was to take; Niall had described them accurately.

At two in the morning the door at the back of the building opened easily, as he expected. The problem began when he was using his pencil light to find the paintings in the dark. He picked one up from the wall as the room lights came on in the area and he heard footsteps in the distance; it sounded like someone, probably a security guard, checking another area of the building. Whoever it was must have switched on a block of lights.

In the room light he saw that the painting he had picked was similar, at least to him, to one of the paintings Niall had directed him to take. But the three he wanted were further along the wall. The darkness and the shape of the hallway had been deceptive. He put the one he was holding on the floor, leaning it against the wall and moved down the corridor. He picked up one of the actual paintings he had come for just as the footsteps became louder. It sounded like solid footwear; the guard had turned a corner nearby.

He stepped back into the office across the corridor and switched off the light inside then pulled out his baton. Hopefully the person would go by and the block of lights would be switched off. He now knew exactly what he wanted.

The footsteps stopped nearby. Colin realised that the stupid sod had stopped to look at the painting he had placed against the wall; he should have put it back, he realised. Then a powerful flashlight beam came into the dark office and the person came in the doorway.

Cheney brought his baton down and then pulled the man in, off balance, sending him flying across the desk. He heard the cry as he landed. Then he heard the guard press his radio button and it crackled alive. He screamed something into it.

Cheney had to either silence him or get out now, he realised. If it had been Glasgow, he would have hit him again, taken him out. But he was very conscious of the fact that he was stuck on an island with limited ways off. A dead or seriously hurt security guard would cause a major manhunt. He dropped the painting in his hand and got out fast.

That Cheney was as analytical and dispassionate about whether or not to further injure or kill the guard went along with his regular work for Dominic Connolly; he regarded himself as a professional. Colin Cheney was one of three people Connolly used to keep his world on the straight and narrow. Colin had been born three streets over from Dominic but much later - he was still only twenty-four.

He remembered his dad; he was just old enough to recall the fights between his parents, the screaming and banging and particularly the bruises and fat lip on his mum on the morning of the last day. After that he never saw his dad again. He had left for Canada, Colin was told. Cheney had dreams of finding him one day, just to hurt him badly.

He had a fight in school with another kid when he was nine. His mum was required to come in to collect him, take him home. He had hurt the other child quite a bit, she was told. If it happened again he would be expelled and they would have to call in the police.

"He is only nine," she said.

"His actions were a lot more vicious than we see in regular scraps between nine-year-olds, Mrs. Cheney," the deputy headmistress said, "Next time you will find the police and child services involved."

On the way home his mum bought him a Mars bar

and told him, 'Stand up for yourself, but use your head, don't let the bastards catch you. Be clever.' It became the pattern of his life.

His mother got into a fight in a pub when he was thirteen and she was sentenced to time in Cornton Vale Women's Prison. For eighteen months he lived with his aunt. She was very nice; he enjoyed that.

When his mum came out she had changed. She had no fire in her. She got a job at Tesco's, first stacking shelves and later she worked on the tills. She drank only at home and kept herself to herself. A life of work, TV and cheap white wine.

Dominic Connolly had come across Colin Cheney at the Black Angus Pub, drinking underage, unemployed. He was then seventeen. He just looked him over and stared into his eyes. "You are Marianne Cheney's boy, right?" and Colin nodded. He had never needed another employer.

Dominic had told him to help Niall out.

~~

Catrin rang Iain at 8.45 p.m. "Hi, do you fancy a drink? I just got back from a meeting at the police station. It has been a long day, Iain."

"You don't drink," he said, "But I was hoping you would call. I'll be right over. Don't listen for the engine, its electric."

"I will listen anyway."

She met him in the lobby. He was wearing a dark blue casual jacket, grey cotton pants and a blue button-down shirt. He's looking elegant again, she thought.

"So where would you like to go?" he said.

She said nothing, took his hand and led him to the lift.

"Am I under arrest then?"

"Let's just say you are a prime suspect in my current investigation. You should give the police your full co-operation."

"Yes, officer, I will."

~~

It was 7.00 a.m. the following day, Friday. Catrin had a visit to Kinnington Church arranged, the church that Alistair Gault had attended. She sat at the table in her room looking again at the note on the plate.

"Thank you for arresting me. I will call. Hugs, Iain."

It had arrived as she had finished showering, a breakfast tray with fruit, yoghurt, toast and a small jar of preserve, coffee and orange juice.

She had woken around 5.00 a.m. needing the bathroom, to find him sitting watching her, wearing the dressing gown provided with the room.

"That's mine," she said, "It's the only one in the room."

"Which is why I am wearing it, until you get up," he replied.

Later he had showered first, dressed and kissed her before leaving to go home and prepare for his own day. He had arranged the tray on the way down and had paid for it, according to the room service maid who delivered it.

She was thinking about how good she felt and, strangely enough, about a conversation in London during the visit of Jian Li, one about love and sex. They had come a long way in their friendship since the days when Jian Li was under suspicion and Catrin was in an undercover role, watching her, presenting herself as a Ph.D. student.

They were in Greenwich, standing near the former location of the Gypsy Moth IV. As part of their day playing tourist Li had put this stop on the list. Being a sailor herself, she had wanted to see the maritime museum.

It had come up during a discussion of how different the final year of an undergraduate university course would be for Li; she would return to Hong Kong to complete her studies to become a lawyer.

Catrin had mentioned how hard a part of the final year at Aberystwyth had been for her, with the breakup of the relationship with her first serious boyfriend, David. Both fine arts undergraduates, somehow his direction and hers had gone from being minor differences for future resolution to a chasm between them, she explained. It had hurt her badly.

She finished, "It was such an intense relationship and suddenly I was alone."

Li had said, "I haven't been in a relationship like that. I always lived at home, even when I went to City University in Hong Kong. I had boyfriends, and I have had sex, but secretly so that my parents didn't find out, but I have not had much of that, either. Do you miss it?"

"Do I miss sex or being in a relationship?" Catrin asked.

"Both, I guess."

Catrin thought. "I miss the relationship with a man in which sex is a normal part of an intimate life together. I would like that to happen again and, who knows what will develop the next time?

"But I just don't want 'sex and a goodbye' for some reason. I have friends who are quite happy with casual sex but it's not for me. I am old enough also not to try and have a relationship with a 'wait and see' about sex either. If it seems right, I go for it, enjoy it. I have dated two guys since I finished with David. In each case I was hoping something might grow... but each time it didn't. Yet I really liked them at the start."

Li said, "I think I am like you, that is what I want too - a good relationship with good sex - but, I am all theory and little practice. And going back to Hong Kong to my parents isn't going to help that much. Any boy I get close to that my parents see will be under careful scrutiny. And, of course, the thing with Wei didn't help."

Wei Chung was another Chinese student at Bangor University who Li had met through the student Chinese Society. Catrin hadn't met him. Li had only mentioned him to her shortly before she left Bangor at the end of the case. Li told her later they had really hit it off and even gone together to Liverpool one weekend. Then she had a message from another friend back at City University. It turned out she knew Wei's fiancée in Hong Kong and thought she should mention it discreetly.

Catrin had coincidentally called Li that lunchtime on Skype to see how she was doing and found her in tears. What was meant to be a quick 'catch up' call ended up as a lunch break with no lunch for Catrin.

Now Catrin was thinking about Iain. This is another 'start', but what will happen? It is life, she concluded; you have to give it a try.

She got herself ready. She was due to take the 3.15 p.m. back to London this afternoon, but she wanted to talk again to Iain.

16 KINNINGTON CHURCH

The tall spire of Kinnington Church dominated the local skyline as Catrin parked the rental car. The minister, Reverend Atkinson, had arranged for a parishioner called Michael Hart to be there to assist her. He was the property convener, Atkinson had said, a formal position in the church with responsibility for assets.

"I only moved to the parish two months ago so, to be frank, I hardly know anything about the building; I have been busy getting to know the congregation," Atkinson told her. Hart was also the church historian, he said.

She expected some older man; in fact he was in his thirties. He took her through the church building quickly to a side room with a stained-glass window, talking a little about the building's history on the way.

"But what you want, I gather, is any gift by Alistair Gault. He left us this small stained-glass window, quite beautiful. He designed it and paid for the installation. And he left us three of his own paintings.

"Two are in this room here, the third is in storage," he

said, leading her into an adjacent room.

"These are quite different in style, I know, but they are both of churches, one of them being ours, obviously. The third painting I could dig out…"

Catrin was looking carefully at the paintings and said, "If you would. It is quite important."

They had chosen these two because both had churches as central features, she saw. The one of Kinnington Church itself by Gault was clearly a later work. The earlier work was in the style of Peploe, very similar to a landscape of his from the Hebrides. She would need to re-check.

Hart disappeared and came back in about five minutes, brushing his coat free of dust. He held a painting wrapped in a velvet sleeve that someone had made for it, itself in a clear plastic storage bag. "Probably not the best way to keep these, but that is the way we store items here, to keep the dust out."

He unwrapped the painting and placed it face up on the table. Catrin examined it closely and like the others, took out her camera and took several shots. She then examined the back and again the front, carefully photographing the signature as she had done with the others.

"Do you mind if I ask an art expert we have available to come and examine these?"

Hart responded, "Are they valuable then? I mean, commercially so, more valuable than we hold them to be given Alistair was a member of the church. I am only thinking of insurance purposes."

Catrin replied, "I don't know yet, but I think it would be in your interest to have our expert look at them. And please return this one to its safe storage."

She passed him the Peploe-style painting.

"Perhaps the one that was in storage should be displayed for a while, for a change? The two paintings are about the same size."

As he walked her out she asked. "You would be too young to know Mr. Gault, no doubt?"

"Well, I do remember him briefly as he was an older man from when I was a child here, but I was very small. But I know him much better through my predecessor in the role of property convener, Donald Davis; they were great friends. Donald has passed on now but he spoke often about him."

Catrin asked, "Without discussion of this further please, can I ask was Mr. Gault the sort of man to be involved in anything underhand, do you think?"

Hart looked at her. "I really would doubt that. You know, I think you can tell good people, by and large. What he did here, the way her participated, the way Donald thought of him. None of that is consistent with any shallowness of character or lack of faith. So no, I doubt Alistair Gault would be anything less than honest. But I didn't know him well."

"Thank you Mr. Hart. You have been very helpful. A Dr. Susan Hetherington will be in contact with you about the paintings."

She phoned Iain. They both said how last night had been special. Catrin said, "Look, I am due out to London on the 3.15 but…"

He said, "And we didn't talk and should have, I guess, but I am tied up this evening and tomorrow in a community sports event. I am on the team representing the bank. It's a charity fundraiser. One of my events is swimming in a relay wearing a clown hat that I have to keep on for two lengths, I gather."

"Wish I could be there, with my camera," Catrin laughed.

"Catrin, let's do this more… normally. Dinner and so on, before you see me look like a complete imbecile. I don't even swim well. I should be in a tennis game not waddling down a pool."

She laughed again. "I'll be back on Sunday evening; I go to the Hebrides, to Lewis on Monday."

"I will call you after work later this afternoon," he said. "Don't sit in the quiet zone car where you can't talk."

She hesitated. "I won't and… I really do like you."

"I like you too, but I am at work. My nosy friend Madge is looking at me knowingly. Wait until you see the photo of the clown hat before deciding on what you like."

He blew her a kiss over the phone and said, "There, that's got Madge talking," and closed the line.

On the train she sent an email to Jean and Melanie. "You pair of witches can stop stirring your cauldron. He is gorgeous. I am collecting the platter tomorrow morning and, if the final glazing is as perfect as Jean says, I will tell you more. Otherwise you are out of it. I am taking the platter to Liz for her and William to decide on. And, if you are free, I am cooking dinner."

The response from Melanie was, "dinner tonight or tomorrow? We can eat late. You sound happy."

"Tomorrow," she answered, "I am still somewhere near Chester on the train. And I am happy, tell Jean."

She started looking through photographs of Colourist paintings. Susan Hetherington had asked someone to prepare a set of all known Colourist images for her; the woman had been exceedingly helpful. She had already asked Susan to photograph all the Gault painting she went through at the Gault home next week.

'I know what this is about, I think' she said softly to herself.

Next week she would be back in Glasgow; and seeing Iain; and taking a trip to the Isle of Lewis in the Hebrides. She was feeling good.

~~

"I like it," said Liz Marshall, owner of 'Liz's Place', as she assessed the platter. "Although you did promise me another vase similar to the one that Simon Williston bought, one of my very good customers, I might add. I reminded you about it already. He has phoned, wants one for a friend."

Liz's mock severity was her hallmark.

Catrin smiled. "I blame Jean," she said. "The woman is just plain lazy."

Liz looked unimpressed.

"I was round at the pottery while you were away gallivanting in Scotland. I wasn't snooping, just taking an American client who wanted to see art markets in London. She bought a complete coffee set made at the Kiln and is having another finished to something she agreed with the two of them, also to be shipped. And I noticed that the bisques for two vases just like the one I want are in the workshop gathering dust, you vicious rumourmonger."

She looked searchingly at Catrin. "You are as bad as Keith."

Liz was Keith Marshall's sister. It was through his curiosity about Catrin's art work that she and Liz had met.

"No I am not. At least I produce art as well as run around playing a police officer."

Liz responded, concealing a smirk. "I meant, over-working, too tired. But I can see you have a spring in your step."

Catrin looked at her. "You have been talking to Jean and Melanie, I can see."

Liz turned conspiratorial. "Come to Sandi's for coffee; William can look after the shop. I want to know more about him."

William Esquith, happily retired from corporate life in the city and the much-suffering husband of Liz Marshall, at least according to him, just sighed. "I will mark down Catrin's stuff for the fire sale while you are out."

"I will set Jean on you, she is both lazy and cruel," said Catrin, as she followed Liz out the door to head across the cobbled alley to the café; she was going to face some really expert interrogation.

Later, she shopped for the things she needed for dinner. She had checked with her flatmate Helen if she wanted to join, but she was going out to a party. "I will have a glass of wine with you all beforehand, but will eat out."

Their arrangement as flatmates was that either could have the kitchen/dining area for guests if the other was invited or offered to go out. Helen had already said she had more than a fair share of the run of the flat in the last two weeks.

She had already told her friends more about Iain and the dinner they had with Marjorie early in the week.

"She likes you," said Melanie, "and is over the moon that you and Iain are dating."

"We are just going out, see how it goes," said Catrin. "This was while you three were sitting around the virtual cauldron, then, I take it? It must be much easier on Skype than meeting in person in a howling wind in the wilds?"

But she was happy with the banter. The question now at the back of her mind was 'what next, if anything?' The Glasgow case would come to an end at least for her, probably in the next week or two, she suspected.

"I am back up there next week, heading to Stornoway for part of it. Perhaps I will get to see some of the pottery there. I actually need to take the train up tomorrow evening."

"Don't spend too long there, on Lewis," said Melanie, "You need free time in Glasgow."

Catrin's plans to return to Glasgow were put on hold on the Sunday morning, with a call from DI Marshall.

"We've broken the Bournemouth case, but there is going to be a lot of work to do and I need you in here; sorry."

Catrin was going to be working with Aina, preparing case documents, re-checking and cross-referencing the statements coming in from the interviews with the file material in ACU's possession. The last thing they needed was to make some record slip-up in their documentation that later caused a problem in court. It would let down the hard work by both Marshall and the Dorset Police.

It will be a long process to bring two men to justice for the coin robberies and the assault, Catrin thought. Television drama never covers the grind of dealing with documentation, everything happens so fast. In real life it was a lot of hard, concentrated work.

Worsley had informed Sinclair, who did not seem too bothered. He was a busy man with other cases, too. It was agreed that the Stornoway interview should take place this week, though, so it was set for Friday.

Catrin had texted Iain once she knew she would not be back on Monday and they talked at some time each weekday. The texts he sent her at other times cheered her up. But she wanted to get back and spend time with him.

Once she knew that she was travelling up on Thursday and flying to Stornoway for the day on Friday, she gave him a call.

"I will see you Thursday evening. We will have the weekend, too," she added, "even if I have to be back at work in London on Monday."

That expectation wasn't to be met.

17 FINISHING TOUCHES

John Dalton stood back and admired his handiwork on the Cadell signature. F.C.R. Cadell. Thank God he didn't sign with his full name, Francis Campbell Boileau Cadell, John thought.

Oil paint takes decades to fully harden. John had tested the finished area for hardness, and also that the microscopic dirt and dust level in the area matched the main painting well. He knew it wouldn't stand up to major forensic scrutiny but that wasn't the objective. As it was, he thought it would fool a lot more than Niall's client.

The first person to use artificial hardening successfully had been Han Van Meergeren, the Vermeer forger, with his use of Bakelite, an early polymer, mixed into his paint, then baking the painting in an ordinary oven. Thing had become a little more complicated and sophisticated since that time.

John never had formal art training at school. The thought of the school he attended in the Gorbals having art classes for boys made him smile. In those days any boy showing interest in art and music was likely to get bullied; it was best to stay with football and woodwork.

He started messing with paint out of boredom, working at a factory where some of the men were given the job of repainting walls. It was supposed to be the same colour as the underlying old paint, the company colour, but the walls had darkened over the years with the atmosphere created by machines running two shifts a day.

There had been a girl on the packing line he fancied and, as he painted the wall, he left areas unpainted, in what his mate working further along the wall took to be a weird pattern. But across the room several of the women on the line stated talking.

"That's you, Sheena, look."

From a distance, his workmate saw, it was a good drawing of the girl's facial features using the lighter and darker shades to show her facial structure.

"You have a talent there, John," he said.

"You had better fill in the bloody holes in the paint job," said the line foreman, "if His Highness catches you, you will be for it."

'His Highness', the plant manager, already had and had been watching from a gantry way.

Company policy was that the managers wore suits, so the chance of relating in any meaningful way to hourly staff was virtually zero. He left it a day then spoke to John at a break, saying that the company would support night classes if he wanted to take them. John was quite surprised by the man's support and took him up on the offer.

It didn't last long; the company went under a year later but John had by then got the basics of composition, sketching and oil painting under his belt. He was hooked.

The back of the painting had become the best part of the fraud, he felt, with the French dealer label. It was genuine and only ten years younger than its alleged date.

He and Paul-André had dug out the box of labels still in the back of the gallery shop in Avignon. They had first come up with the con years ago - no several decades ago now - how time flies, John thought! It was in their heyday of selling forgeries together.

That was before everything went pear-shaped, as they say.

After seeing Niall and travelling south, John had walked into Paul-André's premises in Avignon, Galerie Deniaud, seeing how it had been modernised. Somehow it still felt the same. Paul-André was sitting, reading *Le Figaro* at the large desk. John had stood still inside the door until the owner realised that the person entering was not an anonymous tourist having a quick glance at the paintings for sale.

"John, my friend, so long… I didn't recognize you at first."

Later, over dinner and a good bottle of Meursault, Paul-André responded to John's question.

"Like you, I am old and I can't do time again; there is too little of my life left to waste that way. If you had come a year ago I would definitely have said no. But now there is just Michele… and she struggles."

His daughter had gone through a messy divorce and worked now in Avignon, trying to paint again. Her father sold her paintings in the gallery. It was spotty; her work was not 'chocolate box' appeal. Yet every now and again a customer would get passionate about it.

"The guy down the road with the electronics store

wants my location and the gallery is having difficulties financially. People spend their money on fooking video games instead of art these days."

John had burst out laughing. "You threw that 'fooking' in for the hell of it. It is more than twenty years since I heard you do your 'archetypal Maurice Chevalier'; you were doing the sale to that Irish couple."

Paul-André smiled. "So for the right price I will do only the validation, no more. I can get out of that if they take you off to the Old Bailey or hang you this time. You do the label and, if you get caught, John, you swiped it while I was busy with a customer. Is that a deal?"

"It's a deal, my friend, if you let me have three of those wonderful old labels. There are others I may do and I think that there could be another legend from France; I am not sure yet."

Paul-André said, "No John, two only; and the second one will be the one I took myself from that gallery in Lyon that time, remember? It is now out of business. Then at least I can appear a victim only one time."

"That will work perfectly; even better really."

Paul-André said, "Tomorrow we will look through the records but tonight we will finish this good wine."

18 STORNOWAY

The forty minute flight in the small Dornier commuter jet was uneventful and Catrin had a good view of Stornoway on the final descent. She had been told to take a warmer coat than a light raincoat; it was a good distance north and still could be cold and wet in May. She still took her light coat and packed a sweater that would go with her business suit, if necessary; she had by then had enough of her winter coat over the last months.

As she walked into the 'Arrivals' area a man in casual clothes stood next to a young uniformed officer. They introduced themselves as Detective Constable Alan Fergus and PC Stella Reid. Reid had been first-on-scene in response to the incident and would also drive them to the campus. Her patrol car was parked outside, next to the building.

"You are on the evening flight back?" asked Fergus.

"Yes, I allowed the full day, not being sure what to expect." She pointed at the small backpack. "And I brought some overnight things, just in case."

"Well, if we're done early and it's OK with my boss,

we will go back to the station and collect my car. I will give you a bit of a tour this afternoon. The forecast is fine for the flights today so you can probably get back this evening without problem. Let's see how it goes. Have you been to the Hebrides before?"

"No," said Catrin. "This is actually the furthest north I have ever been."

"We are going first to see the campus building and the break-in. Then we are seeing Robert Halverson, the security guard. I have copies of his statement and the incident report for you."

They were winding their way through town. Stella said, "So you are from Scotland Yard, an Art unit, then, DC Sayer?"

Catrin talked about her role and suddenly realised that the young PC in front was almost in awe. How fast you forget the newness of it all, she thought.

"So Stella, how long have you been here, in the job?" Catrin asked.

"I am from the island. I am still a probationer, coming back home after my training at Tulliallan and first assignment on the mainland. I've been back four months and a police officer a year now."

Tulliallan Castle, Catrin knew, was the training headquarters of Police Scotland.

"I'm Catrin, by the way. Is it nice to be back, Stella?"

"Yes, to be with the family."

Catrin saw her eyes wrinkle in amusement through the rear-view mirror.

Stella continued, "And to give some of the boys from my schooldays a hard time; payback time." She laughed.

Catrin kept putting Iain out of her mind; she had to concentrate on her work. He had met her on arrival at the station yesterday and she had spent the evening and most of the night with him at his flat. Then she had gone to the hotel and dropped her luggage before leaving almost immediately for the airport.

"We have asked the person responsible for the college art collection to help; Dr. Saunders. She wasn't around at the time of the incident," said DC Fergus as they arrived at the building.

The older woman who turned out to be Saunders led them to an area off the library, a long wall in the main building of the complex. "A number of the paintings here were off the wall, we found," Stella said.

Catrin turned to Fergus and Reid. "Which ones specifically, did you note?"

Stella had been diligent; she gave a rundown of the paintings found and their locations.

"So these two were being handled?" She looked. "Any fingerprints taken?"

"Of the frames and backs, yes," said Reid, 'but the security guard reported that the intruder was wearing gloves. We didn't find anything which raised flags in the database. Quite a few staff and students must have touched them at times."

"Dr. Saunders, these paintings are by Alistair Gault - the AG signature in the corner, right?"

"Yes, indeed. So you know Gault's work? That is interesting."

"Why?"

"Well, he was not a known artist. He worked at the Kelvingrove Museum and painted as a pastime. So I wouldn't have expected others to know him. We have his painting because several of my predecessors knew him - he taught here for a time - and he donated them to us. They are actually quite good, typical of the early twentieth century style. We also have several that are not displayed; nor framed, actually."

Catrin had seen in one painting that had been removed from the wall an element that fitted exactly the theory she had worked on during the train ride south on the last trip.

Again Catrin looked carefully.

"Dr. Saunders, I am going to ask you to remove the Gaults from display and, with the others you have, place them in a secure location, at least for the time being. I can't tell you more but it is in the best interests of the university, I think.

"Also, I would like to photograph each one before I leave here, including the ones not on display, if that can be arranged. I have a small camera."

"Well, Detective Sayer, we can do that, and perhaps a little better than that. I have high quality photographs of all our artwork prepared by our staff photographer. Would you like those? On a USB drive; they are quite big files?"

"That would be wonderful. Do you have the backs photographed also?"

"No," said Saunders, puzzled. "There are no dealer stamps or marks. They were given by Alistair directly – the college framed them, I believe."

"I need that confirmation too, if you could, in time. I would still like to see the other paintings with my own eyes. Photographs never do full justice, do they?"

Dr. Saunders smiled. "You must be an art lover or an artist masquerading as a police officer."

The three police officers were later directed to the coffee shop in the building. Sipping the coffee, Catrin suddenly thought of something and phoned Susan Hetherington.

They were now on first name terms. "Susan, when is the funeral for Andrew Gault? You said you would be attending?"

"It's now next Tuesday, in Oban. Apparently a relative from Australia is attending and they waited the extra time for his arrival."

"And you will be collecting the Gault art afterwards?"

"Yes, Dr Bryant will leave following the funeral but I decided to stay over and do it myself the following day. Elizabeth and Mary are on board with that; they say keeping busy will help."

"Thanks. Do you have Elizabeth's phone number to hand? I don't have the file with me."

As they left the college she phoned Elizabeth Gault.

"Miss Gault, this is Detective Constable Sayer. You mentioned, I recall, that you had been wondering what to do with your mother's possessions, the ones that are not needed in the accommodation she is moving into. Will you be moving things to your home?

"Some of them, yes, and some to Niall's. He had offered earlier and has room."

"Right. Have you talked to Mr. Irvin since our visit?"

"Yes, he was a bit surprised in the interest in our art by Mrs. Hetherington and the Kelvingrove Museum but was quite impressed that the museum followed up, I think. He has offered to store paintings and other items. His plans, he said, are to have some of the paintings cleaned and framed or re-framed nicely for family members, as a memory of Alistair.

"I think he, like me, was quite excited about the possibility of the Museum hanging one in due course, once I explained that they would be returned after evaluation. He offered to stay and assist after the funeral, if he could – as a lawyer, he is quite busy, I think. I told him that the museum staff would be doing that the day after the funeral. He said it was probably best if he came another time."

"Thank you, Miss Gault."

They were stopping at a house as she finished the call and she soon found herself in the front room turning down the offer of more coffee. The museum guard, Robert Halverson, was part of a contract security group at the college. He had his right arm in a cast. He looked fit, active.

They went through the preamble of introductions and Catrin said that the attempted theft of the paintings may tie into other lines of investigation. Halverson expressed his surprise. "None of them are Picassos. Some they have around the college are downright weird, I think."

Catrin questioned him about his report.

He had been on routine patrol and had no indication that there was an intruder. It was not a response situation; if so, the operating rules would have required him to call the police immediately before going anywhere nearer, he said.

"I came around the corner by the wall with the paintings - have you been there?"

Fergus said, "Yes we have just come from the site."

"I saw a space on the wall. I had just put the lights on; we switch them on and off at certain points in the building on the check. Then I noticed a painting on the floor. Unusual, but could just have been a careless finish by the staff. I was going to check with Terry - he's my teammate who did the first round - but I saw that a light in the office across the hall was off when it should have been on. It was part of the set I had put on earlier, so I shone my torch in there.

"His arm came down as I went in and I felt my wrist go as I was shoved inside. I actually landed on the same arm, so I was in agony, I tell you. All I could say is that he is tall, solid, and had gloves. I saw one of his gloves clearly.

"And he knew how to get in without setting off the alarm system. I pressed the button on my personal radio and called out, I was in pain. It must have scared him off. By the time I got up he was gone."

"Where were the paintings?"

The one on the floor by the wall was left where I first saw it. Another, from another space I saw, had been dropped on the floor outside the office. I didn't pick it up and when Terry got there I told him to make sure no-one else did."

"Well done," said Catrin, "so you think he just ran off, not taking anything?"

"Yes," said Halverson. "From the sound of his feet he didn't think about stopping, he was gone."

Catrin asked, "I know it was fast but, how did he move, push you, do you recall? You look fit, so it wouldn't be easy for him, I think."

"Let me put it this way. I was in the Royal Regiment of Scotland. He knew how to take people out, I think."

"What did he hit you with?"

"It was some sort of baton or stick, not long but with weight. It just took my wrist out. The doctor said that I was lucky, given the break, it could have been worse. He could have crushed or splintered a bone, he said, when I told him about it."

They wrapped up with Halverson and left. Catrin asked about CCTV recordings at the college.

"There was nothing useful for the building," said

Fergus, "and nothing standing out so far in the review of nearby coverage. It's a campus and there are some tall students, so we are still working it through."

"What about the ports of entry?"

"We haven't looked that far," said Fergus, a little reactively. "It was a break-in, with nothing taken."

A man's arm was broken violently, thought Catrin, but she just said, "Right. Do you think you could check any coverage for the ferries going out the following day for anyone tall enough to fit? And perhaps also the airlines – they will have footage."

"Sure," said Fergus, "if my boss approves. This sounds a lot bigger issue than a simple local robbery."

"It could well be. And violence is involved. There could be more of this if my guess is right. And any 'possibles' you find, can you send them directly over to this officer, PC Kevin Shortt?"

She gave Shortt's number. "I will give him a call, let him know. Alan, Stella, I would love to see more of the island but another time, I think. I need to head back."

Fergus said, "I will call the airline. We know everyone here. You will be on the next one out, but I hope you do come back and I can show you round. I love your accent, not having one myself." He grinned.

Stella said, "DC Fergus, what a sweet-talking policeman you are. I will tell Carol; that's his wife."

She winked at Catrin.

Catrin laughed, "You are in trouble now, Alan. And anyway, I have met a nice man in Glasgow, would you believe?"

In the departure lounge she reported to Worsley her findings and conclusions. Jane said she would phone Sinclair. "When do you get back into Glasgow?"

Catrin told her.

"Sinclair will call you; plan on returning to Govan and giving an evening briefing to the team if we can get enough of them together. Otherwise it will be tomorrow morning."

"Yes ma'am."

She closed the call then saw the text from Iain that had come in earlier, querying her availability. She was about to call him when the boarding call came. She didn't want to talk to him sitting on the jet next to someone with their ear twelve inches from hers. She left it until her arrival in Glasgow. It was going to be one of those 'sorry but can't explain' moments again.

19 UNRAVELLING THE WOOL

It was 7.15 p.m. on Friday. Sinclair had just asked Catrin to update the team. Catrin was nervous now. She had expected Worsley on the discussion by conference call but she had just heard her announce that Worsley's own boss, Superintendent Jack Taylor, was sitting in also. Taylor had a raft of responsibilities in Serious Crime Command at the Met. While he considered this little Art Crime Unit his own, as indeed it was, why he was spending part of his Friday evening listening to this development worried her.

To add to her nervousness, DCI Strachan said as she arrived, "This had better be worthwhile, Eric, pulling me away now. You know what is going down."

We don't though, thought Catrin. You won't tell us.

"Our assigned part of the Gault investigation was the potential theft or fraud associated with a list of fourteen Scottish Colourist painting," she began.

"Reverend Andrew Gault wanted a meeting with the Kelvingrove Museum because he had concerns, but not proof, that that his father Alistair Gault, a former conservator at the museum, had paintings by at least two of the Colourists, Cadell and Peploe. I now suspect he thought they were stolen during the course of World War II and his father had put his own signature on them.

"My investigations have led me to the conclusion that Alistair Gault did not steal any paintings or produce fraudulent copies.

"What he did, I believe, was make minor conservation repairs to some of these paintings, perhaps. They were relatively new at the time, almost contemporary pieces. The movement of the paintings as part of the vast collection at the Kelvingrove was a major undertaking. If some paintings were damaged we will not know; there are no records to this effect that Susan Hetherington can find.

"Gault clearly loved the works by these artists. Whether associated with actual repairs or not, he reproduced exact copies of some sections of at least fourteen Colourist painting on the list that Reverend Gault possessed. He then finished new paintings on these canvasses, with other areas totally new, not copied, and then he signed them with his own name. This is a perfectly legitimate process, particularly so if he publicly acknowledged the origin or inspiration at the time. But that is all in the past."

Catrin began to feel is she was giving a lecture, but there wasn't a sound, she clearly had their attention.

"These paintings form part of his overall collection. He never sold paintings. They are currently in various places; the late Reverend Gault's home, the home in Fort William of a former work colleague, now deceased, and some are in the college on Stornoway. There are also, we know, some in the possession of Niall Irvin, a lawyer associated with the Connolly gang. There maybe more, of course, including three paintings we know of in Kinnington Church here in Glasgow.

"These fourteen specific paintings, with adjustment to the signatures, could be turned into extremely convincing 'new finds' of each of the major 'Colourist' artists. There is nothing quite as effective as a familiar feature by an artist turning up in a painting sent for validation to convince the appraiser of an association."

She paused and took a drink of water.

Strachan had calmed down and softened a little. "Sayer, this is interesting but you said these works are not 'first team' value… not big money, so that's a lot of effort."

"Yes ma'am. And the person closest to this overall investigation that knows of these works and is indeed trying to acquire them is, I think, Niall Irvin. The person who might also be interested in these items is Francis Milne in Edinburgh. He bought a number of legitimate originals at auctions, the most recent being only a couple of months ago. And I understand from your earlier comment that he is a person of interest associated with the Edinburgh drug gang activity."

Strachan nodded, "So these would be used as 'tokens of good will' between the two groups as they build a new business relationship?"

Catrin said, "Or payment in part or whole for drug shipments. They are increasing in value. We are talking one or two million pounds in perceived value here."

"And," poked in Sinclair, "we know Milne is an avid Scots Nationalist. It will appeal to his ego to own paintings by these artists."

Catrin said, "I think, ma'am, Irvin already has some of these paintings for use in such transactions that he obtained from the artist himself, ones that may fit the style and could be re-signed by a good forger. He and Connolly may well be happy to find uses for paintings they currently think are unknown and valueless in a drug deal."

"That's a dangerous game for them, Sayer, if you are right," responded Strachan.

Worsley's voice came over the phone. "It's a timing issue. If these forgeries come to light only years later, who will know when the fraud took place?"

Catrin continued, "But it won't come out. It is all behind the scenes. I think that Milne will be keeping these paintings for his own pleasure, not re-selling them. For a painting fraud to be successful you need two things; a convincing painting and secondly a convincing story, a history of where it came from, where it has been. That normally involves documentation. The label on the back of the painting or the documentation provided with it is as important as the quality of the alteration to the painting itself.

"It's here that Irvin has the advantage. There haven't been art dealers or other museums involved, which happens with many paintings. He hasn't had to forge anything, perhaps, other than family documents and old Kelvingrove or other museum documentation. He will tie everything to his access to them through his uncle and Alistair's ability to fix the original records. Irvin will likely bleed these in slowly to Milne over time, a customer who cannot get them authenticated through any legitimate channel."

She paused, looking at Sinclair. "I am almost done, sir."

He responded, "That's fine Catrin, we need this understanding. DCI Strachan knows this has bigger implications."

Catrin continued, "First they want to be sure that they get as many of the fourteen that most resemble established works as they can. If they get other Gaults they could be for future use, or simply to just keep the other paintings by him from the market and retain his invisibility to the public.

"Irvin must be re-thinking his plans, now that he knows of the interest shown by the Kelvingrove Museum; Elizabeth Gault passed that on. It may have been the reason for the burglary at the college.

"Given that the major set of Gault paintings is in Oban in the household of Mary Gault and there are also a small number in Fort William, these homes are now targets - and we know that the burglary in Stornoway resulted in a vicious assault. Then there are three paintings in Kinnington Church and I am sure at least one there is one of the fourteen. He will try to get these before the Kelvingrove does a major review of the work, I am sure. We need to prevent these burglaries if we can.

"I am done, sir."

Sinclair stood to take back control of the meeting.

"So let's concentrate. We have a lot more now on the paintings issue. We have a potential stronger link to the 'placebo' issue for Eileen's group to deal with, when they can; Irvin clearly had a strong motive for removing Alexander Gault from the scene, with his control of the paintings and his worries about forgery.

"We also have three locations we know of that could be subject to burglary. When Catrin called me from Lewis she had already established the time of the funeral of Alexander Gault. Our minds were on the same page; the burglary risk in the home of a deceased is highest around the time of a funeral or immediately afterwards, we all know that. The houses are often empty or there are unusual comings and goings. Neighbours aren't surprised and they have a natural reserve about interfering, given the unhappy events.

"We are going to assign surveillance to these locations; Oban, at the Gault home; Fort William, at the Thompson home, and the church in Kinnington. Although, I have to be honest, there is a limit to the budget for this."

Jack Taylor's Yorkshire tones came out of the speaker. "For the next week, at least, until DCI Strachan's current operation is complete, you can have what you need, I will fix that. Just keep this confidential, keep it clean, and keep it safe. If it goes belly up, there is a lot more than a broken wrist at stake."

Strachan said, "Superintendent, it is not simply about payment for resources; I also want to ensure the minimum number of officers are informed, given our main issue at present. Even Police Scotland is not watertight on this, as you will appreciate.

"I support this operation going ahead, nevertheless. If DC Sayer is correct and Irvin and Connolly are trying to cheat the Milne's in this manner, it gives us some interesting opportunities in the future. I appreciate that the bottom line is that we want to prevent any injuries to people, but for me, above all, this surveillance must not compromise our larger operation. I hope that is clear."

Jack Taylor said, "You are right, Eileen. As usual. Work it as you see fit."

I knew it, thought Catrin; they have someone on the inside of whatever it is. And it is big. That's why Taylor is sitting in on this briefing.

20 GALERIE DENIAUD

Daniella Milne was visiting Niall Irvin's flat in central Glasgow. She admired his taste in décor. There was a woman's hand here, she felt, but no photographs of her. An unknown woman in Niall's life intrigued her.

Even more than that, though, she was captivated by the painting of the vase and flowers with the signature of Cadell at the bottom. She had already examined the frame and back closely. To her eyes, the backing was the original and showed no signs of disturbance.

Neil stood next to her. "As I told you, a relative gave this painting to me, told me to keep it. One day it would be valuable, he said, adding 'just don't talk about it to people until you are old enough to appreciate it'. There may well be more mixed in with his paintings at my late uncle's home, I believe."

Daniella said, "How many?"

Niall looked thoughtful. "You know, I can't really say. I can't exactly go trammeling in searching at this time. Some may come to light now my aunt has allowed the Kelvingrove Museum have a look at Alistair's own work.

"To be honest, I am a bit out of my depth. It's not my area at all."

When he had delivered the painting, John Dalton had told Niall not to sell it to the buyer at all; it would sell itself. The customer has to find the solution and she will see it, and then work out herself how best to check its provenance. Providing she did that - and that was all she did - he was home free, John said. He just needed to keep his fiction as close to the truth as he could.

Daniella said, "Assuming this is genuine, Niall, this would be worth, probably, £200,000 or perhaps much more in an auction, these days, I would think. Really top works by the Colourists are going for about half a million. But if you put this in an auction it would mean, I suppose, exposing your uncle... which I take it you don't really want to do."

Niall just shook his head.

She added, "And if you did, you would not benefit from it anyway if it became the subject of a legal dispute over ownership."

Niall looked pained. "While Aunt Mary is alive, I don't want my family embarrassed. I tried to stop my uncle from pursuing this issue but he had a mania for the truth of it - he went to the Kelvingrove himself to talk to them and was so worked up he had a heart attack. After Aunt Mary dies, I don't really care about the publicity, frankly. My cousin Elizabeth will be shocked. As to legal disputes, I think we can hold our own there but it is a drag on time and it will be costly."

Daniella said, "Look, I have a solution. I will do some discreet checking on this painting. If it turns out to be genuine, Francis and I will buy it from you at a fair price – we can agree on that as part of the larger negotiations with Dominic.

"Nothing is then visible; we get paintings to keep that we collect and, in years to come, we can find a way to make them public with no exposure on your part. If you are able to find any more that your family... obtained, we will agree to take them on the same basis."

Niall nodded. "I should get the opportunity to see what's at my uncle's place after the funeral while I am in the home. I think this is a very elegant solution you have found, Daniella, seeing as you like these paintings. It's only when Dominic said Francis had bought something by a Scottish artist called Cadell that it rang a bell...."

He paused, looking worried again. "You will be discreet in these enquiries you need to make, I take it?"

"Very much so. It is in both our interests." She had photographed the dealers label on the panel on the back of the painting. It looked as old as the frame.

Niall knew she was going to pose her questions to Galerie Deniaud.

"Daniella, I really value your expertise and thinking on this. We all could benefit."

~~

Paul-André had seen the car draw up and the man get out, talking on his mobile phone as he looked at items in the window of the shop. A few seconds after the window shopper closed his phone, the business phone on his desk rang.

Her French was fluent but the Spanish intonation came through. She introduced herself and wanted to verify information about a painting with a dealer stamp number that she was buying.

"That is a very old number in our system, Madame. It

could take some time. Yes it is possible to do so, of course, our records go back much further than that. We have been established in Avignon for a very long time."

He listened intently, as the man outside came in and, seeing him on the phone, shook his hand to indicate there was no rush. He took himself into the gallery, examining other paintings.

Paul-André continued, consciously keeping his voice at the same level. "Yes Madame, indeed, Avignon is not Paris. A number of Scottish and Irish artists in Paris did sell works through us in the past when they worked in France. My grandfather had a special contact with the Académie Julian in Paris; his brother taught there. A number of artists from Scotland were students there, I believe, and we sold some of the painting of the students to help them pay their way, I think."

"But Madame, we are a gallery, not a library. We do appraisals, sell art. I have no time to go searching through our ledgers at present. Perhaps next week I can look. A customer has just entered the store."

When John Dalton had visited him and they had worked out a suitable ledger entry to use, John had said, "Make it difficult, but not too difficult. The target is female but she is linked to Connolly somehow; so you don't want a break-in."

"My appraisal fee… for what, Madame?"

"Yes, Madame, for an appraisal fee I will look in my ledgers now. Thank you for seeing my point. Can I have a name and credit card number after all… it is a phone call."

He wrote down the details.

"One moment, Madame Milne."

He looked at the customer and mouthed an apology, but he simply replied, "No problem, I am not in a rush."

He was local, Paul-André could tell, but looked tough, would be the only way he would describe him.

While he knew what he needed to say to the woman, he went into the back room. He took his time before pulling out the appropriate ledger, taking it to the desk in the main area and opening it laboriously to the right page.

"Madame? Yes, I am checking. It is noted as a sale on 23 February 1903 to a Madame Cynthia Jacquet of a painting in oil on canvas by an artist with the initials F. C.; that is the way we recorded the artist then. It was mounted in an ebonized frame with gold trim and… please, a moment, Madame."

He paused, turning a page forward then back.

"Three paintings sold to Madame Jacquet over a period of eight months were returned the following month, I see, including this one. It does not say why but it was a long time ago; perhaps she had a financial problem, who knows? I am looking through further. I see no more information on the sale of this one in the next months. I can only assume that the painting was probably returned to the artist if it remained unsold; that would have been standard practice. So I do not think I can help you with a purchaser after all, I am sorry."

He listened.

"The artist initials will refer to another ledger, Madame. That is the way we operated here then, with everything being hand-written. The ledger is in the back, I think, the one for this period. I can get it for you to verify the name but, as I say, I do have another customer waiting so could I call you back?

He listened. "What, no need, Madame?"

He had been carefully searching the following pages for the benefit of the 'customer' who had him in his peripheral vision.

'Thank you Madame Milne. I will charge your card two hundred and fifty euros, my fee as agreed, Madame. I am very grateful; it is very generous. Do you require an image of the ledger entry sent to you for your own records, as that would be included in the cost? No… well then, thank you for calling and I am glad to have been of assistance."

He put the phone down and said, "Sir, my apologies for the delay, and how can I help you?"

The man came forward as Paul-André closed the ledger. "The work in the window, the ladies with the parasols, is it an original watercolour or a print? I did not see a print number on it, just a signature."

"It is an original, sir, by Miss Michele Souverain, a local artist, and it is very nice, if I may say so. I think it is very collectable."

They discussed price and the man bought it. Paul-André affixed a modern computer-generated dealer label to the back.

"We label or stamp everything we sell, sir. A dealer label always helps with the future valuation of any work and my family has been in business here for one hundred and forty years. If you ever have this re-framed, retain the label somewhere, I suggest. We have a good reputation."

He waited for a further thirty minutes after the car outside departed before using his mobile phone to call the number John Dalton had given him.

"John, the call came as you thought it would. It was a woman, a Daniella Milne, sounded Spanish but fluent French. She did not visit in person but there was someone outside at the time who then came in and listened. He did not really know much; it may be someone she organized to give her feedback on things from my end.

"I don't think there were any problems, though. The register entry for the painting by Frédéric Carron worked out well; I did not even have to find and confuse the entry in our artist register, she was in that much of a rush.

"Good day, my friend; it was good to work with you again."

He had made a handsome profit from his friend John, plus a small *cadeau* from the mark herself and he had sold his daughter's latest painting for a very good price. A good day's work.

~~

John Dalton called Niall and told him.

"So now I will start on the next three paintings, Niall. These will appear to be from the same estate in the Highlands, donated at the time the museum started moving their items back into the Kelvingrove. I will probably need some more expense money during this phase if I don't find a property with the right profile first time, please tell Dominic, but so far I am OK. When can I have the paintings?"

Niall said, "I have two, the third should come my way in the next week."

"Right, let me know."

The following morning Daniella called Niall.

"Two hundred and fifty thousand, Niall."

"For the painting, Daniella, good grief, I mean, that is more than generous, I must say. But you know the art, not me. I take it that it all checked out, however you did it."

"Yes, Niall, it checked out. It was sold through a gallery with links to the art school Cadell attended in Paris then returned by the purchaser; the dealer sent it back to Cadell and I guess that is how it ended back in Scotland; probably he brought it back with him.

"I like it, Niall, it's an early work and probably wouldn't be top notch at auction but I want it for our collection. Francis says he likes my idea of receiving part of our terms in paintings, but doesn't want any… cheapness with Dominic and you. He wants to do this right.

"So that is our offer for the first painting, to show goodwill, and we will pay a straight one hundred and fifty thousand apiece thereafter for any more you find, providing each one is a recognized Colourist artist and we like the painting. Nice round numbers and it keeps it simple, don't you think?"

Niall smiled to himself. John Dalton had been right on the money. By leaving her to find the solution she had taken ownership of the findings, scant as they were for a purchase at this price.

"Thank you, Daniella, that sounds wonderful to me; I will let Dominic know. And my best wishes to Francis and Steve. I will get the painting to you as soon as possible. And, certainly, I will look out for any others after I attend the funeral. You never know."

He called Dominic, who sent Kevin, his driver, over to collect the painting and deliver it in person to the Milne household.

Dominic just saw it as a block deal; if they all went through it was around £1.5 million cost reduction off uncut heroin and cocaine. His mind turned that into the downstream profit at street level. Not bad really, for a few Scottish paintings by someone nobody knows, he thought.

21 SURVEILLANCE

It was just after midnight and into Saturday morning when Catrin reached her hotel room.

She and Peter McPherson were assigned as a team, to pull alternate twelve-hour turns with two other officers from Govan. They were assigned to the Kinnington Church stakeout. McPherson, she learned, had family commitments which wouldn't let him go to Oban at present.

She had hoped for the Oban stakeout, which she saw as the primary target. Strachan had said candidly that Catrin's Welsh accent would be noticed less in Glasgow than in the smaller locations and she already had some familiarity with the church. Worsley had agreed, so that was that. Sinclair and Shortt were looking after Oban and Fort William with a number of local officers in each city they knew were reliable.

"Not ideal, I know," said Sinclair to the group, "but it minimizes the communication flow and is only for a few days. If nothing happens by Wednesday, we will review it then."

Catrin was not going home this weekend but she would not have a lot of free time, either.

On the table in her room was a bowl of fruit delivered by the hotel with a note saying 'Any arrests pending? Iain.'

She realised he was talking about himself and that she hadn't phoned him as promised. On arrival back in Glasgow she had spoken to him briefly, explaining her need to go into the office. She had also told him she would call him later from there, but hadn't done so.

She sent a text. 'Sorry, I forgot. I was up to my eyes. Thank you for the fruit. Will talk tomorrow… or now?'

He called her right back and they talked for a couple of minutes when he said, "Catrin, you sound dead on your feet. Go get some sleep. Do you fancy breakfast?"

"At the hotel, say seven a.m.?" she asked.

"In the restaurant?"

"No, in my room."

After making love they decided, after all, that a breakfast in the dining room made more sense than trying to get room service.

He had arrived expecting Catrin to be free on Saturday. She explained that part of her current work was now surveillance and it would be shift work with another team. There was no real time free at all.

"It really is a different life in the police," he said. "I was going to apologise to you because I had to pop into work this afternoon myself for a short while. But you are my first copper, so I guess it is a new experience."

Catrin nodded. She wasn't going to apologise for her reality.

"What does Laura do?" she asked. He had mentioned

the name of his former fiancée during their Chinese meal, talking about the holiday in Thailand.

"She is in insurance. Now she's training to be an actuary; she has a degree in maths. Insurance, banking, downtown work; we had similar hours and lifestyles. So that's why I find your work hours to be a bit strange."

He looked at her. "I think it is a bit of a change for both of us, right? You with your job and your ceramics, me with my life at the bank and helping at the shop. We just need to take it easy and see how it works out because we like each other."

She held his hand and smiled. "Oh, yes."

The older couple seated at a table across the restaurant, people watchers, concluded they were honeymooners.

~ ~

Saturday turned into Sunday and Monday. The stake-out location chosen for the church was an observation van placed in a row of cars parked diagonally across from the church entrance. Kinnington Church sat on a crossroad junction with two sides, including the main doors, facing roads. The van was parked next to a high wall; it meant they would not have neighbours watching the comings and goings from the back of the vehicle.

They had clear view of two sides of the church adjoining the roads but no coverage of the two alleys that went behind the church, forming the two remaining sides of the perimeter. On one of these there was a solid brick wall but the other one on an alley had a double door that was locked.

They solved that problem with a small black box; a compact, temporary surveillance camera pointed down the longer of the two alleys. A police technician clamped it to a telegraph pole on the side road and fixed a video feed back into the van. It wasn't perfect, as traffic at the crossroads often backed up to obscure the view, but it was the best they could do.

Everyone involved had been involved in stakeouts before. It was one of the few times when working at Brixton that uniformed officers could work in plain clothes, so Catrin had experience of the boredom of it all before.

Catrin and Peter worked well together. What they were instructed to do was clear; unless other circumstances dictated, they were to observe only, photograph and document the intrusion and exit of the perpetrator(s). Only if they received specific instruction from DCI Sinclair that normal procedures could be followed should they make any arrest, if that was feasible. And Catrin knew that this would only happen if the delicate operation that so absorbed Strachan was out of the way.

At dusk on Monday, two hours before the shift change, Catrin was convinced the next robbery would take place on Tuesday in Oban during or after the funeral - and she would miss it.

She was wrong.

PART 2

CHURCH

22 LANGMUIR

Langmuir set his class straight into the case examples; there was no preambular lecture. He wanted them off-balance as they went into the Kinnington Church incident.

He started handing out slim briefing books.

"Most of you know something about it. What we are not going to do is re-analyse the event; after all, it was relatively fast and straightforward. Nor will we repeat the review by PIRC."

PIRC was the acronym for the office of the Police Investigations & Review Commissioner, the watchdog group that investigated serious incidents involving the police in Scotland.

"What I want from you are two things. First, I want your assessment of the disciplinary actions, if any, that should have been taken, with whom and why. I will interview each of you on that subject, playing the role of the Crown representative; and it will be taped. Second, you will be expected to make a statement on the incident to BBC Scotland, which is why we have Paul and Sharon here. It won't be a gentle interview, will it Paul?"

"It will be just like the interview I did at the time," smiled Courtney.

"What we will then do is have everyone watch everyone else's performance and discuss what went well and what did not."

He could see the expressions on some in the group starting to grow a little more apprehensive.

He walked to the front of the room again, opening his own copy of the briefing book.

Langmuir continued, "No incident that goes wrong goes to plan; so something in that plan was wrong or was missing. Like all so-called accidents, often it is the combinations of small issues that create the final problem, the one that you, as a senior officer, have to explain to the press and your superiors. Generally you have to do this with incomplete information and little time to prepare. So let's look at it."

He held open his binder, showing the page.

"We start with DS McPherson's written report, from the file. It is page seven in your binder. Something like this, probably in more garbled form, would be the first news that you, as a senior officer, would have received."

Langmuir read the report aloud.

'I was returning on foot to the observation post across from the church after a brief absence for personal needs. I saw and heard people in distress in the immediate vicinity of Kinnington Church. I ran over and saw a man's legs sticking out of the main door to the church; he was lying inside the doorway. DC Sayer was in the middle of the pavement in front of the church door, swaying slightly with a Maglite torch held in her right hand. Her phone was open in her left hand. In front of her was man with his hands on a vehicle, standing by the rear nearside passenger door, complaining about his finger. The rear passenger door was open and a mobile phone was in the gutter. The man later identified himself to me as Mr. Niall Irvin.

'On the ground beside DC Sayer was another man, face down, handcuffed with his face in a pool of vomit. He was uttering threats. I recognized him as Colin Cheney. By him were two paintings.

'I approached DC Sayer who told me she had arrested but not cautioned them. She asked me to secure their mobile phones and complete the arrest. I could see that DC Sayer was injured; the side of her face was covered in blood, as was her sleeve. Blood was coming through a hole – a long slash in her left cheek - and also from her mouth.

'She looked unsteady. I therefore relieved her of the Maglite and handcuffed the man by the car, sat him on the ground and retrieved his mobile phone. I turned round just as DC Sayer collapsed.

'I checked DC Sayer's pulse and airway then placed her in the semi-prone position as per my First Aid training. I checked the condition of the man inside the doorway and determined him to be unconscious with damage to his head. I used my jacket to prop the man's head inside the door, checked he was breathing but did not move him. I did not know the identity of this man. I heard sirens approaching and picked up the mobile phone DC Sayer had dropped. It was an open line and I heard DCI Sinclair's voice and so I advised him of the situation.

'I then saw on the ground by Cheney a baton of some sort, with some blood on it. I did not touch it.

'DCI Sinclair said he had just instructed the attending units to silence their sirens as soon as possible. He commanded me to make sure that the persons arrested were brought directly to Govan Police Station and I was to be personally responsible for ensuring that they had no communications with each other or anyone else until Sinclair's arrival at the station.

'I cautioned each person, placed then in separate vehicles with similar instructions to the officers transporting them after I had first searched each man for any weapons or communication devices.

'DCI Sinclair had instructed me to report immediately to Govan Police Station once the prisoners were on their way. I handed over the incident scene to Inspector Robertson who had just arrived, briefed him, and then obeyed DCI Sinclair's instruction."

Langmuir looked up at the silent group. "It was obviously much more complicated than that, of course. But that is your starting point. What do you ask for next?"

There was silence in the room. Langmuir didn't wait, his voice became harsh. "Come on, people, the press will be getting news of something soon, some neighbours saw it happen, so look lively."

One said, "I want to talk to Sinclair, now."

Langmuir said, "He is not taking calls, he is making them. He is already on the road back from Oban and is talking with DCI Strachan. He doesn't speak with senior officers, one way or another, until he gets to Govan. Sorry, you are out of luck. Other answers, please."

One of the three women on the course, a woman of Indian ethnicity, said, "Then get my bloody car here; we are going over to Govan, right now."

"Right; right," said Langmuir, smiling, liking the way she had settled into the scenario and then looking at the others, either flicking through the briefing folder or looking uncertain, "It's your patch; you own it. You are not an outsider. You need to be there. So what else do you do; quickly now, please?"

They weren't looking so relaxed now, he thought.

23 THE KINNINGTON CHURCH INCIDENT

Niall Irvin and Colin Cheney had worked out a plan to take paintings from the Kinnington and Oban locations sequentially. They had decided to leave the Fort William site alone completely at this time; Niall was not very comfortable with the fact it was a woman alone who did not go out much and that probably the neighbours kept an eye out for each other.

Connolly's people had all kinds of contacts wanting drugs, including people working in private security firms. While Catrin and other police officers at Govan were meeting to decide the next steps on her return from Stornoway, a man in a uniform passed a newly-cut key for a Yale lock to the side door of Kinnington Church to a woman he knew. Two hours later Cheney had it.

It had been the same set-up at the university in Stornoway; it was an unidentified colleague of the security guard Halverson who had abetted the break-in with a swipe key and a security code.

But after the botch-up there, when the primary

painting had been left behind by Cheney, Irvin took the plunge to accompany him and check the goods that he brought out. He had seen the two paintings in the church and one was useful but he would take both. He wasn't sure if they had more by Alistair; the parishioner he had casually asked after attending a service had no idea.

Accompanying Cheney was a risk, but one he felt he needed to take. Cheney worked to instructions but had no idea, really, what to take.

Niall had dropped him further down the road and parked. This should be quick, he thought, and then they would head out to Oban. Cheney was going to meet with someone up there who had a small van. Niall had a reservation at the Caledonian Hotel on the waterfront so that he was close by for the funeral.

On Tuesday he would go to the Gault home early. He would re-check the painting locations before they went to the church for the funeral service and would call Cheney to let him know. There were three specific paintings he had picked out on a previous visit. He had a set of 'sticky dots' with him; one on each painting edge should make it work for Cheney, he hoped. Irvin had already decided to leave his aunt's favorite in place, as much as he would like it; its departure would be too noticeable. He would work on that one later on.

The rest of Alistair's paintings could go through the evaluation process at the Kelvingrove Museum, he thought. Who knows where that might lead? He was not sure whether the decision by Alexander to go to the museum would turn out to be curse or a blessing in the long run, but he couldn't change it now. The three paintings he had had in mind would be enough.

Cheney had no reason to suspect that the church was under surveillance, it was just his natural caution and past experience that made him wait until the traffic flow at the cross roads involved a large van. It blocked the view to the alley beside the church. People would focus on the van and the driver, he thought, as he apparently ambled into the alley. A quick check, then he inserted the key and entered the side door without a problem. He closed it carefully, stood still and listened for the silence to reassure him that the church was empty. He didn't need to hang around but he was in no rush. He knew where the two paintings were located.

~~

In three days of surveillance Catrin and Peter McPherson had covered a lot of conversational ground. They would never be friends but they understood each other and got along. McPherson's son had a bad stutter, he had told her, his progress in treatment seemed to stall or reverse whenever his father was away for work reasons. He was appreciative that DCI Sinclair always tried to keep him close to home; hence the reason why he had not been selected for duty at Fort William or Oban.

Around 5.45 p.m. a sinus headache that had started in the afternoon was bothering McPherson so much he told Sayer he would walk to the chemist's shop nearby and get something, visit the toilets in the café they had been using and bring back fresh tea for both of them. Each shift had to cover the bio-breaks in this way, it was nothing unusual. He picked up the Thermos flask and headed out.

As he walked, he used the time off-watch alone to call home, check up with his wife and say goodnight to his younger child, who would be in bed before he finished his shift.

The service at Kinnington Church had been well-attended on Sunday and Michael Hart had been busy talking to people afterwards socially, rather than on church business. It was only when he got to work on Monday morning that he realised he had left his leather-bound business planner, with all his notes, address book and plans for the week ahead on the side table in the office he shared with another church staff member. He got through his working day without it but knew he would need to collect it on his way home. He was on the road for the next two days and it was a vital tool for him, for professional work as well as church responsibilities.

He parked in the clergy parking spot at the church, not even locking his car. He knew it would be deserted at this time. As he rapidly unlocked and opened the main door and entered, a tall man was standing there, two paintings held in one hand, a mobile phone in the other. He was talking to someone and apparently had not heard the church door open. They looked at each other.

Michael could only say, "The church isn't open now," before he realised that the man was an intruder; these were the paintings the police officer had spoken about. The man dropped them and, instinctively, Hart bent down to pick them up. It was as if his head exploded and he felt his shins scrape as his legs slid down two of the entrance steps - and then it was blackness.

At 5.51 p.m. Catrin saw Michael Hart drive into the car park, unlock the main church door and enter. She photographed his entry and noted the time before calling McPherson, but his phone was engaged. She had placed Sinclair, McPherson and Worsley all in her speed dial.

Within seconds, she saw a movement at the door but did not see Hart come out. She checked with the binoculars. Hart's feet were just extending out of the door; he must be prone on the ground and he wasn't moving. He could have fallen, but…

Catrin grabbed the large Maglite torch from the storage bin it rested in and ran from the van. She pressed the speed dial on her mobile for Peter again; it was still engaged. As she ran, thinking of possible scenarios, she had the fleeting thought that the heavy, metal torch could serve as a light source and baton if needed.

She pressed the number for Sinclair before she crossed the road. As he answered she told him she needed backup at the church urgently, she was entering the premises as a man was collapsed on the floor in the doorway and she was alone. He had no time to ask for more as she was nearly at the door and had closed the call.

In the failing light and the darkness of the entrance Catrin switched on the torch then slowly pulled back on the door handle, wanting to see Hart more clearly before proceeding. Just behind her she heard a car pull up, so she turned her head round to see who it was - just as the heavy church door burst open hard, pushing her back. Catrin looked back towards the door to see a body, then part of a hand - and felt the blow. It was as if the side of her head near her cheek and teeth had been crushed. She went over backwards.

It was fortunate, it turned out, that she was entirely off-balance on the steps as Cheney's baton connected. The force of the blow sent her whole body-mass down the short flight of steps to the pavement below and she dropped the torch as she fell. Her head, hip and a knee took heavy bangs and she ended on her back, shocked.

Then, given she was face up, she saw part of a painting go past. It was the sudden realization that it was a painting that brought her into action. It was being carried towards the car by the man who had just assaulted her.

In his haste to reach the car, Colin Cheney didn't see the black torch on the step in front of him as it rolled beneath his shoe. With a metallic scrape on the stone his forward foot trod on it, then his leg slipped sideways from under him. He tried to recover his balance but couldn't get his trailing leg forward far enough. He went down face first on the steps, arms pushing forward to break his fall. The paintings went flying.

Catrin had rolled to her knees and saw him go down. "I am arresting you," she said, almost automatically, but it didn't come out clearly, there was a blood in her mouth suddenly as she stood up. She spat it out, bending to pick up the torch which had slid closer to her and, in one motion, brought it full force on the part of her assailant she could reach, his ankle.

Colin cried out in pain; his ankle felt unresponsive. He moved his foot slightly. At least it wasn't broken, just painful.

Catrin heard the man yell, but he continued to struggle to get up.

"Stay on your front, on your front, NOW," she panted.

She had shouted it loudly and found more blood coming out; again she had to spit it and saliva clear. Her face was feeling warm, wet. She must have cut her head badly on the steps, she thought.

Cheney had been thinking, if he could get up he would deal with her. He looked at Niall Irvin now standing, opening the back door and their eyes met. Irvin wasn't going to mix in with the policewoman, he saw, but clearly he wanted Colin to get up and deal with her.

It was the look on the face of the man by the car that gave it away to Catrin. She saw the sudden tension in the legs of the man on the ground. He was still going to try to resist, she realised, as she closed in on him, handcuffs now in her hand.

Catrin was in sensible, comfortable work shoes for her shift. She took a well-aimed kick between the spread legs of her assailant, her weight giving full force for the toe to connect with the genitals - and she connected with his body hard. Then she came down full weight on one knee on the base of his spine as he screamed.

"Arms back," she yelled.

She grabbed his arm then cuffed his left wrist and stood up, wrenching the arm over as the man vomited. Catrin stood there, swaying, dropping the Maglite on his back as she pulled the free cuff to the extended right arm – and he was contained, thank God.

Catrin felt like she was about to pass out. She was in worse shape than she thought; she realised, but was feeling happier to have cuffed her assailant.

The man by the car was frozen, looking on in shock at what she had just done. She picked up the Maglite and approached him.

"Hands on the vehicle, NOW."

Her teeth felt strange. One tooth at least was broken and pain was replacing the numbness. Her coat and shirt were splattered heavily with blood now.

Niall Irvin said as evenly as he could, "I am a lawyer. You need help, I need to call."

One side of her face was now completely red from below the cheekbone to the chin, he saw. He was wondering, hoping in fact, that she would collapse from shock or loss of blood.

He reached into his coat. "I am getting my phone."

He needed to reach Dominic and let him know that if the Gault paintings were blown then the police were all over them.

As he pulled out his mobile he felt the blow to his hand and the expensive phone slammed into the gutter. Irvin cried out and reached for his damaged fingers with the uninjured hand as she hauled his shoulder round.

"I told you once, hands on the vehicle, NOW!"

Catrin knew she had no clearance from Sinclair and inside she was in anguish over how this had gone down. Woozy as she was feeling, she knew this incident needed containment. Nothing could get out while Strachan's operation was in progress. And she needed help badly.

She pulled out her phone again and pressed send again. Sinclair answered first ring.

"What happened, Catrin?"

"I have arrested two men at the churchyard. I need help. There is another man here with a head injury and … I have been hit on the head…"

As she spoke, Peter McPherson came running over and stopped.

"Christ, Catrin, what happened?" he cried.

Then she saw him looking at her face, his eyes reflecting his concern at what he saw. Damn it, she thought, it really is bad, then.

He took the Maglite that she was brandishing as she said to him there was a man, Michael Hart, in the doorway injured and he needs help. "Caution these bastards and take their phones." she mumbled.

After that she blacked out.

The next time she woke up, she remembered again first the painting moving past her head, she felt the pain in her cheek and then had the strange thought that she would need to make a written report. There were flashing lights and a woman was bending over her checking her pupils with a penlight, telling her to lie very still. Then she was being moved on to a stretcher.

24 THE INFIRMARY

Catrin's next recollection was of being in the ambulance with a technician. She had a cold compress of some sort against her head and a big dressing was stuck against her left cheek, it was as if she was glued to a cushion. A penlight was waved across her pupils again.

Her head was in some sort of brace, so she thought she couldn't move it anyway. She just lay there thinking, "What will happen now?"

The ER crew at Glasgow Royal Infirmary were more worried initially about concussion and head injury than the damage to the cheek and jaw. Catrin went through X-rays and an MRI scan and was being checked every few minutes, or so it seemed to her, about the day of the week, where she was and her name. Each time her answer was mumbled but they seemed OK with it.

A young Asian doctor had frozen her left cheek and removed two pieces of broken tooth embedded inside it.

"Mr. Leiss is coming in," he said.

Whatever that means, she thought, it means more

problems.

Catrin felt that she had a lump of string in her mouth but had no idea why. She looked at the drip they had placed in her arm. She was lying still; the drip was directly in her line of sight. For some reason, she felt as if she had no energy to move. Shock, she thought; is shock like this?

Sometime later two older men swept in.

"Miss Sayer, I am Angus Leiss, a surgeon here. This is Dr. Anderson, our senior dental surgeon."

He gently examined the cheek inside and out and pulled back.

"Harry?"

The dental surgeon made a similar examination. Leiss, she saw, was studying the case notes.

"Catrin," said Leiss, "Your tooth snapped laterally with the impact and made a fine razor edge. And the blow from whatever it was pulled the cheek forward so the tooth cut through both outward and on the return. So the hole is little bigger than just the tooth coming through the cheek. We are going to take you into surgery and I am going to do my best to make your face have as little scarring as possible and Dr Anderson is going to put the bits of the tooth back together with his fancy Swiss glues."

Catrin started to realize this was a little bigger an issue than she had thought, but just nodded gently. He asked her to sign a form and lie still then said, "The least we can do when young Welsh police officers get hurt by our countrymen is fix them up again."

They disappeared and Catrin lay there. A nurse had already checked on her last meal time and what she had had to eat and drink. In a little while a Chinese woman in surgical attire came in and told her to relax.

She had a brief recollection of the recovery room, like a dream. Eventually she found herself in a single room, with more checks by nurses waking her up. A young female doctor came in and said that the good news was that the concussion seemed to be minimal, but she would need to be checked out for some time. Her cheek was looking clean, she said.

Catrin had been looked after, she said, by one of the top cosmetic surgeons in Glasgow, who had come into the hospital when the ER physician had called him. She must do no exercise, make no sudden movements, nor do any work until approved by a doctor. She could sleep now, she said, and gave her an injection into the cannula sticking into her left hand. It sent her right out.

Then it seemed, it was the middle of the night and she was being woken again for another check. And afterwards she had another sleep.

~~

She was sitting up in bed, exhausted. It was now Wednesday morning, she had found out. A nurse had just helped her to have a shower without getting her face and head wet but the effort of even doing that had worn her out.

The headache had diminished but had not disappeared entirely. Her face felt very lop-sided, swollen and sore right up into the scalp. Her backside and hip hurt all along the left side; she could only see a little of the bruising as she was showered. There was also a minor-looking scrape on her left wrist that hurt way out of proportion.

She had wanted her hair washed but was told it would have to wait, the nurse said. They could not get water near the dressing on her face. Her hair felt really dirty – she knew it still had bits of blood and gravel in it.

Mr. Leiss had been back in earlier to examine her. He had shown her the facial scar in a mirror, an angry two inch red line on her left cheek starting one inch from her mouth along her upper gum line towards her ear. There was extensive bruising and swelling along the same side of her face up into the eyelid and, further back, into the hairline. An abrasion on her forehead was clean, but without a dressing.

"You'd best see it now, get it over with," Leiss had said quietly. "The surrounding bruising and swelling looks awful but will fade fast. You have good bones, Catrin. The cheek bone doesn't even have a hairline crack. We thought that it was going to be a lot worse than that, initially."

He had applied the fresh dressing himself.

He smiled encouragingly at her. "The scar line will fade to pink if we keep it free of infection and then it will fade in time to white. There are some post-operative measures to reduce it again, perhaps, meaning more surgery if you so choose. However, I am not sure it will give much of an improvement on this finish and the cosmetics you may choose to use once it is properly healed. It really is as fine a line as you could hope for. So don't knock it at all."

Catrin said, "It was a lot worse, wasn't it?"

He nodded, "I wouldn't have shown you your face earlier, I must admit."

"Thank you, Mr. Leiss - and thank you to the other doctors and nurses. I never expected to be here, but ..." she ran out of words.

He smiled. "Constable Sayer, I am glad to help. You are one brave young lady, I hear."

He stood up and left quickly.

She lay back thinking she would just drift back to sleep. How long, she wondered, will my face feel sore and so 'big'? It felt so awkward.

She had been told keep her tongue away from her cheek inside; it was harder than it sounded.

She was half-asleep when Worsley entered with a bag. Catrin sat forward.

Worsley just said, 'Catrin'. She sat on the bed took both her hands in hers and asked how she was feeling. Catrin started to ask what had happened and she held up her hand to stop her.

"You are being discharged. Mr. Leiss has just authorised it providing the first thing I do is get you to a surgeon back home. But here is someone to see you first."

She went to the door and Catrin thought, 'it must be Iain.'

But it wasn't, it was Jian Li Yeung, all the way from Bangor, dressed like she was on her way to a class at the college. She came in and hugged her.

"What are you doing here?" said Catrin, shocked.

"Jian Li has been here last night and yesterday evening," said Worsley, "sitting out there. I called your parents. They called your friends. I had told them all to stay away, that I was getting you back south but Jian Li turned up anyway, came straight to the hospital.

"She is obstinate," added Worsley, with a smile.

"Chinese people don't take kindly to being told what to do." Li smiled. "But Jane says we are going now, so get dressed. I will help." Catrin saw that the bag contained clothes from her hotel room.

Catrin thought, 'Jane', not 'Inspector Worsley'? They

had obviously been talking. The last time they had met had been in Colwyn Bay. It had been a lot more formal and strained conversation between the two women at that time, Catrin recalled.

"Where are we going?"

"London. Home," said Worsley. "We are dropping Jian Li near Crewe; she has exams to prepare for."

Catrin recalled that Li's year-end exams were due next week. Worsley had the phone to her ear and turned away and said something.

Catrin got dressed slowly as a female officer and nurse entered with a wheelchair and joined Li in helping her dress. As she started to absorb what was happening Catrin found herself being wheeled outside and realized that there was a police guard at her door with an automatic carbine. He smiled at her and then he followed the human train that Worsley was leading. Down in an elevator, out a side door to what Catrin recognized was an Audi Q7, a big seven-passenger vehicle in metallic grey.

"Meet Henry and Jim, from my old group," Worsley said.

Catrin knew that Jane Worsley had last been a Chief Inspector in the Diplomatic Protection Service. She had irritated some politicians by arresting someone that thoroughly deserved it but had muddied political waters in the process. Jack Taylor had given her a lateral transfer in the newly-formed Art Crime Unit.

The two large plain-clothes officers were surveying the area as she was helped into the back seat. She found herself sitting next to Worsley. Li was sitting in a middle row, diagonally across from her. With a little wiggling Li turned sideways to keep her eye on Catrin, who had automatically buckled in.

The officer getting into the passenger side front seat

said, "We have your case and all your belongings from the hotel in the back, DC Sayer. Everything is shipshape."

"Thank you," she said.

Then she realized how sumptuous her surroundings were. The vehicle was now gathering speed yet was quieter, she thought, than Iain's electric Peugeot. Ahead, clearing traffic with lights and sirens was a Police Scotland Range Rover.

She thought of Iain and wondered what to do to contact him. Her mind went back to him meeting her at the train station.

"I thought we would be going by train again."

Worsley looked at her steadily. "Catrin, you took out a high-level enforcer from a drug gang, violently. You also arrested Niall Irvin, the legal counsel that the Connolly gang has relied on for years at the time they need his work the most. Strachan's operation was quite successful, by the way. She had you under a security guard almost from the time your ambulance arrived at the hospital. You won't be riding on trains anywhere for a while."

"Strachan?" she thought. What about Sinclair?

25 CONVOY

Worsley was emptying a large travel bag as if she was dealing with her weekly shopping. She had files on one side, a laptop and an iPad Mini on her lap and a plastic bag with a tube of pills and various medical wipes down by her feet.

"We will go through all that after we drop Jian Li," she said.

Catrin took the hint; confidential business later.

"Now, first things first," Worsley went on, pulling out the iPad Mini and tapping away. "You are to talk to your parents; I promised them I would arrange that once we were on the road. That and Li's discussions with them were the only way they would stay away. It's the same story with your pottery friends. I told them all that by the time they got here I would have you out."

Jane Worsley passed over the iPad, now with the Skype connection live. "Just pretend there aren't three police officers and a former 'person of interest' present."

She spoke to her parents in Welsh, trying to reassure them all was well, but her mother cried when she saw the face. Belatedly she wished Jane Worsley had connected without video or just given her a mobile. But she was happy to see them.

Her dad held it together better. "Chief Inspector Worsley says that you saved that man's life. We are really proud of you, Catrin."

The doctor who had checked her after surgery had told her that Michael Hart was still in critical care but was showing early positive signs of recovery from the head trauma. "But if you hadn't called when you did, I doubt he would be alive, frankly."

Her parents told her they were coming to London soon to see her.

When she finally closed the call she said, "I don't have a mirror."

Li passed her one from her purse and she saw again the dressing covering her cheek and the swelling and bruising spreading above the cheek bone into the scalp. She thought of Iain again and said, "Li, did you get to meet Iain Simmons. I was out of there so fast..."

"Yes, I did. He was there for the first few hours I was there, Catrin. We overlapped."

Catrin saw her friend's face, which she could now read well and knew immediately. "It's over, isn't it?" she whispered.

"You need to talk to him. He is going to call you once you are home," Li said. She stopped and, turning to Worsley, said, "So much for my Chinese inscrutability."

Li turned to face Catrin fully. "He works in a bank and at a pottery shop. He was having difficulty getting used to your world and... now this." She waved her arms. "There's more, but the two of you will need to talk it through.

"Catrin, I think it was partly my fault too, I have to

say, and I am sorry about that. We were sitting there talking about you and he asked how we met. I made the mistake of telling him you saved my life when... you know. I thought it would help him understand how good a friend you are to me but all I must have done is resolve in his mind that you are a Welsh female Arnold Schwarzenegger - or someone like that."

Catrin heard Jim or Henry snort at Li's comparison. She saw how upset Li was with her confession and was reminded how Li's choice of English at times was unique. She had plenty of examples.

"Rubbish," Catrin said as she forced a smile. "I am more like Uma Thurman, I'm blonde."

They all laughed but Catrin felt close to tears.

She turned to look out the window. Li looked at Worsley and Catrin caught from the side of her eye that clearly her friend was holding back, probably at her boss's request. Catrin knew it would have to wait.

Yet another patrol car was passing, talking to Jim on the radio she realised, then for a period leading the way in front, lights flashing, clearing the fast lane of the motorway. It had happened through Glasgow and now several times on the M74 motorway. She felt her world had just turned on its head. It had only been a few days with Iain but it had so lifted her spirits to start a new relationship, it felt magical ... and now all this.

They were silent for a minute or two then Henry, the driver, spoke.

"DC Sayer, the car in front says, 'hello and well done'."

Catrin sat up slightly and looked, then waved through the front windshield at them. "Tell them thank you."

How did they know? She assumed everything to do

with the Kinnington Church mess would be hush-hush.

Henry continued, "Every police car we have seen so far has been saying the same. And probably everyone on duty on the M6 and the M1 will be doing likewise."

Henry had been listening and glancing in his mirror. He thought the young DC needed some cheering up.

Worsley said, "Did you fix this convoy thing, Jim? I know I didn't organize a circus."

"No ma'am. We asked for help clearing Glasgow, that's all, we didn't want any unnecessary stops there, if you take my meaning. This… this is traffic police talking to each other. You know what they are like, bloody road warriors."

"But we are making very good time, ma'am," said Henry. He knew they had been one of the fastest vehicles on the road south so far.

Catrin just put her head back into the pillow that the hospital had provided to think about everything. She was asleep in seconds. Li, Jane and the two security officers kept it quiet.

~~

Jane woke Catrin as they pulled off the M6 on to the A54, just before the Audi headed down a side lane. "Li is leaving us here. And it is time for you to take the painkiller that I was given for you, the strong stuff, once we are inside."

They pulled into the gates of what appeared to be an old country house and came to a halt in front of a police car waiting there with another vehicle next to it. Henry and Jim exited simultaneously, eyes sweeping the surrounding area. Catrin could see their professionalism; she had met officers with this training before, generally those on VIP special duties while she served in Brixton.

Worsley said, "We wait until they tell us to get out."

The two uniforms came forward showing their warrant cards to Henry. It was obvious that he didn't regard this as a perfunctory task. Henry nodded and Worsley said, "Now we go in for the loos and some lunch, for those who can eat."

It was obvious that the two officers were to watch the Audi while they were all inside.

Out of the other car came Detective Sergeant Idris Bowen from the North Wales Police Service, a colleague that Catrin had worked with on the Yeung case just months ago. He was wearing one of his badly-creased, old-fashioned suits and beaming at her.

He gave her a hug and said in Welsh, "You look shocked Catrin. Dafydd and the folks say hello and we are proud as hell of you. He also said ·you shouldn't be working with those northern vandals, you should be with us. So any time you want a good job, love, call us."

He was looking at her face carefully, neutrally. All this was going to get back to Dafydd Powys, the DI she had worked with in Bangor, she knew.

She was so pleased to see him and then realised. "You are taking Li, right?"

He nodded. "Jane organized it. Did you think you would drop her off at Crewe Railway Station?"

Catrin had already concluded that her boss, with her former life in Diplomatic Protection, had a stack of places like this around the country. You can't exactly take a VIP whose life is in danger to a cafeteria in a motorway service area.

They went into the house for coffee, tea and food provided by a woman who was never identified to Catrin. It was obvious though she had been briefed. "Welcome,

DC Sayer," she said and talked for a while with Jane. Clearly they knew each other quite well.

Catrin realized she had not even caught up at all with Li's recent news. She had last Skyped with her on the train north on Thursday last. It felt like a lifetime ago. She talked with her friend and Idris as they ate and she drank tomato juice with a straw. For some reason it tasted really good.

~~

Later, as they started out again with just Worsley and Catrin in the back seat DCI Worsley was all business.

"Now for the difficult stuff, Catrin, as if you haven't had enough. Are you up to it?"

"Yes ma'am."

Worsley pulled a newspaper out of a set of files. "Police Scotland is new, as you know. So it's a new set of politics, new dynamics and different forces all coming together. And Scotland has a different system than England under the Procurator Fiscal and the Crown Prosecution Service. And, frankly, not all of it is good news. That's why you are back south so quickly."

She paused.

"You will be interviewed in due course by the Scottish authorities to see if any recommendations of disciplinary action or criminal charges against you are warranted arising from your actions at the incident."

She was watching Catrin's reaction, gauging how far to go.

Catrin just nodded and said nothing; she was shocked.

"I was on the phone earlier while you were sleeping, listening into a discussion between the two services. Police Scotland is not happy that you are out of Glasgow.

Sandra told them she would let you go back north of the border when they were ready to give you a medal, and not before."

"You two," she said to Henry and Jim, "you didn't hear that."

They were smiling at each other. "No ma'am," they said, almost in unison. Then Henry says, "Not a thing said in this car goes outside, ma'am; you know the rules."

"The Assistant Commissioner, she said that?" said Catrin.

This is crazy, she thought. It was an arrest, I got hurt but... to end up involving an Assistant Commissioner of the Met on a small incident seemed bizarre to her.

"She put a gag on Jack Taylor, he was so angry. She did the talking. It's all about this." She passed over *The Scotsman*, folded at an inside page.

'Scottish Legal Expert tries to help at an incident; attacked and injured by a London Police officer', ran the article by-line.

The article recounted how Mr. Niall Irvin, a prominent Glasgow defense lawyer, was passing Kinnington Church and saw an incident in progress. He stopped to help and was attacked and arrested by a Metropolitan Police officer from London, there assisting with enquiries. She was seen to physically attack a suspect prone on the ground, kicking his body and then she attacked Mr. Irvin with a heavy torch as he tried to assist.

"I explained to her that I was a solicitor and wanted to help, as she was hurt, but she just turned on me, hitting my hand with a heavy metal torch as I tried to call 999... I was in agony, a bone is cracked and I became very scared. She was holding the torch up. I thought that she was going to hit me again."

"I had recognized the person she was apprehending, a

man I had represented in the past, a troubled individual I think. I don't know what he had done but he was already under arrest on the ground, I believe, and she laid into him, kicking him. He screamed with pain and was vomiting, but there was nothing I could do to help."

"I am really shaken by the whole matter and by this unwarranted police violence. I will be filing a formal complaint about my improper and inappropriate arrest at the scene and the way the prisoner was treated. It is intolerable."

It was this morning's paper.

Worsley let her absorb it then continued, "Niall Irvin fixed the interview as soon as he was released and he has also filed a formal complaint this morning to the Police Investigations and Review Commissioner for Scotland, PIRC. Strachan got the press liaison to pull your name before the press publication, covering it in the D-notice with all the officers involved in Operation Finisterre. I will come on to that shortly."

"But your name is out there, if not in the media, certainly for the Glasgow and Edinburgh gangs to know. And Dominic Connolly, who Strachan was after, is angry and vicious at the loss of the heroin and a supply route they had worked to build for months. There is street noise that he is prepared to pay anyone who kills you or the undercover officer in Operation Finisterre. Taking out Colin Cheney, one of his enforcers, has also damaged his control structure at the worst possible time for him.

"Irvin has given two television interviews that we know of so far, one this morning on STV's Scotland Today. And in each one his damaged hand is front and centre, strapped."

She moved forward slightly to make sure Catrin was looking at her face.

"The bottom line, Catrin, is that every police officer north or south of the border is on your side. But there are influential people in Scotland who consider that you assaulted an upright citizen, a lawyer, and viciously assaulted a suspect when he was already under arrest. They think an enquiry is warranted; some of them think you should be charged.

"None of them know the circumstances and some wouldn't care anyway. The complaint by Irvin has been accepted by PIRC. They have their own investigators who will doubtlessly want to interview you. They are the counterpart of our IPCC."

She was referring to the Independent Police Complaints Commission.

"I did the best ..."

Worsley said forcefully, "Stop right there. You have no justification to make to us. We know the circumstances and the Met will do nothing but support you, from the Commissioner down. Eric Sinclair was ready to tender his resignation and take early retirement when he heard about the in-house reaction that Police Scotland couldn't quash this. He says they are pandering to some Scots Nationalist politicians listening to Irvin's media bullshit, pardon his French. Strachan asked him to stay on, to help her fight back from the inside.

"Peter McPherson is suspended indefinitely and may well leave the force, voluntary or mandatory, it's not sure.

"The person who is working most effectively to address this is, in fact, DCI Strachan; despite her growling at us early on and being unhelpful, she is a good officer. And we are under strict instructions to know nothing about it."

Worsley straightened herself up and sat back in her

seat.

"Sorry to be the bearer of such news, but you needed to know, particularly as probably everybody else knows the bad news already including, I should add, the man you had just started to see in Glasgow. I asked both your parents and Li not to say anything before I got the chance to talk to you."

Catrin looked out of the window, not sure what to say or if she could bring herself to say anything. It was bad enough to be injured but this felt so... unjust.

Worsley said, "You may also want to read the article on the front page about 'Operation Finisterre', the Connolly gang heroin seizure. That was the reason for the secrecy, as you gathered, and you were also right about an inside operative, a French police officer who is now back in his own country. Eight million pounds of heroin at street value, twenty-three arrests made in Finisterre, Eire and Glasgow. It will hit Connolly's operation a significant dent, but not cripple it, we think.

"You and I and everyone that matters know that without your containment of the church incident, this could have all been fouled up. And as bad as it seems now, it won't be forgotten. So there are guards on you until Strachan says that the Connolly gang does not pose a foreseeable threat to you. Those are Taylor's orders.

"We are trying to ascertain the significance of the threat level, but are being cautious. Hence Henry and Jim and a few others. I told Sandra I wanted the security team I know. Even if you aren't a diplomat."

Catrin said, "I don't think I will ever be one of those, ma'am. After all, I haven't exactly been very diplomatic, have I?"

They were passing Coventry, nearing the end of the

M6. They would soon be on the M1 heading to London. Yet another bright police car came past, flashed it lights as Jim said something to them. Catrin smiled at them but inside she felt devastated. The car took up station ahead of them and turned into a Christmas tree of lights as they cleared a way through the building traffic.

"What about the man I arrested, Colin Cheney?"

"He was in the same hospital as you for a while having his ankle and genitals inspected," she said dryly, "You did him some damage to the latter. I am not sure how much, nor do I care. He was uncooperative until his solicitor, a minor satellite of Irvin, saw him. Now he is negotiating for the lowest sentence possible with a plea, but has also supported Irvin's statement. He said he had no idea Irvin was there and the last time he saw him was on his last court appearance.

"He hit you with a modified three-section ASP baton. The weapon ties in also with the statement by the security guard Halverson on Lewis. Cheney had the two outer sections of the baton fused together with something so it did not extend fully. It's a lethal thing; he should go down for attempted murder of Hart and you, but I doubt it."

Catrin asked, "So where do we go now with the cases, ma'am?"

"The ACU is out of it, Catrin. We are going to have to leave all that to Sinclair and Strachan and trust them to follow through. You did a great job of identifying the fraud and the reasons for the thefts, but it's with them now."

It was the final straw. On top of all the things Catrin had heard on the drive south the loss of the case by ACU hit her hard. She tried to hold back and Worsley put her hand on her arm and said, "It's OK," as the tears streamed down her face and she sobbed.

"You are making your dressing soggy," said Jane, gently.

Jim passed back a box of tissues but Worsley got out the medical wipes; they didn't shred.

26 FORGERY REVISITED

John Dalton had followed the news of Irvin's arrest and the press interviews. When he got the call from Niall informing him that he was still bringing three paintings over, he was surprised. He said nothing, though, until Niall was in his flat. He still had strapping over his hand, as John had seen on the news clip.

"Niall, was the Kinnington Church item related to our activity?"

Niall looked at him. "They had two Gault paintings I needed, yes, and we didn't get them, no. In fact, I think these that I have are all I will get now, at least for a while. I need to wait on the museum returning the paintings they took from my uncle's home. I hope it won't be too long.

"You will have to work with these."

John looked the paintings over. "This one, it's a Gault, but a throw-in, right? You didn't intend to use this?"

Niall nodded.

"Niall, the police know; that's why they had the church staked out. So why do you want to go on?"

"What the police know and what they can act on are two different things, John. And what they know about is the Kelvingrove concern raised by Andrew Gault. Neither relate to the private transaction of the art. They are not linked."

"Have you talked with Dominic about this?" asked John quietly.

There was a tension in Niall's voice. "No, John, I haven't and I won't. Dominic is up to his eyebrows in it, sorting out a bigger problem. Eight million pounds in inventory and a new supply route have just disappeared. He will have no time for this. And I should get back; there are preparations for the defense of a number of the people involved that Dominic wants me working on."

John nodded, weighing his next steps. He should tell Niall the truth; it was over. But he said, "Leave them with me; I will do the best I can. Same story we talked about and perhaps a little more than two weeks, three at the most. OK, Niall?"

Niall nodded, grateful. "Call me when they are ready, John."

When Niall had gone, John Dalton surveyed his flat for the last time, packing only clothes and some practical and sentimental items. He included the three paintings in his larger suitcase and all the special pigments and some favorite brushes; other art supplies he could buy anywhere.

He drove across the Pennines down to Manchester, to a service station run by man he had served time with, Les, whom he asked to sell the car and let him have what he could from it later on. He would let him know where to send the money.

Les looked at him and offered him a fair price there

and then. "I take it you need this, John?"

He nodded. "I have to get out of the country, Les."

Les went into his safe. "Here is a thousand down. I can send the rest once I see the car sold, I promise."

John then asked him for one more favour; a ride to the railway station. He bought a ticket to London and another on the Eurostar to Paris. At the nearby bank he lowered but did not completely empty his bank account, taking cash and traveller's cheques in Euros.

In Paris he had a day to kill before the twice-weekly charter flight from Orly airport to Máo, the largest city on Minorca. He had chosen it as a small airline that catered to tour groups but sold unused seats at the airport on the morning of the departure. It might be harder for others to track him that way than the regular scheduled flights to the island, he hoped.

He spent the time waiting by visiting the Quai D' Orsay and L'Orangerie museums, lost in paintings he knew well. In the back of his mind was the thought he may be seeing them for the last time.

He ended up in a discussion with a copyist at L'Orangerie on the subject of reproducing green foliage. He was a student, doing a fair reproduction of Alfred Sisley's *Le Chemin de Montbuisson à Louveciennes*. Then Dalton reined himself in and moved on; he hadn't come here to gain any visibility.

Later in the afternoon he took the Metro to see an artist he knew from the old days, to restock on some powdered pigments he would not be able to get in any art store selling new bright modern tubes of paint.

He was ready.

At Orly he cashed in the remaining traveller's cheques

in a currency exchange, in a line-up of arriving tourists. They all wanted Euros too. He took a beating on the agent charges. At least all his money was now untraceable.

His last step was to call Dominic from Orly airport on the phone he had been given. The answering machine message said simply, "I am not available, leave a number and a message."

So he did.

"Dominic, I am going to the place you know. I will finish the three items Niall wants, if you want me to. But I think this is going belly up; you know why. You have a lot on your plate but watch this side of things; if the police know about this it could unravel for you and for Niall. You know what they are like. Good luck, lad.

"Call me back and let me know what you want me to do."

On arrival on the island he stayed in Máo for the first evening at a small hotel recommended by the welcome desk in the airport. The following morning he contacted the people on the sheet of paper that Dominic had provided and by lunch time, after a 25 mile bus journey and a short taxi ride, he was in his new apartment. Dominic had been good at his word about his fee.

But Dominic never returned John's call. Nor did he get to paint a portrait of the Connolly family.

And he never heard again from Niall Irvin.

27 A PLAN

Detective Chief Inspector Eileen Strachan felt she owed Catrin Sayer every help she could give her, not only because she was a fellow police officer injured in the line of duty and now facing a review of her conduct. The containment of Irvin and Cheney for even the few hours it took to process them proved to be the balance between success and failure for Operation Finisterre.

Strachan had led an operation resulting in a set of arrests in northern France, Eire and Scotland. Key to that operation was an undercover French police officer. If Connolly had suspected any surveillance at all, he would automatically have re-checked the operation and people in it. Sayer had kept the Kinnington incident contained knowing that there was something big in progress, Strachan knew. While Eileen was receiving accolades from senior management, Sayer's situation played on her mind.

She left much of the tidying up of Finisterre to her subordinates who were astonished by their boss's 'hands off' attitude. She wasn't known for it. Strachan spoke with Sinclair, now in a holding pattern pending the review of his management of the stake-outs. She first talked him out of taking early retirement.

She told him baldly, "Eric, that's the easy way out. It's giving in."

He came back angrily. "Giving in; who to, Eileen?"

She said softly, "Do you really want the complete list? To them."

She meant the political lobby exploiting the situation.

"To Cheney; the bastard injured a young officer under your local command... but above all, to the old Eric Sinclair. The one who used to slam the office door and grab the bottle in the bottom draw."

He looked at her and took a deep breath. She had known him both as a drinker and in sobriety.

"You are as bad as my AA sponsor, Eileen. Thank you, I should say; as honest as him, really."

She said, "So, take the crap, the review meetings and the waiting. But let's start to do something constructive to get Sayer feeling good about what she did. We owe her that. We need to keep Peter McPherson from the wolves looking for scapegoats and try to stop him resigning. I need you on this."

Then she re-read the Gault file, went through it with Sinclair. She called Susan Hetherington at the Kelvingrove Museum. Susan had seen the newspaper item and Strachan asked her to come in and take her in detail through the painting issue that DC Sayer had uncovered.

The two women got on well, it turned out. Strachan suddenly said. "Look, if I come up with something to move this forward, can I count on you and the museum for support?"

Hetherington was unconditional in her response. "Let

us know how we can help. I'd be happy to do so."

The thing that had been missing from Sayer's analysis, Eileen Strachan realised, was the insight into the leadership of the Edinburgh and Glasgow gangs, something she had intimate knowledge of; and hadn't shared, she knew. She had an idea, the beginnings of a plan, one that could not only address the Irvin claim of his innocence but cause a further blow to Connolly.

~~

Catrin had been taken directly to University College Hospital on arrival in London and examined by a surgeon, Mr. Weldon, who told her that all looked well, the wound looked clean. He dressed her cheek again.

"Angus did a good job, DC Sayer," he remarked. "But you must have no sudden movement of the face, nothing to touch or disturb this area, otherwise your scar line will widen. In about four days I will see you again to remove some of the sutures; others that Angus used will dissolve in time but I will want to check everything, so I may need to see you again afterwards."

Henry had taken Worsley back to the Yard and Jim waited with Catrin while she was attended to at the hospital. The car returned and the two Diplomatic Service officers, sensing she was exhausted, spoke softly as they whisked Catrin to her flat.

"There is a duty officer outside, on rotation, and our people have been through your place. There is a panic button installed and so on."

Jim saw her to her door and verified that her flatmate Helen was home, that everything was in order and then he shook Catrin's hand.

"Good luck, Catrin. Henry and I think it has been a

privilege. Look out for yourself."

In her flat, with an armed, uniformed officer now on duty outside, she had to talk to her flatmate.

"Helen, I'm sorry for the fuss and for putting you in this situation."

Helen told her again that a security officer had spent half the day at the flat and two window catches had been replaced. They were both looking at the panic button module on the coffee table. There was another in Catrin's bedroom.

Helen had made Catrin tea and said she had got off work early to be here when she arrived. Someone at the Met had apparently talked to someone in high places in the British Library and Helen had been told to take any time off that she wished; it would be covered.

They were sitting down and she had already offered to cook dinner but Catrin told her that Jean and Melanie were coming over; they had sent a text message to her phone on the ride down.

"They are bringing soup and things they think I can handle and a homemade lemon meringue cake, because it's my favorite. To be honest, though, I am still tired, not hungry, even though I have been sleeping a lot of the way on the drive, it seems. I feel bad about you having all this at the flat."

Helen said, "Catrin, if you didn't pay the rent or left the place a mess, I would have something to complain about. But doing your job... if they hadn't told me that the news article was about you, I would never have thought it. I didn't realise what my new flatmate really did, I guess, and how brave you must be. I am in awe."

She thought of Iain Simmons and knew she must call him, but tomorrow. Awe was better than fear or rejection but none were just normal.

Catrin said, "So can I intimidate you enough to help me wash my hair without getting this lot wet?" She pointed at her face. "It's driving me crazy."

When Jean and Melanie arrived she was asleep again, so the three women ate and talked. At some point Catrin heard voices and it woke her enough to realize that she needed to go the bathroom, after which she joined them. The look on Jean's face when she saw her brought home the impact her injuries had on people.

"It's not that bad, Jean," she said.

She saw that her imperturbable friend was on the verge of tears and had been crying already, by the look of it.

Jean said, "Well, Catrin, it's not that good either," and she came and hugged her tightly. "I came and looked at you while you were asleep."

Melanie did the same then then said she would make more tea.

"And lemon meringue, cut up small, if you please." said Catrin, as airily as she could manage.

She filled in for them what she could about what happened.

"We saw the policeman outside and he stopped us. We are on an approved list, it seems," said Melanie.

"So am I," said Helen, "So I can stay in my own flat."

There was a pause and Catrin suddenly thought of Iain. "Have you talked to Marjorie?"

Melanie looked at Jean as Catrin said, "It's OK, Li gave it away. Her inscrutable Chinese face told me."

Jean said, "Yes, she called us. Iain had talked to her after he left the hospital. She was quite upset with him, apparently, as she took to you big time. She didn't say much but hopes he... gets it together. I don't know. She thinks somehow he can't handle it and hopes he will come round when he talks to you."

Melanie said, deadpan, "I think Marjorie Simmons wants to steal our decorator from us, that's what it is, she knows she works cheap. It's a plot."

Catrin smiled. "My price is going up, right now."

Then she said, "I'll talk to Iain tomorrow. Li also said we two have to sort it out. But, you know, Li is my friend and she came up to see me right away. Jane Worsley told me the only reason you two didn't shut up shop and come up was because of her and Li talking to you. The same with my parents. Iain was on the doorstep and didn't stick it out.

"I really think that is where it's at. I am a police officer. I didn't choose to get clobbered but when I did, the people in my life who matter were there for me."

Including a whole bunch of men and women in police cars down the motorways, she thought.

Catrin looked around. It didn't seem as if she would be getting much argument from the others in the room.

~~

On Thursday morning she started afresh. First she took her tablets. She looked at her face for signs of the bruising growing fainter and saw nothing other than the colours appearing more vivid. If anything it was darker around the eye, she thought. She unpacked, knowing that the clothes she wore at the church were still in Glasgow in the evidence materials. Then she remembered the envelope that Li had given her in the scramble at the lodge near Crewe on leaving.

In it was a printout of an electronic ticket and a

handwritten note.

'Dear Catrin,

'I talked with Jane in the hospital. She now lets me call her that, even if you have to call her 'ma'am'. Remember the promise in Bangor? I said if you bought an economy ticket to Hong Kong, Cathay Pacific would upgrade you to First Class. Mr. Lin had fixed it for me. You would need to clear it, you said.

'Well, I know you were saving for the trip, but I go back home in a few weeks. And the events of the last week have brought home to me how good a friend I have and I want things clearer. Mr. Lin organized the ticket. Jane has OK'd it as a personal gift. I want you to come to see Hong Kong and meet my family and for us to spend time together.

'Don't worry about the cost. I have much to tell you. We have guanxi, remember?

'Love, Li.

'p.s. Jane also approved the vacation dates for you – but you have to complete the entry into the system, though, she said.'

Guanxi, Catrin knew, was the Chinese expression for a specific connection between people, about dependence of one on another, reciprocation of a special relationship. Catrin had first thought it meant friendship and had used it in that context.

It was only later that Li explained it more completely and its cultural importance. 'It's more than friendship, Catrin. If I was never to see you again – which I sincerely hope is not the case – and we each lived to be one hundred years old, our guanxi would be unchanged. And already I owe you my life.'

The eticket was a First Class return from London to Hong Kong on Cathay Pacific Airlines, travel dates separated by two weeks. She looked at the ticket price. She was dumbfounded.

28 AFTERMATH

Worsley had told Catrin to stay at home on Thursday and not to say anything to the press if they called. Dr. Herrington, a police psychologist, and DI Keith Marshall would be in touch.

In the myriad of activity, Skyping with her parents, thanking Li for the wonderful surprise and sending emails and texts to people, Keith Marshall called her work mobile number about 9.30 a.m.

"You up yet?"

"I am not an invalid, sir. I have been up since 7.30."

"No exercising though, I hear," he said.

"Right. Although my left side is telling me that anyway, it's pretty sore."

"From what I heard, I am not surprised, which is why I was asking if you were still in bed. Jane filled me in on yesterday. And she outranked and out-sexed me on coming to get you myself. She said you needed a woman travelling companion back, not a boss to talk about cases."

"She was very good to me, sir, but I half-wish I had

been talking about cases, compared with what we did talk about," said Catrin, "It's such a mess."

Marshall was businesslike. "Well, you can't. Can I come over in an hour and tell you what we can talk about?"

"Yes sir, I would love that."

"And Catrin, the mess isn't yours. It's Police Scotland's mess and the Crown's mess; they are all being stupid sods on this one. Don't wallow in it, it doesn't suit you. Got it?"

"Yes, sir."

He closed the line. Wow, she thought, it's good to be back in a normal conversation with someone.

Dr. Herrington called shortly afterwards and talked to her after first checking on any physical effects, headaches, nausea or disorientation. She had a slight headache; that was all, she told him, but was taking medication and it was manageable. Her left side was sore in a lot of places, but she could walk slowly, she said.

He needed her to come in for an evaluation for trauma. This will be a preliminary evaluation only, he explained. Catrin could not return to active duty without his evaluation report and that would also require some further hospital checks. They set a time for Friday.

She decided not to put off calling Iain any longer. Something Keith Marshall had said resonated with her. She called him on his mobile and he picked up immediately saying, "Catrin, I am sorry. I was going to call today."

"Iain, Li didn't tell me anything, really, I just read it on her face. Yesterday wasn't that good for me. In fact, the last few days weren't really."

She stopped, waited.

Iain said, "I came to the hospital as soon as I heard. Jean called my mother and she called me but I wasn't allowed in to see you. None of the police staff knew me and there was a guard on your door. Then I met a police officer from London who turned up, one of your bosses, who told me a little of what happened but said you were under tight security. Then your friend Jian Li came and… I couldn't believe it all. It's a different world you live in, Catrin. I don't think…"

She cut into his explanation.

"Well, I don't do this on a weekly basis, Iain. But that's not the reason for the call. I wanted to tell you how my last week was wonderful with you. I thank you for that. You are a caring, sensitive person and I really enjoyed it; I would have liked it to continue. But I am a police officer and I am proud of my job and the way I do it. I just want to wish you well and hope you find someone who is better suited to be a partner for you."

She stopped. What would he say? She half-hoped he would insist on taking the train down to London to see her and to talk it through, to fight her closure of the relationship.

"And I wish you the same, Catrin, thank you. I enjoyed it too. You have such diverse talents, obviously. I feel bad, but it would have become worse if it had gone on."

"Good luck Iain."

She put the phone down and checked herself. I am glad that discussion's over, she thought, then found she was crying. She felt she had to clean up before Keith Marshall arrived and then realised how stupid that was; blotchy eyes from crying were the least of her facial concerns.

Keith Marshall had given her facial injuries a quick inspection on arrival, his face neutral. "The bruising will clear up soon; you will look like new, other than that." He pointed at her cheek, which still had a dressing on. "And that will get sorted out too, take my word, I know. It will be fine, Catrin."

Now he was watching her as she moved, she saw, noting the stiffness. She remembered that Marshall had been an army officer and had at least one bullet wound, she had discovered.

Once they had coffee and sat down at the table, Marshall said, "So your statement on the incident is the work item we can discuss, Catrin. Some people in Edinburgh are demanding it and posturing about you leaving Glasgow before giving it.

"We have said you were concussed, that we know they are looking at disciplinary action against their own officer and prosecutorial action potentially against you, so your statement will not be made until we have sign-off from our medics that you are free of symptoms of concussion.

"I have also asked for Evelyn Carter, a member of the legal firm the Police Federation uses, to prepare you for the interview with the Commission. We are sure they will want an interview once they get your statement."

"Evelyn, the one everyone complains about?" said Catrin, astonished.

She knew that in the legal team that the Federation used to represent police officers in enquiries or claims, Carter was the solicitor that higher levels in the Met rolled their eyes about. She was very combative, she had heard.

"She is a good lawyer and tenacious. Catrin, I think she's what you need. Besides, it will be the Scottish brass she aggravates. You know well enough the process of witness statements and officer's logs. Your last log entry was the note on the arrival of Michael Hart, the church member. What you write in due course is your decision, of course, but Evelyn will go through it carefully, I know.

"So what else am I going to do then?" Catrin asked.

'Well you will come into the office tomorrow - with the security team - to meet with DCI Coltrane and myself and go back through all the art-related aspects of the Colourist case; what you found and what you suspect."

"With Neville?"

Her voice showed her surprise. The case didn't belong to Art and Antiques, was her first thought.

"Yes, with Neville Coltrane. My former boss may be a conceited pain in the arse, but he is always there for his team. He is royally annoyed; royal is a probably good choice for Neville, I know, about your treatment in Scotland. Coltrane is a Scottish name, Catrin, and his family roots go back there a long way, even if he has always lived in Mayfair. He went to Jane and Jack and offered to help in any way, Jane told me. I was quite surprised.

"So he is now working with Strachan. And once you brief him we are out of it. Hand on heart; we will say ACU knows nothing of whatever unfolds."

"And what else should I do?"

"Get to the Cwmbran Kiln and make some scintillating items. I wish I could say it was simply good therapy; which art is, I have experience in that area, remember; but Elizabeth told me the last platter you gave her sold yesterday to Sir John Vale. Neville apparently told him he could buy your pottery at Liz's gallery."

"He is a character, if you don't know him. He paid the asking price and then remonstrated with Liz for selling it so low. He left and a few moments later walked back in with a message. 'Tell her I bought it for the art, not because she is a brave woman; that would be an intolerable perception of one artist by another'. Then he walked out without another word. Just like that, Liz said."

Catrin thought I may not have had my name in the paper but word is getting around. Then she thought, Connolly and the other villains know anyway.

"Yes," said Catrin, "I only met him when I covered for you at the last Coordination Meeting - and he is a man who gets straight to the point. He was interrogating me on the finer details of ceramic decoration within about five seconds of saying hello."

After Keith left she changed the dressing on her face in the mirror by herself in accordance with Mr. Weldon's instructions. Catrin took her time and was careful, inspecting yet again the new feature she would need to get used to. She also had to go to the dentist that afternoon to have the repair to the broken tooth checked, she had also discovered.

She walked out of the flat and talked to the DPS police officer on duty, to confirm he had her home and mobile numbers and said if they wanted coffee or anything, let her know.

He laughed. "Thanks, but you know how it is."

His eyes were on the environment, not her, but he pointed at her face, "And you know how fast situations can change. There are three of us on at present; I drew the 'visible bobby' role, my partner is floating around and we have a relief for rotation.

"So with the three shifts, that's nine of us, all from DCI Worsley's old unit. So that's a lot of tea and coffee you would be making."

She laughed, "I can handle that."

"Best get inside though, we stick to protocol. In the

Diplomatic Protection Service we have to. But we are real chuffed, all of us, to have this assignment, I can tell you that, looking after one of our own this time. Andy, he is on nights, has a sister in in the force in Dunfermline, part of the old Fife Constabulary. We know more about what's happening in Police Scotland than the brass at the Yard do about your case, I think. You take care, DC Sayer."

She blushed and went inside. That's what they should have had at Kinnington Church, she thought; adequate resources, with reliefs. Strachan had objected to expansion of the team size.

She dug out her mobile and called Sinclair.

"I probably shouldn't be calling, sir, but I wanted to say hello and thank you."

He sounded delighted to hear her voice. "Catrin, I don't care if you shouldn't be calling, it's lovely to hear from you although the line may be a little crackly."

It may be monitored he was saying.

"I wanted to get Peter's home number and say goodbye to him also, if can you give me that."

He did, and then asked "How is the face doing?"

She told him that Angus Leiss had done a good job.

"And you understand why I couldn't come in to the hospital to see you, lass."

"Yes sir, DCI Worsley explained it fully."

"You will be fine, Catrin, you are a damn good copper."

"Sir, one question. Do you still go to that church I saw you at after the first meeting?"

He thought, then laughed, "Yes, love, I do. Now I understand the discussion in the car to Oban a little more. But I do indeed."

"Glad to hear it, sir. You keep well now."

"You too, DC Sayer, and I hope we work together again sometime."

29 EVELYN

On Friday morning the security detail took her by car to New Scotland Yard, straight inside, underground. On reaching the ACU area she was able to spend a minute or two with Aina and promised to see her later. DI Marshall came to collect her and they went up to Coltrane's office.

"When do you see Dr. Herrington?" he asked.

"This afternoon, sir; he is seeing me at his office. I have your Evelyn Carter first, here, after the meeting with DCI Coltrane. She contacted me yesterday afternoon, she was right on it."

He was checking how she was walking, moving, comparing it with his observations yesterday.

"You were pretty badly bruised up, I know, but you are moving better already," he said.

"I am not sitting for too long and I keep walking a little, keep moving. I think these painkillers help a lot but... if there is a cushioned seat in DCI Coltrane's office, it would be nice if I could sit on it."

Keith said, "We will fix it. Even if I have to bring a cushion in that makes him wince about the clash with his furniture."

Neville Coltrane was affable but business-like. To his credit, he had thought about Sayer probably needing a comfortable chair at the table; he had already wheeled over his Herman Miller Aeron desk chair and when they arrived he fussed with adjusting it for her.

Looking at the meeting room table Catrin could see that DCI Coltrane had been reviewing the images of the Colourist paintings and Gault's work before they went in.

"I think I see this, Sayer, and it is good work that you did. Gault has captured the styles of Cadell and Peploe exceedingly well, as you said, and picked up on elements from their paintings. But you take me through this from the beginning, as you worked it out."

The next fifteen minutes were spent with Catrin talking softly. She realized that it was getting harder, making her cheek sore. So she mentioned it and they stopped her then.

"Did it occur to you that Irvin is planning to win either way?" said Coltrane.

She smiled, "I thought it, sir, but I had not mentioned it to anyone."

Her eyes showed she was impressed by Coltrane's analysis.

He looked at Keith. "You know too, I think, Keith."

Keith said, "You mean, to forge the Gault's as Colourists, get the value. Then later, if the forgeries are spotted by others or he leaks the news, rake it in off the newly-discovered trove of Gault works, a painter that has now become highly-collectible?"

Neville nodded. "I think the selection of paintings and his eagerness for more than the original fourteen all tie in with that."

He closed the file and looked at her. "Good work, Catrin. That's it. Strachan and I will work on it."

He looked at her sympathetically.

"Sorry you face is in such a hell of a mess, but it will get better, I am sure. Does it hurt much?" he asked, as they stood up.

"It hurts when I laugh, so not very often. Thank you, sir."

She looked at Keith; he was smiling. 'That's our Neville' was the message in his eyes.

As she went to the small meeting room assigned for the discussion with Evelyn Carter, a number of other officers came over to say hello and ask after her.

Bling, thought Catrin, looking at the Federation solicitor. And she needs her roots done. The woman who came into the meeting room at the Metropolitan Police headquarters had obviously just had a smoke outside.

"Evelyn Carter, Catrin," she said without ceremony, examining her client as if she was assessing damages to be claimed in court.

So this was the scourge of Met tribunals into police behavior, Catrin thought. She had heard of her as an institution of the Police Federation even when she was in training college. Keith had wangled her into doing this, she concluded.

The woman was overweight, fiftyish and her hair was as dyed blonde as Catrin's was natural. She began with what was obviously her standard introduction.

"Catrin, you are to call me Evelyn. And you are going to tell me everything that happened. How you felt, what you did, what you think you should have done but didn't, your fears, whatever. And I am going to tell you what to say in the interview to the questions they ask and hopefully I will cover all the bases, although this is a bit different for me, seeing as it is Police Scotland. I don't know them as well as all my friends at the Met and the IPCC."

"I thought I was to write a report first, Evelyn," said Catrin.

"I asked them if they were going to interview you anyway. They said yes. I told them to stuff the idea of a written report; they could ask what they need at the interview. They have McPherson's formal report and they know you were injured. So no written report from you.

"Which hasn't exactly made PIRC warm and fuzzy towards me, I must admit."

She did not sound at all contrite.

"And the interview will be down here; your Assistant Commissioner insisted on it, I gather, which is good. You don't need to be travelling or near the villains up there, I understand, and I am too busy to be wasting time on trains or planes to Glasgow or Edinburgh.

"Remember, they will start out with the allegation. It's not a charge but you will suddenly feel very much alone. You will be made to feel a private citizen who -"

She looked down at the paperwork.

"- attacked with a weapon an unarmed, reputable lawyer and placed him in fear for his life."

She looked at Catrin, then back again at the paperwork.

"- and in the presence of the same lawyer, you committed an assault causing bodily harm on a person already under arrest. You will hear these accusations and wonder 'what planet they are on, don't they know the truth?' Which is what you are thinking right now, I suspect."

She was watching Catrin's reaction.

"The only way to stop this turning into a charge is to show that your actions were entirely - and I mean entirely - within the remit of your powers as a sworn police officer under these circumstances. The answers I will work with you to prepare will not be lies - I have never counselled a client to lie - but they won't necessarily be the ones that come straight to your mind. We have lot to do here, dear, so let's get started."

Catrin looked at her.

Evelyn smiled. "But it's not that bad, either, given Cheney's confession. And while I think about it, can you check with your doctor? I would like the scar to be visible during the interview, if at all possible. I am sure it will be wonderful evidence of what you were really doing at the time."

~~

Catrin had realized on the drive over to the Yard that she was very glad to be in a car and not on the Tube. She realized how self-conscious she felt about her face. The dressing over the scar was bad enough but the bruising and swelling really made her feel uncomfortable with strangers.

Working in Brixton she had seen women with similar bruising from beatings by their partners, family members or strangers and she always felt for them. It always looked so ugly. Now she looked like someone coming out of the wrong end of a domestic dispute and it wasn't sympathy she felt, it was embarrassment. She wanted to hide away.

After the meeting with Evelyn Carter she had gone for lunch in the cafeteria with Aina who had sat her down and brought her food over to her. Somehow being among other police officers made it more acceptable, less embarrassing because they would know and understand. Again, some came over to see how she was doing. But she also got some glances that made her realise how bad her face looked.

Her appointment with Dr. Herrington was in his surgery, in a building close to University College Hospital. One of the DPS detail accompanied her inside and waited in the anteroom as she entered Herrington's office. The DPS Officer was in plain clothes but she could see the familiar bulge of his sidearm under his jacket. She had no idea where the others were but it felt a little surrealistic; here she was in London, being protected by an armed police officer from an unspecified threat made by a drug baron in Glasgow.

Dr. Herrington was in his mid-forties, she thought, with prematurely greying hair and what she thought of as a 'BBC English' accent. He sat opposite her in one of two easy chairs, relaxed, with a file folder on his lap.

"Catrin, it's my job to assess whether you are ready to return to work, given the experience you have been through. Anything you tell me will be protected by client confidentiality, of course, but equally, if I say you are not ready yet, no one is going to ask the reason why. They will take my word at face value unless it goes to some sort of appeal.

"I always say that at the beginning, because it is important for me to know your mental state. Not, I should add, to be convinced that you are one hundred percent over the experience but I need to be assured that you have come to terms with it and have a system of coping and recovering."

Catrin nodded, "I understand, but to be honest, I feel just fine. Physically sore and worried how the scar will look but otherwise I'm OK. I want to go back to work."

He said nothing to agree with her, just looked at her.

"So let's begin. Tell me what happened and how you felt while it was happening."

I have been through this once already today, she thought.

When she finished, Dr. Herrington said, "Do you remember being scared?"

"Not as such," said Catrin, "more a sense of 'What have I done?'. This was meant to be a covert surveillance operation. I had no permission to do what I did. That worried me."

"And now?"

"My superiors have explained I have their support – it was the right thing to do."

"But how do you feel?"

Catrin paused, thinking. "I am glad I did it for Mr. Hart. They say he would have died if I hadn't called for help."

His voice was soft. "But you could have called for help from the surveillance point, a request for an ambulance? You saw his legs on the ground, and so could have called for back-up and awaited instructions, right?"

"Yes," said Catrin, "I could have. I tried as I ran to call my partner, as the closest officer. Then I spoke to the officer in charge but had no time to talk to him, I was near the church door.

"But looking at it now, looking at it when I was in the hospital, yes I could have ... but not then."

"So how do you feel about that decision?"

Catrin's voice developed a shake. "I still feel a bit guilty, to be honest. All this trouble between the Met and Police Scotland, the security coverage, my face. I wish I had done it differently, somehow, but I am not sure how."

He nodded. "So now, why do you think you acted the way you did?"

She took her time answering. "I saw Hart's legs appear and knew he was down and I thought Cheney could be in the church after all. During the Stornoway attack he had hit the security guard in Stornoway with something. Now we know it was a baton, but I didn't know that then. So I thought perhaps he had hit Hart; which it turned out he had. I felt I had to get to Hart and see how he was."

Dr. Herrington said, "If you had called for backup you would have been told to secure the scene and await other officers; that's the procedure, right?"

"Yes."

"So all you have to do is decide; did you go in to the scene with the right motive – to help Hart – or the wrong one, don't you think?"

"Yes."

Again it was all she found she could say.

"And only you can know that, in your heart. So think on it and we will talk again on your next visit."

"So I am coming back?"

Dr. Herrington stood up. "Yes, Catrin, you are. I will tell you now I think we have a way to go yet, but don't despair. Recovery is a road, not an event.

"And tomorrow, Saturday, there will be a further medical check up for you at the hospital here for any lasting effects of the concussion. If the results show no change from the last assessment in Scotland, I will declare you ready for your interview and your report preparation. Not because they are pressing me, which they are, but I believe it is something that you need to get behind you, for your own recovery; not pleasant, I know, but necessary."

She found herself in the outer office confirming her next appointment with the medical secretary there. 'I thought this would be it; one visit, just a sign off', was on her mind.

30 MEDIA

It was Friday afternoon. Superintendent Jack Taylor, Assistant Commissioner Sandra Hunt and DCI Jane Worsley were seated at the conference table in Hunt's office. The Met's Public Relations Director, Tony Johnston, was there also to review the media coverage trends for the Kinnington Incident enquiry.

Johnston said, "The most problematic item now is the interview yesterday with the ACC; the coverage was trending down until he gave his second interview on the case. According to Bob Stewart, my opposite number in Police Scotland, Assistant Chief Constable Andrew McKillop went right off script; and he is known for handling media interviews really well so it was no accident. Here it is."

He pressed the remote and the wall screen came to life.

They watched silently. The press interview with McKillop came after two clips, one of two Scottish Assembly MSPs calling for answers to the enquiry established by PIRC and a summary of the accusations made by Niall Irvin.

"We understand that the officer concerned has not yet provided a statement?" was the first question.

McKillop ignored that one.

"The conduct of the enquiry is the jurisdiction of the Review Commissioner," he said, looking around the press and pointing.

"Do you believe an enquiry is merited?"

McKillop answered, "Personally, no, I believe all officers acted properly within their mandate in response to a violent crime. But we will co-operate fully with the enquiry by the Commissioner. As will the Metropolitan Police."

He pointed at the STV reporter.

"The Metropolitan Police are clearly not cooperating; they are looking after their own. What if the shoe was on the other foot, a Scottish officer under review for an incident in England? What would you do?"

McKillop paused and then responded. "The PIRC investigation is proceeding normally, I understand, so I don't know where you get that inference. Police Scotland would cooperate of course with any enquiry by the English counterpart, the IPCC, should that situation arise. It hasn't."

Then he added, unnecessarily, "Of course, my shoe size is a little larger than the Met officer attending the scene at Kinnington."

Tony said, "And here are later runs of the same interview. Look at the image changes."

Later replays of the footage showed the ACC exiting the interview and the camera panning to his shoes. The message was clear, given the earlier coverage. "Assistant Chief Constable McKillop seems to have some sympathy with the officer who assaulted Mr. Cheney, it appears," said the STV reporter in a voiceover of the exit scene.

Johnston continued. "It has caused more howls and McKillop is in it deeper now with the wolves. It will take longer for the whole thing to die down."

Hunt nodded, "He called me about it. Said he had done it; this politically neutral stuff was eating at him."

Johnston continued. "The other point is that certain sectors of the media are deliberately eliminating any references to the police officer being injured. They say they are waiting on details of the injuries and we are not, of course, going to mention anything specific about Sayer's injuries to avoid any identification.

"The Welsh media, though, all say that the officer received substantial injuries in the line of duty. This has caused some questions back to the BBC and ITV social media sites about their coverage."

Jack Taylor said, "That's Emrys Howell's doing, poking Scotland in the eye, I suspect. He gave Sayer a commendation after the Bangor incident."

Howell was the Chief Constable of North Wales.

"Those Welsh stick together," he added.

Jane said, "Not like Yorkshiremen, Jack?"

Taylor went po-faced. "We Yorkshiremen are known for our discerning objectivity."

All business, Sandra said, "Thank you, Tony. Jane, what's the status of the threat level against Sayer and the French officer – any change?"

"No ma'am. We still don't have any more substantive evidence of a specific basis for the threat, only the word through informers. DCI Strachan and her team are not seeing any unusual financial transactions from any Connolly or Milne accounts they are able to monitor and there is nothing new on the streets. They doubtlessly have other financial holdings, of course.

"However, there is some chilling news. The French police have found the body of Sophie Rousseau, the person who they compromised to get their officer into the Finisterre operation. She had been tortured before she died, it appears."

Hunt said, "By locals, I assume."

Taylor answered. "We assume so. Strachan checked the whereabouts of the main players in the Connolly and Milne gangs and they were all here, with the exception of Daniella Milne, Francis Milne's wife. She was in France, shopping in Paris, we gather."

"Do we think so, just shopping?" Hunt asked.

"No," said Jack Taylor, "I don't believe in coincidence on this at all. We will never prove anything different, I think."

"A woman though, involved in torture," Hunt said. It wasn't a question or a statement, more a reflection.

Taylor said, "Daniella Milne is Colombian; her father is in the higher levels of the drug trade. She probably has had some family tuition."

There was nothing light-hearted about him now.

Hunt said, "So we continue the current level of security, for now." It wasn't a question.

There was the constant cloud overhanging the security issue that, other than senior officers, only Keith, Jane and the Security team were aware. Catrin only had a basic understanding of the issue and was never privy to the details - but she understood the implications for her.

Strachan and others were trying to get clarity on the contract value that Connolly had placed on the hits for the French officer and DC Sayer, without success. It had been Worsley and Taylor that had decided on the current security arrangements for Sayer, as they gave Catrin a more normal lifestyle. It was based on the assumption that Connolly was relying on loyalty or a contract fee for work by his own people.

If they found that the money offered was significant, or had already changed hands, everything would change; they would then be in the ballpark where a professional contract killer could have been engaged. Catrin and the French officer would probably be moved to secure facilities and cut off from all regular contacts.

In the end, that clarity never came, nor was it needed. But the potential for it gnawed away at Catrin. Her world could be wrapped up in an instant, to be replaced by an unknown hotel room or apartment and an indeterminate period of isolation.

~~

Catrin had problems sleeping after that first interview with Dr. Herrington. She would awaken once or twice a night with a bad dream about standing, holding the Glock 17 pistol that she trained with at Milton before joining the ACU, frozen in some sort of anxiety attack on the steps of Kinnington Church. She knew she would have to cover it with her psychologist but was dreading it, dreading the consequences of doing so; it was bound to damage his confidence in her ability to return to work.

She was still astonished how quickly Dr. Herrington had driven the interview into penetrating her fears.

Catrin had arranged for a discount rate for her parents at a small tourist hotel about five minutes' walk away from her flat. Jean had agreed to meet them at Paddington Station as Catrin was not allowed there, even with her security detail. Melanie had walked over from their place to Catrin's flat so she would be there when they arrived.

It was only when they came through the door with carrier bags and luggage and Jean saying, 'I tried to get them to take this stuff to the hotel first' that Catrin realized that her parents had never met Melanie, only knew about her. They had known Jean from almost her toddler days.

Catrin introduced Helen first as her flatmate and then introduced Melanie, who was making tea. Catrin's dad shook Helen's hand and then turning to Melanie said, "Jean, you chose a cracker here, it's nice to meet you at last." He just went forward and gave her a hug.

Catrin smiled. Her dad was usually the quiet one. Her mum did the talking, but he could rise to the occasion. And it was true what he said. Melanie was as eye-catching good-looking as Jean, quite simply, was not. At least there wasn't any awkwardness about them being gay with her parents, she thought.

When her mother had entered the room Catrin had instinctively checked her out, her eyes, her movement. Not that she had any thought her mother would be drinking again but it was a habit deeply embedded from more painful times. What it did this time for her, and she looked across at her dad too, was bring home the stress her parents were under.

Her mother sat close by, just looking at her. The dressing was reduced in size and some of the bruising had faded a little, at last. The swelling was coming down nicely, too.

They spent the evening talking and eating after Jean and Melanie left and Helen went out. There were tears from her mother and later from her and at one point her dad choked up on what he wanted to do to the man who did this to her. There was anger in him that surfaced that Catrin hadn't seen since the worst of her mum's drinking days. But it evaporated or re-buried itself quickly.

She could see they were tired from the journey and she was also worn out from her own day. She had checked with the security detail but she wasn't allowed to walk them to the nearby hotel. The uniformed officer made a quick call on his radio and another DPS officer appeared and walked them over.

Before leaving she said to them, "Tomorrow I have to go to the hospital for a check-up in the morning with the security team, to declare that I am free of concussion. Then we three will have lunch in the market and can go to see the Cwmbran Kiln, and later I have something special for you," she said. "Tickets for the London Philharmonic Choir at the Royal Festival Hall. I can't go but Melanie is taking you."

She knew her parents would probably be fine going to the concert by themselves, but they were also the sort of people if they got lost, they could run into difficulties. Pontypridd was their home and they found Cardiff to be a big place.

"But we came to see you," said her mother.

"And so you are, and we will spend the day together and Sunday morning, but I want you to have something special as well while you are here."

Her father had sung in a male voice choir for years until his voice went. She could see he was pleased.

"Melanie is a soprano, she sang years ago in her school choir. She will enjoy it." Catrin's fingers were mentally crossed behind her back as she spoke; Melanie was doing this, she said, "as a labour of love."

By the time they left on Sunday afternoon, insisting

they could get back to Paddington themselves, Catrin was glad to have had the time with them but she was looking forward to a quiet Sunday evening. Next week was going to be as busy as the last one, she knew, one way or another.

~~

At The Cwmbran Kiln on Monday, the security detail had worked out a different setup, so as not to disturb any customers. The uniforms weren't in sight but a plain-clothes policewoman called Jackie, who Catrin never saw otherwise, stayed in the shop sitting with Melanie while Catrin worked in the back with Jean. The PC and Melanie got on well and she, at least, accepted coffee. It was Jackie who confirmed to Catrin on the Wednesday that the decision on Peter McPherson and herself by PIRC was due in a little over a week – on the Thursday. "Through our source," she said enigmatically.

Despite the security protection and the whole weird life at that time, Catrin threw herself into the pottery work. Jean made blanks, both greenware and bisques, to meet Catrin's requests, joking about the opportunity to reap a harvest of pottery at the Met's expense. But it was clear to all of them that they were working to keep Catrin occupied.

That it had a therapeutic element to it, as Keith had said, was not in doubt. Later, Liz was to say that the finishes she applied to those pieces made a series quite different to her past work; and it was a theme she came back to in various other forms in later years, during times she was troubled by other issues. 'It has a quite a cold tone,' thought Liz's husband, William. It sold well although some of the customers for Sayer's work said it did not seem typical of her and it did not appeal to them.

So the week went by. In a work context, Catrin saw only Dr. Herrington for her second appointment and had another meeting with Evelyn Carter. Both Worsley and Marshall called to ask after her and also for comments or details on other cases she had been working on.

Aina became her source of information on what was happening at work, as far as she could tell; nothing about cases from her, but the movements and goings-on at the office gave her a sense of continuity that Catrin sorely missed, she realised.

Evelyn told Catrin that she had heard that the PIRC interview was due next Tuesday. A formal call from Worsley the same day confirmed it. Not a lot of time between the interview and the decision date, she thought, but probably all the other interviews and preparative work had been completed.

Evelyn Carter told her, "I talked with someone I know in the Scottish Federation office. The PIRC investigators are McLellan and Strang. McLellan is senior, fair but sharp she says. Strang is a woman, sounds about your age and is a go-getter. So I want you to be very careful. Don't identify with her when they start, right? Remember what I said."

Evelyn had explained that investigators knew the training and experience of police officers and would not be trying any sort of shock or deceptive tactics, particularly with Federation representation present. But they would work on the collegiality and on professional common standards.

"The next thing you know you have slipped out something you would tell you colleague or a boss - but not a lawyer for the opposition. And that's what they are, Catrin, the opposition."

31 ALL ABOUT THE BUSINESS

"Finally, we would like to know what Niall was doing with Cheney at this church thing. Just what we needed, the additional visibility," said Daniella. It was the first agenda item she had spoken to before Steve, as their lead negotiator, had provided the Milne position.

Dominic has specifically told Niall not to attend the meeting because he knew this would come up.

"It was my doing," he lied, "but with good intent."

The Milne brothers had brought Daniella to the business meeting for the first time. He was there with only Shannon, the accountant, and Carmichael, his head enforcer. He could see clearly how instrumental Daniella was in their organisation. She wasn't the daughter of a Columbian drug dealer simply to enjoy the good life, it was clear; she knew the business and was heavily involved in making the supply line side work efficiently.

The great mitigation for Dominic on this issue and the reason why he knew he was in control of the meeting was that the Milne organization was to blame for the fiasco. The leak and entrance point for the French undercover officer had been through the Milne operation. In the bald, business-language discussion between the accountants for each side they talked about relative losses and terms of adjustment through future inventory allocation. Connolly had come out of it with only a $2.3 million portion of the $8 million street level loss resulting from 'Operation Finisterre', as the media dubbed it. The lion's share was to be borne by the Milne operation.

Given he now had a strategic advantage over them - it was their mess - he was calming down about the money side of it. But the people loss angered him, good people put in place in Ireland and built up in Brittany.

Colin wasn't really a loss at all; he had just put him in key position in the internal prison supply operation, which was no small market. He had given Colin and his mother enough money to make them both smile and a promise to the man that he would get something moving on early release once he was sentenced and they knew where to head next.

He smiled inwardly. The media were howling about the damage to him. All he had to do was steer through this last bit. Daniella was all ears as he spoke.

"It's my fault because I should have stuck to my own business. Niall mentioned to me that you were really pleased about the painting and he was working on finding more for you, Daniella. He let drop that his relative had attended that church and given a window and some paintings there. It was my bright idea to check to see if any were your Colourists and I sent Colin along to get access. I even asked Niall to go and check on the paintings he brought out.

"Niall said he was no expert and not too happy about being there, being a lawyer, but he would do it as he had seen how the first one was so well-received."

He looked at Francis.

"Anyway, that went as belly up as the Brittany thing. We had no idea that some police art group were going to such lengths over the death of Alexander Gault after his blabbing to the people at the museum about his own dad stealing paintings. He must have got someone fired up enough to bring a police officer specializing in art all the way from London."

Daniella was still looking at him intently but Francis said, "It was a nice gesture, Dom, but it back-fired. We should both just stick to our business, I think, and forget about these paintings. Another group of snooping scum is the last thing we need."

Dominic nodded as Daniella said icily to her husband, "No. If Niall still finds access to more paintings I want them and on the terms we agreed."

Steve looked at his brother and sister-in-law; he had been the main Milne spokesperson throughout the negotiations until the church thing came up.

"Let's move on, family," he said.

He looked at Dominic. "We need to work together on the route we shelved through Denmark. Now, let's talk about it. Volumes, people, payoffs needed. Let's get some real work done here. We have mutually beneficial businesses to run."

Dominic agreed and nodded, glad to be through Niall's screw-up.

Daniella looked down at the table, getting her cool back, controlling her breathing. She is so explosive, so intense, Dominic thought. Part of the reason Joan would have nothing to do with 'Madame Muck' was that she was no fun at all, but there was also the behavior she had just shown.

"She's not normal, Dom. I don't want her around

Jason, Angie or me."

Daniella, not Steve or Francis, had gone over to Brittany to meet with the people dealing with the person who had turned the operation over to the police. She had been extreme, even by Connolly's own standards. His rule from the time he did his own enforcement was you hurt people commensurate with the damage they did, so they learn not to repeat the mistake. If it was past that, don't mess around, just kill them quickly. His enforcers abided by the same rule.

Daniella came from a different camp entirely.

~~

It was Catrin's third appointment with Dr. Herrington on the Friday of that week that was the breakthrough. He said afterwards in his report that few trauma incidents of this type had moved to positive resolution so quickly in his experience of police work.

As usual, he asked her to spend a minute relaxing, thinking of something serene, positive. In Catrin Sayer's case, it was something to do with the Menai Straits, she had said.

Catrin had told him about the night anxieties at the second interview. She felt she had to get it off her chest.

"Catrin, we are now going to deal with your bouts of waking up at night that you mentioned last time. Tell me how you feel when you wake up?"

"Anxious, scared."

"Close your eyes. What do you see at night when you wake up?"

"I am back at the church each time but with a gun drawn, pointing at Cheney. It's the weapon I trained with, the Glock."

213

"Describe the surroundings, the light, what you see other than either Cheney or Irvin."

Catrin's eyes were closed. She talked about the church wall and steps, the vehicle in the road and the shadows in the failing light as darkness approached. Herrington noted in the comments the emphasis of detail of what she could see from her right side, consistent with the after-effects of a blow to the left side of the face. She was there.

"What do you do in your dream?"

"Well, I wake up then."

"No before you wake up, there is something. What is it?" His voice had taken on an insistent edge.

"I ... I am angry, and sometimes I think I ...shoot him."

"Sometimes or every time, Catrin?"

She paused, eyes closed, swallowing nervously. "Every time."

"Where exactly do you shoot him?" Herrington's questions were coming faster, right on the heels of each answer, demanding.

"In the head. Then I shoot Irvin.... in the face, He is looking at my face and I shoot him. Then I wake up."

She opened her eyes. Tears were running down both cheeks.

"And how do you feel then?" Herrington's voice had softened.

"Guilty, ashamed, guilty.... it's awful." She sobbed and wiped her eyes with the tissue he proffered from the box on the table, and then she blew her nose.

"Did you hypnotize me?" she suddenly asked.

Dr. Herrington smiled. "Hypnotize you against your will, without prior permission? No, that's not how it works, nor would it be professional of me. Someone with your artistic imagination doesn't need hypnosis, at least not for this sort of thing; it is not deeply blocked, is it?"

He was inspecting her carefully. "And how do you feel now?"

"I'm not sure; really anxious, I guess. I was anxious about telling you about the dreams last time and now … what is in them is so bad. Telling you that I felt like shooting them so violently. I am not ready for work, am I?"

He smiled at her. "On the contrary, you would be surprised how soon you will be back at work, but let's talk about what to do when you have these dreams first."

He looked down at a document he slid out of the folder on his lap.

"This is a professional psychiatric opinion on Colin Cheney that I requested from his prison assessment. I asked for it for your health, not for his, so it's confidential. I can't share it with you; you just need to accept that I know. I am not speculating.

"He is not only a dangerous man but, to my mind, a very sick one. Sick in the sense that from childhood the only ego-building he has received has always related to violence, generally violence he perpetrated and in which others encouraged him or rewarded him. Everything else, his upbringing, the abuse he suffered as a child, just about anything that he spoke about with the psychiatrist there was all destructive."

"In summary he is a very dangerous man, but very damaged. And here you are a successful college graduate, a police officer, an artist, with a good family base and good friendships. You are from a different world."

"I tell you this because when you wake up at night and see him, I want you to think immediately about how weak and damaged he is. Not to engender sympathy, but what it will help to do is put him in perspective, put the anger you feel in perspective, diminish his impact on you. Then we will talk about what you do next as this dream changes or simply disappears.

"Catrin, your guilt is so natural associated with the dream. It is about the anger you feel about the damage to your face that we talked about previously. You weren't armed at the church but I am sure that if you were, you wouldn't do the things in this dream. You were never trained to shoot people in the face, were you?"

"No," she said, "I never finished the training, but we were to fire at central body mass, that's what I practiced."

Herrington said, "What you did do, without firearms, was to manage an almost impossible situation arresting two men, one of them violent, single-handed."

He paused, assessing how well she was absorbing the information.

"The people who go through events like yours who do not recover are the ones in denial - the ones who can't identify with guilt or anger for something. Everyone is saying to you did the right thing and you smile and say 'thank you' but inside, you are wondering what you could have done different, better. Well, what you did is… what you did. It was fine. You are just having trouble accepting it.

"I am going to recommend you return to work on what I will call 'light duties'. You need that for the face anyway, right? I want to see you next week to talk about the dreams again and I plan to see you at fortnightly intervals to begin with, for the next two months. Also you must contact me if you find these anxieties are getting worse, not better. I am going to trust you to do that."

Catrin gave a big sigh. "Thank you, Dr. Herrington."

"When is your interview with the Scottish investigators?"

"Next Tuesday."

"Recognize that you will be anxious about that, too, and it's natural to feel so. Call me shortly after the interview; we can talk about it, OK? Catrin, you are doing very well, just remember not to be so hard on yourself."

Ryan, the security officer waiting in the anteroom, saw Catrin's face when she came out and said as they walked out, "Good for you, DC Sayer. From that smile it appears the doctor has let you go back to work. Right?"

"When Superintendent Taylor agrees, I think, yes, Ryan. But first I have the PIRC interview."

They were outside, approaching the car. "At least you have Evelyn on your side; she is good, I hear," he said.

32 THE PIRC INTERVIEW

The interview of DC Catrin Sayer under the authority of the Police Investigations & Review Commissioner of Scotland was conducted by Investigators McLellan and Strang on the following Tuesday, two weeks and a day after the Kinnington Church incident. Everything about it was formal, from a Yard staffer escorting the PIRC investigators to the interview room, right down to the PIRC team's reception of Evelyn and Catrin. They were kept waiting, sitting on two chairs positioned outside the room, for some time after their arrival.

The door opened. Strang invited them in, smiling, and offered them coffee, tea or water from a side table.

"No thank you," said Evelyn and pointed Catrin to the vacant chair opposite the senior investigator. She wanted the younger woman from Scotland opposite her, Catrin realised. The chances of Strang bonding and identifying with her client still bothered Carter.

They had started, of course, with a request for her version of events, which Catrin gave exactly as agreed in language she had gone through with Evelyn. With clarifications, it took over three-quarters of an hour for the run-through. Their questions were fair, balanced, Catrin thought. Perhaps Evelyn was over-sensitive about this interview.

Then they had jumped straight to the kick into Cheney's groin.

Why do that?

She explained. They seemed indifferent about her explanation, going back to it from different angles, while showing disdain and disappointment with her action. Catrin ignore the implied guilt, as Evelyn had warned her, and withdrew mentally her earlier thoughts about her solicitor having overreacted.

Finally McLellan said, "Do you accept, at least, he was already under arrest, DC Sayer, when you kicked him?"

"He should have acted that way instead of resisting arrest," Evelyn said, interrupting.

"He denies it," said McLellan, irritated that the answer did not come from Catrin.

"Can we take a break, please?" asked Evelyn, looking at her watch. An hour and a quarter had passed. "My client needs a break, I need a smoke and it's starting to feel like Disneyworld in here."

Evelyn was a different personality in the room, Catrin thought, one she could see would give the lawyer her reputation with the Met. Abrasive, short or rude in her responses at times, unaccommodating of any leeway by the Commission investigators when they asked open-ended questions. Catrin had been told to ask for such questions to be re-phrased more clearly and the first time she did that she could sense Evelyn's approval. Catrin did not feel alone; there was a sharp, battle-hardened person on her side.

After the break they started on her attitude to Irvin, about it being excessively hostile and threatening without any need to be so; she had agreed to a question earlier that he had not been combative at all.

Catrin said, "He was clearly part of the crime; he was collecting the art, that is why the rear door of the car was opened by him. They were going to put the paintings in the car."

"He was unarmed and non-threatening, correct?" said McLellan.

"He did not move towards me, no. But part of the reason I reacted to Cheney's movement was seeing the looks exchanged between them. His look was supportive of Cheney. I took that to be threatening."

"That's your perception of their exchange, DC Sayer. Irvin says he had just recognized Cheney as a former client. Did you misinterpret a look of recognition as something... conspiratorial, perhaps?" He was sounding collegial, understanding.

"I know what I saw, I understood the look, I acted accordingly," said Catrin.

"Your perception," said McLellan again.

"I was there, you weren't."

I am beginning to sound as belligerent as Evelyn, she thought. She looked at her Federation representative. Evelyn was staring coldly at McLellan, liking Catrin's responses.

Then they went into a twenty minute exercise on the theme of how disorientated Catrin had been, given the severity of the blow, and whether she really felt it was appropriate to attempt the arrest rather than observe, call for back-up or, indeed, just let them get away and deal directly with the injured victim. Had she really overstretched herself? It was an area Evelyn said would be covered in great detail.

Catrin gave the responses they had agreed and when they came back at it again Evelyn had cut in. "Officer Sayer has already stated that she felt capable of making the arrest and securing assistance for the victim promptly. She did so."

Strang turned a page in the materials that the two Commission officers were using as their reference set.

"Let's talk about your training, Officer Sayer. I see that apart from baton training you also later commenced firearms training at Milton but did not complete certification as an Authorised Firearms Officer."

She looked up at Catrin. "Fortunately, you were not armed at Kinnington Church."

They will bait you if they are getting nowhere, Evelyn had said. Neither Sayer nor Carter said anything. Strang could say the moon was blue for all it mattered, Catrin thought.

"Please describe your knowledge of procedures in the event of the use of your baton during an arrest." Strang asked the question softly, almost routine.

Here it comes, thought Catrin. She described the procedures she had been taught and exercised on as if it came from the manual.

Strang nodded. 'DC Sayer, is that the sequence you followed on May 6 at Kinnington Church?

Catrin answered, "I responded as best as I could with the target areas available to subdue a hostile and aggressive assailant."

She had wanted to say she didn't recall when Evelyn went through this beforehand; her solicitor would have none of it.

Strang sighed. "Shall I repeat the question, DC Sayer? Did you follow procedure?"

"I believe so; it becomes instinctive with the training received, but I was recovering from a blow to the head at the time."

Strang leaned forward, more aggressive in her question.

"I remind you I am not talking about your use of the torch on Cheney. In fact, he says you hit Irvin without due warning, is that correct?"

"No, I had already commanded the man by the car to place his hands on the vehicle. He did not comply and tried to make a call on his mobile. I had to stop him making any outside contact. That was consistent with my orders."

"Your orders were to observe and record unless otherwise instructed; you had already disobeyed those, hadn't you?" said McLellan.

"No," said Catrin, "My orders were to observe, photograph and document the intrusion and the exit of the perpetrator or perpetrators unless other circumstances dictated. A man suddenly collapsing inside the church door was, I believe, consistent with that order. Circumstances had changed."

Strang said, "Back to hitting Irvin. We have been trying to establish if your use of the torch as a surrogate baton was proportionate and reasonably necessary. That is what the law prescribes in the use of a weapon and I fail to see how striking Mr. Irvin fits that, frankly. What was going through your mind when you hit him?"

Catrin paused then gave the answer she and Evelyn had gone through. "All I recall is not spitting then. I let the blood run out of my mouth instead as I wanted no head motion, as I was unsure I could stay upright. I was concentrating on how to get help, how to keep these men secure and isolated in accordance with the primary instruction, to protect the police operation now known as 'Finisterre'. That is all I recall."

That was true. Evelyn had established it with a series of questions much harsher than the one posed by the PIRC investigator.

Strang's voice showed her disbelief, "Cheney was there and saw you make an angry and vicious attack on Irvin from less than six feet away. You were standing up, recovering from his blow, a heavy blow. Are you saying his recall of the events is less accurate than your own?"

Carter cut in sharply. "Don't answer."

She leaned forward. "DC Sayer has answered the question to the best of her knowledge. Don't continue to ask her to speculate on the honesty of the bastard who split her face open. Are you two done, or what?"

They weren't, but it was downhill from there. At the end they thanked her formally for her cooperation and closed the recording. Carter grabbed Catrin's arm and wheeled her out without another word, not even a goodbye.

Evelyn had said beforehand, if they can show that you used the torch like a baton out of anger and violent retaliation, they have a case. Whether there are extenuating circumstances is immaterial; potentially that is a matter of law. We are going to give them no case whatsoever from your statement.

Catrin was going back to her floor afterwards to talk with Keith; he wanted to know how it went, he said. She walked Evelyn to the front entrance of Scotland Yard, shook her hand and then, impulsively, she gave her a hug.

"Thank you again. I now know what you meant about feeling alone, but with you there, I wasn't."

Evelyn had said on the way down that she had done very well and she would be keeping track of developments.

"Now, I need another smoke." said Evelyn.

Her parting comment was, 'Your cheek is healing nicely."

~~

Catrin had called Peter McPherson's number after the brief discussion with Sinclair and left a message. He had never called back. Back at her desk, on impulse, she called him again and left a new one.

About fifteen minutes later she got a call on a mobile phone different to the number he had used previously.

"I hear that they will decide on my fate and yours at a meeting on Thursday, Catrin, and the Commission people will interview you before then."

"They just did so, Peter. How did it go with you?"

"I told them I should have been there but was away on a break, which was true but they hammered me over my phone use and not being contactable when you were on watch alone. They had the records. Said I was acting in contravention of regulations.

"I hope it goes well for you, Catrin, I really do. I feel so bad about not being there for you when it went down. I am not sleeping well, to be honest. And I am seeing a police psychologist; Federation orders."

Catrin heard the emotion in his voice. "Peter, I feel bad too that you are in trouble from my actions. It is part of my discussion with my own psychologist here. Don't you think we, at least, should just forgive each other, whatever that means? I really don't believe either of us acted inappropriately. We were just coppers doing our job."

"Well I have no hard feelings against you, Catrin."

"Me neither."

Peter said he had gone in private to see Michael Hart in hospital. He was talking more easily now with the therapy and still had no recollection of the event. The last thing he recalled was entering the church.

"He asked after you, Catrin, and said, 'God Bless You' for coming so quickly."

Catrin started to choke up. "He wrote to me, signed a card, with a longer note from his wife, Peter. It was very nice."

McPherson said, "I am glad you called. Frankly I am giving this job up anyway, the stress and all, you know? I need more regular work, to be around here, help with my kids and just be around for my family."

"Peter, you take good care of yourself. And I hope you make a good decision and everything works out. You are a good officer in my books, whether you stay in the job or not."

She closed the call and looked across from her desk. Keith had been in a meeting with Jane and someone she didn't know in Jane's office while she was on the phone.

The man left and Keith popped his head out. "Come on in. How did it go? We were racing through the last meeting just so we could hear about it."

33 LANGMUIR

Langmuir led them through the videos of their individual performances, making it a group exercise. They would laugh at a botch-up, such as the gem by Inspector Randall, irritated by Courtney pushing the microphone in his face, telling the reporter, "Piss off or I will arrest you."

"You are not the first policeman I have interviewed who has told me that," said Paul Courtney, "but the ones who do usually don't get to be Chief Superintendent."

Courtney had picked Wright's interview as his choice for the best response. Wright had insisted that they imagine the venue for the interview was the Kinnington Church steps, he said at the outset. Despite some effort by Courtney, he stuck to the message he had developed.

"Two men were arrested in association with an attack at the Kinnington Church here, in which it's parishioner Michael Hart and a police officer were seriously injured. We send every prayer and good wish for their speedy recovery.

"Regretfully one of the persons present during the incident, a Mr. Irvin, was apparently a bystander not a participant in this event. He was arrested but was released immediately the true situation became clear. We have apologised to him already. We will co-operate fully with the enquiry by PIRC into this incident but doubt its value and this use of public resources."

Courtney tried one more angle as Wright listened attentively. Then as Courtney stopped to hear the response, Wright ignored the question and said, "If you will excuse me, I am going inside to be with the family and congregation of Mr. Hart; my focus now is on the victims of this incident." He then turned his back and walked away from the camera.

"Wonderful," said Paul, " At the time it would have frustrated my editor, but you gave me only video and sound bites that showed a responsible, caring police officer and made Irvin's stuff seem… irrelevant."

"The politics were driving that," responded Langmuir, "which is why my choice for the interview with the Crown about disciplinary action is Bala." Other nodded, having already reached the same conclusion. Most had picked one or other officer at the scene, Sinclair or Strachan for some level of disciplinary action.

Inspector Balasubramanian, who everyone called 'Bala', was a small Indian female inspector with a natural intense gaze. She had appeared calm in response to Langmuir's invented anger as he portrayed a senior Crown official wanting to find the culprits who mishandled this fiasco.

"I will not bring disciplinary action against anyone in my team, nor support it against DC Sayer. Were there errors, yes there were. Hindsight is wonderful. But the material outcome of the Kinnington Incident is to confirm our suspicion about the involvement of the complainant, Irvin, in a crime and to arrest Colin Cheney for robbery and serious injury to at least three people. Our investigations are proceeding and I expect more shortly."

"Nevertheless, I am telling the Commissioner that the Crown has no objections to the enquiry requested by Niall Irvin," said Langmuir. He had said that to each interviewee.

Bala had looked straight at the camera. "I can't stop you being a bloody fool and making my life and that of my force more difficult. I can, however, make sure every member of the Parliamentary Sub-Committee on Justice gets a confidential brief on my opposition to this enquiry and its basis. And I will give my counterpart at the Met – she had glanced at her file notes – Assistant Commissioner Hunt – my support and tell her that I personally disagree with any action against DC Sayer."

Langmuir had thought she had finished and was about to close the interview when she added, "Mr. --, I know your power and I know your politics and who you are cozying with on this. Well, here is my position. Deny this request for an enquiry. It is unfounded. Otherwise tomorrow morning the Minister of State for Scotland will be informed of your personal attempt for political reasons to destroy the good working relationship between two police services. I can do that. He is outside your cadre of friends in the Scotland Office and you know who he will brief next himself."

She meant clearly that the Cabinet office in London would be informed.

Langmuir pressed the remote and the screen went blank. "That was good, Bala, and particularly that last point; it may even have had some traction at the time. But it didn't happen, I know that.

"So tomorrow we move on to Module Two. It's been a good start to this week's course. It gets more complicated tomorrow. Have a good evening everyone."

By day three they would be handling communication decisions for a relative marathon; the three-month-long investigation into the disappearance and eventual discovery of the remains of a sixteen year old schoolgirl.

As Langmuir put away his materials he thought about the repercussions of the Killington Church incident. He knew a lot more about it as a civilian than any of these inspectors would give credit. The current Press Officer to the Minister needed a sounding board on really complicated issues, someone who was experienced and whom he could trust. It was a nice private contract for Langmuir.

He knew that the events that unfolded in the wake of the attempted theft at Kinnington Church had far larger consequences than even Bala had stretched her mind to.

PART 3

TRAP

34 THE SET UP

Neville Coltrane was in a videoconference with the two Scottish officers, DCI Sinclair and DCI Strachan. It was Tuesday morning, the same day as the PIRC interview of Sayer. Strachan had assumed control of the meeting and Sinclair said nothing about that; clearly this had been sorted out within Police Scotland, Neville thought.

His role was clear. Offer expertise support from the Met and in doing so see what could be done to bring Niall Irvin down. It was as simple as that. They had the person who had injured their officer locked away and also had no doubts about the accuracy of Sayer's statement about Cheney and Irvin working together at the robbery.

With Chief Superintendent Matheson, his direct superior, he had met with Assistant Commissioner Hunt. She had very much appreciated his offer of assistance after the Kinnington incident, she said. It spoke well to collegiality and support among Metropolitan Police officers, given the background on the formation of the ACU and its role alongside Art & Antiques.

The way Irvin was being lauded in Scotland had to be addressed, was the bottom line, she said. The facts needed to be exposed to vindicate DC Sayer completely. She deserved no less.

Strachan told them that she had a plan to break Irvin's alibi and cause further damage to the drug operations in southern Scotland. She took them through it and Coltrane could see that she was a very strategic thinker.

Critical to the initiation of the operation was the Kelvingrove Museum itself and they were on board, particularly Susan Hetherington, she said.

Strachan said, "Let's begin with the two main drug gangs. Neville, you will need some background here. I will be the first to admit I kept all this under wraps during Eric's investigation, but you can understand why.

"Connolly's group in Glasgow is typical of most of larger drug operations in the UK. If it wasn't drugs, Dominic Connolly would be running some other criminal organisation here, it's the way he is. The organisational structure funnels everything up to Connolly and their operating approach is fear-based, vicious and hard.

"He has three enforcers - well, had, we have Cheney now - who keep things in line and, I have to say, they are effective."

She continued, "The Edinburgh scene is different. Francis and Stephen Milne may be 'Frank and Steve' to the people down the pecking order, but the brothers operate differently. There is in fact little overt violence. Dealers get cut off and replaced for even a minor infraction. If they are pushed out, no-one within the organisation is allowed to sell to them afterwards, even for their own needs; they are quite literally left high and dry.

"If they make a more serious screw-up they get a visit from Steve, who just tells them the way it is. They either find a way to repay the loss or, in the worst scenario, they simply disappear. There are no bodies on the street, nothing for the media to see and so far, Police Scotland has never traced anyone who disappeared. They vanish.

"The Milne brothers are both very bright, both university graduates. Steve primarily runs the domestic distribution operation. Frank handles the planning and supply routes. Socially he prefers to be known as Francis and also has a quite separate legit business in the Exchange district of Edinburgh, all high class stuff, one of these job search and recruitment agencies."

Neville could see she was drawing this all from memory; no notes, no glances at files.

"His wife is Daniella Milne, actually Senora Daniella Maria Ramires Milne. She is still a Colombian citizen and is part of Francis's success. She will be the key to this operation.

"Daniella is the daughter of Estevan Ramires, a retired Colombian cartel kingpin, one who actually got to retire; to somewhere in Portugal, interestingly enough, not Spain. Why he left South America and chose Portugal, we don't know.

"So she has a family history in the 'living in luxury' side of the drug trade. She studied Fine Arts at Columbia University in New York. But don't let that fool you; she is tough and vicious, we hear. We have never caught her involved in anything, though.

"Francis and Daniella are into art collecting. Her husband likes to own items dealing with Scottish heritage and she likes owning art. They have been collecting recently, among other things it appears, several Colourists paintings placed on the market. Sayer did good work there; if her theory is correct, she and her husband are the targets of the Connolly/Irvin forgeries."

"But enough background, let's talk about next steps."

They had to get Daniella Milne into the Kelvingrove Museum for a planned event next week. It was absolutely critical, Strachan said.

"Once I mentioned your involvement, Neville, Susan asked if you would do the main spiel instead of Bryant. He will open up and set it rolling. He was going to then pass it to the Board chairman to say something and Bryant would do the main presentation, but you can do a lot better, we think, particularly with the embedded messages for Milne. I said I would ask."

Neville said, "In principle, yes, but you need to let me know what you want me to do before I can fully agree, of course."

Strachan continued, "The first challenge will be to get Daniella there, given the short timeline. We know they are both around Edinburgh next week, as she accepted Dr. Bryant's invitation, but will she actually come to the Kelvingrove in Glasgow for the event or just cancel out? The Milnes can be quixotic about these sort of events.

"We may have to find fallback dates if she won't play. And remember, we are tying this to a legitimate Museum initiative, so the rest has to be right."

Neville said, "In Columbia University, what did she specialize in?"

"Good question," said Strachan, pulling out a file folder for the first time. After a minute she said, "Her final year project was in the area of sculpture, something about ethnic migration patterns and transferral of sculptural symbolism. Even the title loses me. In fact, the Milnes own some sculptures as well as paintings; that is in the file."

Coltrane said, "I think I can have the magnet you need. It's a big magnet if she is interested in sculpture and it should guarantee to pull her from Edinburgh to Glasgow for the morning."

~~

On Wednesday morning, Coltrane was finishing a meeting with two of his inspectors on a number of cases when his assistant stood in the doorway. His next appointment was waiting.

"Neville, DC Sayer called twice this morning hoping to speak to you. She said it might be important."

Coltrane said, "OK, get her on the line and ask Simon's indulgence for ten minutes, please."

When she came on, Coltrane said, "Good morning, Sayer, what can I do for you?"

Her Welsh lilt came down the phone. "Sir, I thought of something I didn't make quite clear, I think, during my briefing with you and DI Marshall."

"That's hardly surprising, Catrin, you were in not the best shape, but is it really that important – what is it?"

"It's Francis Milne's wife, sir; you know, the Edinburgh couple I mentioned. DI Strachan said they were part of the drug scene there. When I interviewed Professor Murray, he told me although the Milne couple were at the auction, he was clear it was the Latin woman, the wife, calling the tune. She is the art lover, the collector, sir, not the husband. So I think there has to be some focus on her, not just the Milne brothers."

She paused, "It's a nuance, I know, but it could be important for you. That's why I called. And to say thank you for doing this, I didn't say that with DI Marshall there at the briefing but it means a lot, thank you."

Coltrane suddenly saw behind the curtain.

"How did the PIRC interview go, Catrin?"

"It wasn't easy, sir, but Mrs. Carter said it went well, from her perspective and I think it will be over soon. There is a rumour that PIRC will report as early as tomorrow."

"Is that why it was important for to you to talk to me today?"

"Yes sir."

He paused.

"Thank you for the additional information. Nuances are sometimes important so I appreciate the call. What are you doing now?"

I am still on leave, sir. I am actually at the pottery shop where I decorate ceramics."

"I still haven't seen you work, Catrin, I must admit. I must do so."

She laughed. "Well, it's not exactly in your area, sir, I expect."

She always thought of Neville Coltrane lost in chasing stolen paintings by the big names in the art world, the masters.

"Sayer, I personally own three Picasso works, one of which is pottery, a vase he decorated, so don't underestimate my interests there. Ceramics are definitely in my area. So I suggest you get back to using your time decorating some, as you will be busy as hell once Jane gets you back into harness."

"Yes sir. Thank you."

At lunch time Coltrane was thinking back on the morning developments on various items and it struck him how much progress Sayer had made on the case despite

Strachan's reticence at the time. He left Assistant Commissioner Hunt a voicemail.

"Ma'am, I had a call from DC Sayer this morning, with an item she had forgotten in the briefing and handover. She was right on the money on the Milne case, despite Strachan keeping her in the dark.

"But she wanted urgently to get this additional fact to me. I think she is waiting on the PIRC report which, from rumours circulating, she expects to be released tomorrow. If it is critical of her at all, she will resign; that's my read."

He said no more. Hunt didn't like long-winded messages. He knew that there was no way that PIRC would issue a report while Strachan's operation was running. Whispers at higher levels would make the Commissioner hold off on releasing the document; the last thing she needed would be egg on her face if the complainant turned out to be a total liar.

35 ST. PAUL'S CATHEDRAL

On Friday, Catrin was working on a vase when her mobile rang. She answered straight away; she was becoming anxious about what was happening with the PIRC investigation. She had not heard any news yesterday, nor had she heard anything about the operation that had taken DCI Coltrane to Glasgow. Aina had told her that morning that she had heard Coltrane had now gone up north.

"DC Sayer, this is Sergeant Ross, one minute please."

There was a moment's silence then a woman's voice came on.

"DC Sayer, this is Assistant Commissioner Hunt. Look, I know you are not on duty but could you spare me a few minutes? Where are you?"

"At the Cwmbran Kiln, ma'am, a pottery shop in Spitalfields Market. Yes. ma'am, of course I would, where should I..."

She heard the address being repeated by Hunt. "Nowhere. Stay put. We will be there in ...George?.... ten minutes. And relax, nothing is wrong."

The line went dead.

Catrin saw she had a splash of clay slip on her sleeve, now dried, from helping Jean with a piece earlier. She was in old jeans and a T-shirt. An Assistant Commissioner of the Metropolitan Police was walking in to see her in less than ten minutes.

Only Melanie was nicely dressed; she was always that way for the customers in the shop, even if she was working with Jean in the back during the quiet periods. She was the sort of woman who would walk through a coal cellar and not get a speck on her. Catrin thought she and Jean would stand outside the coal cellar and become grimy from just looking at it.

"One of my bosses is coming round in ten minutes."

"Jane?" said Melanie.

"No, Assistant Commissioner Sandra Hunt. I only met her once, very briefly, on a PR visit to some event with Jane Worsley."

Jackie, the DPS officer, looked surprised and spoke into her sleeve microphone; she was clearly already getting some feed from her earpiece.

Both her friends looked at her worried. Catrin felt she was becoming nervous but all she did was get her comb from her purse and run it through her hair.

She said, "It's OK, if they are going to arrest me, they would just send a sergeant or someone."

A few minutes later the door to the shop was opened by a tall male sergeant, armed, in an immaculate dress uniform; Catrin assumed it was Sergeant Ross. Then a small woman walked in, also meticulously turned out in uniform.

"DC Sayer, good morning."

Jackie was now standing, looking alert and talking softly again in her sleeve.

"Good morning ma'am. These are my friends, Jean Hughes and Melanie Farrell. They own the shop and make the pottery. And my security guard." She realised she only knew her as Jackie.

Hunt nodded and shook hands, and for several minutes virtually ignored Catrin, talking with Jean and Melanie while looking at the items on display. Catrin watched as one of the most powerful women in London put her friends at ease.

Hunt turned around. "Will you ride with me, Sayer? I am on my way between a breakfast meeting and a speech in the City. We will fix for your security team to pick you up somewhere."

Somehow it didn't seem like a question.

They headed out the door with Jackie in tow as far as the curb. A black Jaguar limousine with its driver was waiting. They left Jackie standing there as another vehicle came up behind them as they took off.

Hunt began as soon as they were seated.

"DC Sayer, Superintendent Taylor and I were talking this morning before the meeting at the Adelphi Hotel and, first, your clearance from Dr. Herrington is through. On Monday report as usual."

She had been observing Catrin, taking in the reaction and also her scar.

"You will hear this, no doubt, through normal channels, but it's not why I came. I started out to my next appointment and thought, given your situation – and I now see some of your artistic talent that Jack was talking about – and all this Glasgow crap, pardon the phrase, I thought why would you want to stay with us at the Met? And I want you to stay. Hence my detour; simply to ask you to stick with it if you are having any doubts. Are you?"

Catrin looked at her. "About the job, ma'am, no... I like my work and being a police officer. But about my suitability, with the issues I have caused, well, it has made me think, to be very candid."

She paused. "You did ask."

They had turned from Aldgate into Whitechapel Road. Hunt looked at her seriously.

"Catrin, you have caused no issues, you have been told that, I know, and now I am telling it to you. You did your job and did it well. This political thing is being solved. That's all it is, politics. And I am leaving Neville Coltrane and Strachan to sort part of that out, the underpinning criminal aspects. Neville is enjoying it, I expect, and I hope Strachan gets a promotion out of it, given her other success recently.

"That should do it. If not, I will solve it my way. I play politics too and very well. You are not going to receive any disciplinary action from the Metropolitan Police Service nor have any stain on your record, I assure you, independent of conclusions in the PIRC report. Do you understand?"

Catrin saw she was telling the truth and felt a weight lift. "Thank you, ma'am. That means a lot."

They were now driving along Cannon Street. St. Paul's Cathedral was looming on the horizon ahead, partly obscured by the buildings on either side of the road.

Hunt said, "I am popping into the cathedral for a few minutes before my appointment in the City. Do you want to come on in?"

As they walked together up the steps with Sergeant Ross a couple of paces behind them they bypassed the crowd of visitors awaiting entry. Catrin was feeling self-conscious about being in her old clothes going into the cathedral next to a smartly dressed superior officer, but she had said 'yes' for some reason, so felt she had to go to the entrance, at least.

Hunt said, "I come here a lot. I've loved this place since I first came with my Brownie troop as a little girl. George says that if he had five pounds for every time we detoured here he would be retired in Cornwall. But it's a busy life and I find moments of peace here."

They crossed the covered entrance towards the doors as a clergyman in a suit and clerical collar heading out changed direction and came towards them. "Sandra?"

Catrin recognized him from a crowd duty assignment in her probationary time at Lambeth Police Station; he was the Dean of St. Paul's Cathedral.

"Dennis, hello, this is DC Catrin Sayer," said Hunt.

"Catrin, welcome."

He shook her hand and took in her face and the still livid scar. "You should go on in," he said.

He looked at Sandra Hunt. "Tuesday, right? I'll see you then."

He was away as fast as he had approached.

Inside they walked towards the centre, to the plain wooden chairs laid out row by row for the midday Eucharist. Sergeant Ross stayed back, standing to one side near the door, observing the crowd and his charges. Hunt said. "I like to pray here, so if you want to go, your security detail will be outside by now, I suspect; check with Sergeant Ross though first, before you leave."

"Thank you, ma'am, for taking the time with me."

Hunt was moving into an aisle and said, "Are you preparing for your sergeant's exams yet, Sayer?"

"No ma'am, it seems a little early, I have only been a DC for eight months. In time though …"

Hunt turned to face her. "Dr. Herrington wrote in his

report on you, as I recall, 'Her ability to take control of a dangerous and fast-moving incident after a physical trauma and still retain her focus on the primary objective of keeping another officer safe shows a deeply embedded attitude consistent with the core values of the Metropolitan Police Service.' That impressed me. Start studying, Catrin, I suggest. Thank you for the time. Good day."

She moved into a row, sat down and bowed her head.

Catrin sat down herself at an aisle chair a row behind, not wanting to leave yet but uncertain what to do, a little overwhelmed and needing to absorb it all; from talk of her disciplinary review to talk of promotion in a matter of minutes. It was too soon for her to be thinking of promotion, was her first thought. Resignation, not promotion, had been in the back of her mind.

She looked down the nave and closed her eyes. She hadn't gone to church or chapel regularly since her teens. Occasionally she would go with her parent when she home to Pontypridd, but not often.

The first thing that came to mind was the thought of Sandra Hunt as a young girl in a Brownie uniform ordering other Brownies around, which made her smile. It changed to a memory of her own Brownie uniform in a photograph that was one of her mother's favourites.

The noises of the cathedral seemed to diminish, disappear and she was looking at herself, happy as a child with her first uniform standing next to two friends, similarly clad.

She remembered how proud her dad had been of her when she told him about each merit badge earned. It was the beginning of a life in which teams and uniforms still played a part. She looked at the faces in the mental image of the photograph and saw, strangely enough, that she had a scar on the cheek that was never in the original, but it was OK. In fact, everything felt OK; she felt at peace.

She opened her eyes and saw that there was no sign of Sandra Hunt or Sergeant Ross. Her watch told her twenty minutes had elapsed, which surprised her. She got up and walked towards the exit, seeing the now familiar face of Ryan from her security team standing where Ross had been. Then she came back a few steps to the Perspex box for donations and took out her purse. She put a ten pound note through the slot and headed outside with her security guard at her side.

When she got back to the Cwmbran Kiln, Melanie said, "I washed your brushes for you and cleaned up."

"Thanks," said Catrin, "well, that was unexpected. She told me not to worry about the Glasgow thing."

Then she told them about the conversation, about sitting down in St Paul's and where her mind went. Jean Hughes was one of the other Brownies in the photo.

"How do you feel?" asked Melanie.

"At peace, would be the best way I could describe it."

"See, you should come with us to St. Stephen's," Melanie said.

Jean and Melanie had gone to the same church, one actively welcoming gay and lesbian attendance, since they had arrived in London. They were quite active there.

"I don't know about that, but I may be going back to St. Paul's," said Catrin. "I tell you, there is something special about that place."

She didn't tell them the thing that truly surprised her was not the image of the Brownies and the sense of tranquility that she found there, but the thought on the ride back. She had suddenly recalled that Strachan and Coltrane were doing something in Glasgow that affected both her and the Colourist case and she had no idea what it was. It had bothered her a lot over the last week, but now she was fine with it; fine with leaving it to Neville Coltrane, of all people.

36 THE KELVINGROVE
FUNDRAISER

Coltrane had taken the opportunity to travel up to the Highlands on Thursday, to spend a long weekend with friends who owned Strathlewen Lodge, the former home of the Laird of Alton. It had been sold in the seventies to an American couple, owners of an engineering company heavily involved in the North Sea Gas business. They had made improvements to the property.

Neville's friends had bought the place only three years ago and were undoing some of the improvements, one by one, as funds permitted.

Feeling thoroughly civilised by the weekend and the time with the Scott-Johnston family, he drove his rental car into Glasgow early on Monday, arriving at the Kelvingrove Museum on time for the pre-meeting, an hour before the formal event with potential future sponsors.

Everything was in place.

There were around eighteen people in the boardroom

including the museum director Edward Bryant and the Chair of the Board, a person called Colin Hyde. Susan Hetherington, Sir John Vale and Neville Coltrane were sitting next to each other.

Bryant went to the podium to open the batting.

"Thank you everyone for coming today, making the time in your busy schedules at such short notice. When we heard that Sir John Vale was visiting the Lord Provost, we couldn't miss the opportunity to invite him to speak, in addition to our planned esteemed speaker, Neville Coltrane, representing the Coltrane Arts Foundation. Sir John needs no introduction of course, nor I hope does the Coltrane Foundation to this audience.

"What one or two of you may not know is that Neville also spends some of his time chasing down stolen art works – he is a senior officer at New Scotland Yard."

"Our purpose this morning is to introduce you to three artists whom the Kelvingrove Museum will now be proudly presenting as important contributors to Scottish art who, in their period, were not recognized and still have limited or little recognition today. We plan to change that. As much as you know me to be committed to bringing the best of both classical and contemporary Scottish art to public view, I am also driven to find those artists from our past who did not make it simply because they did not gain visibility south of the border, where much of the decision-making about 'what was important art' rested back then.

"You are members of the Scottish arts community who have either an interest in this area or already have become one of our gracious major sponsors on other projects. As you can tell, we need funding to achieve our goal and I am totally unrepentant in my venality…."

Coltrane's position gave him a good line of sight of

Daniella Milne. She was not attentive to the speaker but was making eye contact with Sir John at times. He had been right to bring him in for today.

Bryant closed his remarks. "First, Let me ask Sir John Vale to speak to us."

Vale stood up and moved to the podium.

"Thank you Edward, it's a pleasure to be here and thank you for the opportunity. As you know, I am no longer creating sculptures; somehow the juxtaposition of a knighthood with my 'Madonna' in Barcelona being vandalised told me it was time to stop. My art being turned into bath tub fittings brought home I should do something different, I guess, and a knighthood meant I was getting too old to start again, even if I found something different to do.

"A lot of my time these days is spent in seeking visibility for the unrecognized creativity of younger sculptors. So let me speak to the first of the three artists, Shelagh McCrae. I didn't know of or ever meet Timothy McFadden or Alexander Gault, but I knew McCrae briefly when I was a young sculptor - she taught a workshop I attended quite early on. I could hardly understand her accent, I must admit, but I understood her art, self-taught as it was.

"Unfortunately others with influence and resources at the time did not. All they saw was a woman welding together rusty pieces of old car parts from scrap metal dealers. She died in obscurity, unrecognized. I confess, I had almost forgotten about her too, to my shame, until Neville called me. Which is why I wanted so much to be here… to help redress this wrong."

In fact, he had flown in by helicopter that morning just for this meeting, had enthused about the McCrae opportunity but would be leaving directly after the event.

Neville was looking forward to speaking about Gault and McFadden; it hadn't taken long for him to prepare; this was his milieu.

Vale spoke easily and passionately about McRae's approach to sculpture and her works.

Soon Neville Coltrane replaced him at the podium and talked first about the surrealist, McFadden. His brother Richard liked Tim McFadden's work and had a painting by him in his own home; he had long been pressing the importance of the man's art though few others had seemed to notice it.

He eventually switched the image from a near-lunar landscape to a post-impressionist view of Lewis. Someone in the target audience gave a sigh of relief.

"Now let me move to the final artist of this project, Alistair Gault, who worked as a conservator in this very museum for much of his life. His work hasn't been recognized in large part because it hasn't been seen. To understand why, you have to understand something of the man and his busy role here at the museum and his subsequent transition to a role in education. He became a teacher during the formative stages of the University of the Highlands where he taught part-time at the college at Stornoway for many years. The Hebrides provided much of his inspiration for landscapes. Here is one of his many paintings of an Isle of Lewis shoreline.

"Alistair, as a conservator, also had access to many paintings by near-contemporary artists, of course, including some of the Colourists in this museum. In fact, during World War Two, at a time of crisis for the museum, he was very involved with the protection of the works here. His own work absorbed much of their influence and the paintings of Cadell and Peploe clearly inspired his own creativity ..."

The reception and private viewing of works by the three artists was in a roped-off gallery. Susan caught the attention of Daniella Milne who was now intently examining the Gault paintings rather than the sculptures. She whispered to her, "There are two more you should see," and led her into the adjacent anteroom and closed the door. Neville had entered a minute earlier.

She said, "These two by Alistair Gault are not ours and are not officially on display. One will be returned to his daughter-in-law, the widow of Reverend Andrew Gault, who coincidentally and tragically died here at the museum. The other comes from Kinnington Church, the scene of a recent robbery attempt, you may recall."

Daniella shook her head. Her eyes were moving between one painting and the other.

Susan continued. "Some of Gault's works tie back to inspiration from his work as a conservator here during the war and post-war period, as Chief Inspector Coltrane said. These two clearly have Francis Cadell elements in them, as you can see. There are a number of his paintings based on the work of Cadell and other members of the Colourist School in our possession. We believe he copied elements that particularly inspired him as starting points in a limited number of his own paintings."

Neville had moved alongside Milne and said softly. "In my other role, Mrs. Milne, we understand that some of Gault's work has already been passed off as Cadell and Peploe by someone forging signatures. It's under investigation, of course. But we know you and your husband are collecting Colourist works and want you to be forewarned, the marketplace may be a little suspect at present; care is needed."

He smiled at her.

"Ironically, the new owners may want such fraudulent copies restored to their true identity, as the work of Alistair Gault, if the people here at Kelvingrove are successful in their venture, don't you think?"

Daniella looked at him and he saw she had blushed. She turned and spoke to Hetherington.

"Susan, thank you for inviting me and please pass on my thanks to Dr Bryant and Sir John Vale. It was a great pleasure to meet them. I really do believe my husband and I must look closely at supporting this wonderful initiative by the museum."

She stepped back a pace and looked at Coltrane. "Mr. Coltrane, thank you, for your presentation and the explanations, they are much appreciated. If you will excuse me…"

He thought she did a superb job of trying to hide her embarrassment and anger.

Neville saw that the limousine waiting to take Sir John to the helipad was outside. They had planned to go back to London in the same helicopter. Then he remembered his rental car parked outside.

He took his keys out and held them out to Strachan, who had joined them after the reception. "Eileen, can you get someone to return this for me to the airport; thanks."

She looked at the proffered keys, amused, and said, "Well Neville I would, but you are the registered driver, so I expect that you are the only one insured to drive it back there, I am afraid."

He knew she was joking. Neville just dropped the keys on the table. "Well, if anyone damages it and Hertz say it is not insured, send the bill to the Assistant Chief Constable and tell him I said he could pay it personally."

He waved to Sir John that it was time and they shook hands with the others, making their goodbyes.

They talked in the helicopter. Vale said he appreciated the chance to help; it had been fun to support McCrae. And he liked the young police officer. She seemed a pretty good artist. "Not my medium, you know, but she has the eye and the insight. Anyway I bought a piece by her at Liz Marshall's gallery.'

Coltrane sighed. "I know, John, I am hoping to get her into my unit at the Yard in time, give her some really challenging stuff to do, but we will see."

He still had dreams of bringing the ACU into his fold.

~~

"She came back, went straight home," Coleman said to Strachan, phoning in from the surveillance van parked along the road leading up to the home of Francis and Daniella Milne. A mansion, he thought it was, really. She had called her husband and the surveillance on the office shows he called his brother.

Strachan just said, "Keep on it."

"I will, ma'am, but it's totally unclear where this will go. It's like powering up the fire hose without anyone holding the nozzle down. At least with the Finisterre interception we knew it was going to hit directly at Connolly."

Strachan gave it twenty-four hours then called Francis Milne on his personal mobile, at least the mobile he professed to use. They got through the preliminaries. Despite the Milne territory being Edinburgh she had travelled up early that morning to the city and was in the building where Milne's legitimate business was located. They knew he had turned up there earlier.

"Detective Chief Inspector Strachan, how can I help you?"

"I am downstairs, in the coffee shop. Would you like a coffee?"

Ten minutes later he was sitting opposite her. There was no sign of anyone with him. He had seen the two plain-clothes officers behind her, some distance away at the table in the corner, but still he sat down.

"For the record, I have no recording devices, we aren't capturing this," said Strachan.

Francis opened his suit jacket and smiled. "Neither am I."

"You asked how you can help. I am going to take that seriously, not in the facetious manner it was made."

Milne said nothing.

"Your wife mentioned her visit to the Kelvingrove Museum, no doubt."

"Yes she enjoyed Sir John's company. And the other information she received there. I took it to be police doing, so to speak, given the involvement of that other policeman."

"So I would like any threats against DC Sayer and other officers by persons of interest whom you may know to be cancelled, permanently."

"I don't believe I have made any threats but... I take your meaning. And if they are not, and I hear anything, I will let you know. Is that all?"

Strachan smiled. "Hardly, I think. We have saved you considerable embarrassment and an opportunity to support a newly-discovered artist, wouldn't you say?"

"Yes, my wife sees it something like that; not quite embarrassment, but something like that."

So she told him exactly what she wanted. "I want Robert Cheney to tell the truth about Niall Irvin's involvement in the burglary. And you know who can get him to tell that. I have a man from Kinnington Church, a good man, who may have brain damage and a police officer scarred for life. Cheney wasn't in this alone. I want Irvin - and so should you, I think."

He said nothing. He made no facial gestures. He just got up and went back to the lift.

Francis Milne was not going to tell Strachan that his wife had already gone overboard, wanting a higher price, in flesh. Nor was Strachan going to tell him what chaos she hoped might erupt if Dominic Connolly betrayed his lifelong friend.

For Strachan, the jigsaw was nearly complete and all she needed was the final piece to drop in place - and for the fire hose to start up.

37 THE ARREST

On Monday morning a week later DCI Eric Sinclair and two constables went into the High Court building on the Saltmarket in Glasgow. They found Niall Irvin, as his office had said, near Courtroom 2. He was in a corridor talking with an advocate about a case before the High Court of Justiciary that day. The court session had just broken.

Sinclair did not stand back politely waiting for the conversation to finish but walked straight in.

"Chief Inspector, how can I help you?" said Irvin.

"Mr. Irvin, you can accompany me to Govan Road Police Station to assist us in our enquiries."

"Well," Irvin smiled at the wigged and gowned advocate, "perhaps later. I am rather busy now, in court."

"Now please, unless you want me to place you under arrest."

"I really must protest ..."

He got no further. Sinclair had the basis for showing he had tried to be discreet. He nodded at the constables. They handcuffed Irvin and led him across the main hallway to the exit.

At Govan Police Station they had to wait on Hamish Sanderson, a lawyer with impeccable credentials whom Irvin had stated was his solicitor. Irvin felt he did not really need advice from Hamish but he wanted the man's credibility for the record. After a brief consultation, he expected, he would be interviewed - about what, he was not sure.

He was somewhat surprised to be asked to agree voluntarily to participate in a line-up on arrival. He declined. He was then placed in an interview room until Sanderson arrived, with a police constable watching him.

DCI Strachan and DCI Sinclair came in and sat opposite the two men and went through the ritual of identification into the microphone for the record. Sinclair led the questioning.

"Mr. Irvin, can you tell me your whereabouts on the twentieth of October two years ago, please?"

"Not offhand, I would need to check my calendar."

Strachan placed a photocopy in front of him as Sinclair said, "This is a photocopy of a petrol receipt record against your Visa credit card on that afternoon, from a petrol station in Fort William. Were you driving the car that day?"

"I believe it is possible, no-one else drives my car."

So you were in the vicinity of Fort William that day. Is that correct?"

"I don't recall being there but, if this is correct, that would appear to be the case, yes. It is some time ago and I would need to check my business calendar. I am a busy man, Chief Inspector."

"Indeed. Do you know this man?"

He produced photo of Malcolm Drummond.

"No I don't."

"For the record, I have shown Mr. Irvin a photograph of Malcolm Drummond."

He took out another photograph and placed it in front of Irvin.

"Do you know this man?"

Irvin looked. It was a photo of John Dalton.

"Not that I recall, no."

"Please answer yes or no."

"Not that I recall, no."

"For the record, Mr. Irvin was shown a photograph of John Dalton, a known felon with multiple convictions for art forgery."

Silence. Sinclair waited, looking at Irvin.

Sanderson said, "Any more questions, Chief Inspector?"

Another photo was pulled from the folder and placed in front of Niall Irvin.

"Do you know this man?" said Sinclair.

Irvin saw it was Colin Cheney.

"He is the man at Kinnington Church, when I tried to stop and help."

"That is the only basis you have for knowing him?"

"No, he was a client some years ago, as I said in my press interviews, the man has a troubled past." His mind was racing. "I recall his name is Cheney but I don't remember the case in detail. In any event it will be a court record, as you know."

Sinclair said evenly, "Would it surprise you to know that Colin Cheney has now pleaded guilty to a number of crimes in addition to the Kinnington Church robbery, including a burglary in Stornoway that he now claims was at your instruction. He also now claims you and he were together on the Kinnington robbery and were, in fact, planning a further robbery in Oban the following day."

"I have nothing further to say," Irvin said.

Irvin was analysing the news and trying to control the growing panic. Cheney could not have changed his statement without Dominic's instruction otherwise he would be dead in prison before Niall ever came to trial. He knew that. So what happened? And what is this issue with a Malcolm Drummond?

His counsel said, "We need to understand where this line of questioning is leading, Chief Inspector, it seems to be all over the place to me."

Sinclair looked at Strachan who spoke for the first time.

"Niall Irvin, I'm arresting you on suspicion of two counts of housebreaking, theft and assault and a further intent to commit a crime of housebreaking and theft. You do not have to say anything, but it may harm your defence if you do not mention, when questioned, something which you later rely on in court. Anything you do say may be given in evidence."

In Scottish law there is no crime of burglary; entrance for theft is the crime of housebreaking, whether it is a domestic dwelling or not.

"We are also pursuing investigations into the suspicious deaths of Mr. Malcolm Drummond and the Reverend Andrew Gault. Do you understand these charges made against you?"

"Yes," said Irvin.

Sanderson said, "I would like some time with my client."

"Before you do," said Sinclair, waving at the CCTV recording camera.

The PIRC officer came in. "Mr. Niall Irvin, I am here to advise you that based on evidence provided by Police

Scotland and the subsequent review of that evidence by the office of the Commissioner, your complaint against the parties of Police Scotland, The Metropolitan Police and DC Catrin Sayer has been dismissed."

He passed across a letter and left. The whole process took seconds.

Sinclair said, "Mr. Irvin, having been charged, we are now placing you in a line-up as we requested previously and rejected by you. We now have the right in law to do so. Then you can have time with your counsel before we begin questioning you in more detail. We have kept a potential witness waiting long enough."

What witness, thought Irvin, to what?

Sinclair watched the steam leaving Irvin's demeanour. I'm back, he thought. I really feel I am back now.

Constable Shortt had finally located the server from the coffee shop near Fort William, where Malcolm Drummond had bought his coffee. She was waiting in the station for the identity parade to be over. She had agreed to come along but had told them that she had little memory of the man who handed back the thermos before she gave it to the man who was killed in the accident.

You never know, though, with line-ups, thought Sinclair.

~~

Niall Irvin was amazed at the combination of questions designed to make him provide an unguarded or revealing answer. Professional as the police officers were, this was his home ground. His mind was working on how to compound their error on the Drummond issue, one he did not commit, to ensure that the others he had committed were rolled up into the same raggedy ball.

They could then be tossed out en masse.

The hard part, he thought coolly, might be Cheney and the turnaround in his statement. That Dominic had condoned or insisted on it - after all, it would add to Cheney's sentence - was a given. It would now have to go as far as the courtroom, Niall realised, and there would go his career and standing.

He thought, they must have the art theft and some knowledge of the forgery if they know of John Dalton's involvement and they could only have found that out through Colin or Dominic. He would hear about that doubtlessly in more detail in the later questioning. So perhaps the Milnes know by now and, probably driven by Daniella, they had pressurized Dominic to sell him out.

He started to plan constructively.

The Andrew Gault investigation did not worry him too much; it was all circumstantial, there was no evidence of his involvement. If only the man had had a heart attack in church or at home, as he had hoped for, it would have served his purpose well. Now it was simply a confounding factor.

He had already concluded that the combination of the 'death at the sight of the Dali', as he thought of it, and the stupidity of Cheney hitting that policewoman were really bad luck. The police always get their nose in a wrinkle when one of their finest gets injured.

Hamish was wittering on at him; he should try to pay attention. He suddenly remembered to look frightened and nervous. They would be watching him, wanting to get back in. It was going to be a long afternoon and evening.

~~

It went back to when Niall was nine years old, the

origin of the fraud, he recalled.

He and his parents visited the Gault family regularly at the time for family events. Niall liked Alistair and admired the way in which he painted; he had always liked the fact that he lived in a nice house, away from the Gorbals. He also used to draw really funny cartoons at high speed for him.

His father and Alistair had been talking about life during the war and the older man had commented on the difficulty of finding time and resources for his own painting. Niall had sat there silently, taking in the conversation of the grown-ups. He learned that there had been so much to do at the museum, with its dispersed treasures and the shortages and the bombing raid damage.

Alistair said, "And we had it a lot easier than most. We lost Stephen, in '42. Some families lost more."

He talked about how his own art was his bright spot even though he couldn't get out into the countryside. "I painted some canvases just starting with part of an image from another, mainly those of Cadell and Fergusson, I really liked their work. I copied part to get me going and let my mind work from there."

Niall had asked him how he would know if paintings he saw were from real subjects or just invented.

"That's a good question, Niall, you would make a good detective!" Alistair had said. "I have marked them in my book. Look."

He pulled out a small pocket book and showed Niall the system he used to note the start date, completion date and details for every painting he created.

Nearly three decades later, when Alexander Gault phoned him after the visit of Drummond, seeking advice, he had first tried to ease his uncle's mind, as he was clearly quite upset.

"I don't believe your father would steal or forge anything," Niall had said.

It was later, when Dominic said he wanted to find a way to put an end to the warfare between his operation and the Edinburgh gangs, it wasn't proving productive, Niall said, "Isn't the younger Milne the one with an artsy wife?"

"She's a cold bastard," said Dominic, "for a South American. But yes, she buys art, Scottish art I gather. It pleases Francis."

Niall had the germ of the idea then. He explained it to Dominic, who seemed amused by the opportunity. "But it will only fly after my uncle's death. He won't let any of the paintings go, unfortunately," Niall mused.

They had talked of ways and means, as Niall had no time for his uncle, really. It was Dominic's advice to swap the placebos for the nitro pills. "You can be so effective with that lawyer's tongue of yours. Talk him into a heart attack."

The news of the possible financial cumulative penalties for harbouring stolen or forged works of art for so long was a shock to Alexander Gault. Niall had suggested that he should let him look through Alistair's documents, as this would be covered by client confidentiality provisions. "I won't have to say anything about my findings and we can then decide what to do."

Among the possessions was Alistair's little black pocket book. Niall had looked through it, making a list of fourteen works that had Colourist elements in them. In the end he decided to just keep the pocket book and, in putting papers back, missed pocketing also the list he had made. It ended up on the floor, beside the bureau, later to be picked up by a worried Andrew Gault.

Niall Irvin never knew, but it was the worry from talking to Niall and finding the list that eventually led Alexander to decide to go the Kelvingrove Museum and make a clean breast of it. That was the honest thing to do.

~~

It did not take long for Niall Irvin to secure bail. The day following his arrest a sum of money had been paid and his passport had been surrendered. His reputation as a prominent defense lawyer and his own council's good standing all counted towards bail approval. Irvin decided that it was time to play his final card.

Sanderson offered to drop him at home. Irvin's own car was still parked at the law courts. Instead Niall asked to be dropped at the Hilton hotel.

In the lobby Niall spoke to a concierge he knew and passed him something. He sat down with a newspaper, in full view. A little time later the man re-appeared with a briefcase and a new mobile phone for him. He called Dominic.

"I can't believe you did it to me," was how he began, voice steady, measured.

"Niall, we need to talk, I can explain and we can sort it out. I had no option. Francis and Daniella found out and that was the price to keep the business."

"We have been together since we were boys. Since Rowen Street, Dominic."

Connolly continued, explaining his reasons, but aggressively. He wasn't used to this anger from Niall, warranted though it may be.

"Daniella Milne had already threatened to kill both of us and had called her dad in Portugal wanting all supplies from anywhere to be halted. She is crazy. Francis had to calm her down. He sorted it out with her father but there was a price for keeping the peace. You were to go down for the deception and lose your professional standing. He says Daniella was insistent.

"I knew you'd get out on bail and was waiting to talk to you. Kevin's outside your place now, with that message. We have to sort out how to move forward. Let's get together and work something out."

Irvin laughed. "Work something out? Dominic, I am a dead man if I see you, I think, and if you and Francis think it is in the bloody 'business interest' to provide the woman with a scapegoat if she blows her fuse again. Look at the Brittany thing and that woman. She has probably asked her dad for a hit man already."

There was a silence on the line then Dominic replied, "I put you in the frame for the burglary to save the business relationship, knowing you can run rings round anyone in those courts. We chose to screw them with the forgeries; we have to sort it out. But I am going to make it right with you, you know that. And me, see you done in, Niall; never. And you bloody well know it."

Dominic needed to see Niall and talk him through it, the way he had others over the years, to accept that prison was just a transient stage and he would be looked after well during and afterwards. He wouldn't get a long sentence, he knew.

The fact that Dominic had betrayed him at all overwhelmed Niall. He realised finally that his friend saw him just as one of his team, to be used, not as an equal. The fact that Niall would lose his standing as a lawyer, his occupation, his friends and his reputation meant little to nothing to Dominic.

He just closed the phone. He didn't even say to Connolly that he should have chosen him over the business; that it would have been a strategic decision his accountants would have supported in the long run.

He walked out of the hotel and took a taxi straight to Govan Police HQ. As they approached he made one more telephone call.

He wasn't seen in Glasgow by anyone he knew again.

~~

Worsley put down her phone and called her team into her office.

"I have just been informed that the investigations into the actions of Police Scotland and Catrin have formally been dropped by PIRC as of yesterday; confirmation is being sent out today.

"Niall Irvin was also taken into custody yesterday, having been charged with burglary. He got bail this morning. Strachan says she and Sinclair were working on the Alexander Gault charge, although it was proving a hard sell to the Crown prosecutor, when Irvin called her direct line. He was outside Govan Police Station in a taxi, it turned out.

"He is prepared to turn over every operation he had worked on with Dominic Connolly and what he knows of Milne's operation in return for complete immunity. He also agreed to appear as a prosecution witness, with the proviso that he gets a new identity and his bank accounts transferred. Apparently the Crown is buying the deal, other than any funds Irvin obtained outside of legitimate legal billing."

"He should still be rich then," said Keith.

"What's worse," said Catrin, "is that immunity will get

him off the Gault murder charge."

"Yes," said Worsley, "But it is still not clear that such a charge would have been laid. Sinclair is struggling for evidence on it, particularly about Irvin's access to the pill container. This way the Crown gets a whole bunch of virtually certain convictions and will clean up a lot of case files, I bet."

"Virtually certain?" asked Keith.

"With Irvin's skills and knowledge, I would hate to be in the dock with him as a prosecution witness," she said. "And Superintendent Strachan thinks the drug world across Southern Scotland is going to get a lot messier as others carve up the Connolly turf. As you can also tell, the promotion of DCI Strachan to superintendent was made public today.

"Catrin, it's over. Strachan also confirmed that the potential threat against you and the French officer has been removed, as far as it is possible to know. So I am asking Jack to cancel the security detail; you will have to come to work on the Tube again now, just like a normal person. But well done. That's it."

As they left her office Worsley said, "Catrin, can you stay behind and close the door." She pointed her to a seat.

"Two additional things. Irvin denied any involvement in the death of Drummond. It seems coincidental now that he happened to be in the same area and he also told Strachan the name of the client in Fort William he was visiting - it seemed to tie in, so he wasn't the one in the café. So Drummond's death was probably an accident, after all."

Catrin nodded.

"Secondly, how are you doing - in yourself?"

"Very well now, ma'am, I think. Happy to be back to normal, have this over with."

Worsley nodded and pointed at her face, "And physically."

"My dentist says the fix on the tooth should be fine but I will need a crown in time; the tooth repair won't last forever. And I have the chance for additional surgery on the scar if I need it. But at present, I don't want to go through any surgery; Mr. Leiss said he thought it might not really help, and I think he knows his stuff. The redness will fade."

Worsley paused then said, "Assistant Commissioner Hunt has made it clear that you are to be fast-tracked, assuming you want that. Do you? And it's not an idle question. Fast-tracking generally results in work absorbing your life - and you have other interests. And as much as you like this job now, you would have to be prepared to move around; different places in the Met, probably and different duties."

Catrin knew Worsley spoke from experience.

She said, "I have been thinking about next steps, ma'am. I told you that the AC came to see me and it was clear you already knew. The truth is I do, but I don't want to leave this team and this work at present, I am still in my first year. So if going for my sergeant's stripes moves me away from this, I want to wait."

Worsley nodded. "Thank you, Catrin. Put in for the training. I am going to make it clear that, at least initially, I want agreement from Jack and Sandra that my budget and structure will accommodate any promotion and you can stay here, at least as a sergeant. I think I will get it. And thank you for wanting to stay and be part of my team.

"Neville Coltrane has alluded that you may want at

some time to go chasing Rembrandts with A&A. A 'bigger challenge' he had the audacity to tell me. Has he said anything?"

Catrin said, "No ma'am. And I wouldn't, at least not in the foreseeable future. Although I do, I think, owe him for whatever went on in Scotland leading to Irvin's arrest. And I shouldn't rule out any logical role in the future, I know, art-related or not."

She smiled. "Anyway, he would probably tell me to get more cosmetic surgery; that my face is still a mess."

~~

The raid on the homes and offices of key figures in the Connolly gang was coordinated for the following Friday at 6.30 a.m. and involved over one hundred officers of Police Scotland. It netted 28 people being placed into custody, including Dominic Connolly himself.

As charges were read out and interviews were made, it became apparent to Dominic through the feedback from his new lawyer and from his wife Joan that Niall had sold him out. All the information the police had obtained was supported by hard facts. What turned out to be a confounding problem was that no top-line defense counsel in Scotland would take their cases, nor would any of their standard court 'mouthpieces', their advocates, represent them in court. The man he had now representing him was light years behind Niall, he thought. They were in a new ball game with the odds against them.

Irvin had not only betrayed the group but had apparently got the word around that Connolly liked to make arrangements to kill off his defense counsel. Now Connolly would have to make arrangements to kill off Niall, living up to the lie, so to speak.

The only person on the list they had failed to find in the raid was John Dalton, the Northumberland Police had communicated to Strachan. They had sent a squad to the old man's flat in Berwick-on-Tweed to find it vacant. He had moved to somewhere in Spain some weeks ago, his neighbor said.

Daniella Milne had just returned from shopping in Jenner's department store in Edinburgh when the two cars drew up at the home, waving warrant cards at their household staff. She was taken into custody. She asked what the reason for the arrest was and was given the non-response of 'helping with enquiries'.

Francis said, 'I will call the lawyer' and went back into the house, noticing one car remaining in the driveway with two people in it. They seemed in no rush to get out of the vehicle. When he had called Jeremy, their lawyer, about Daniella's arrest he would go out and clear the vehicle off his property personally.

When Francis found out that Jeremy wasn't there; that his secretary had no idea when he would be available and she was noncommittal when he asked her to ensure that Jeremy called him back urgently, he knew something was wrong. Steve explained it later. Jeremy wasn't their lawyer any more but even before he knew that, he had other problems.

The housekeeper called him to the door. He had more visitors, she said, a Superintendent Strachan with a gentleman. They had finally got out of the car.

He got her to show them into his study.

The person with Strachan was very candid. He wasn't police, he said, he was Immigration, but Francis had his doubts about that. He looked too seasoned, too much like, frankly, the hard cases Daniella's dad knew.

The stranger said, "We can hand your wife over to the French. I doubt that they will be able to prove her link to the torture and killing of Sophie Rousseau but you and I both know she was there and that she steered it. But they will find a way to keep her a long time, I am sure."

Francis said nothing. He looked at Strachan who made it clear by her silence and demeanor that she was only sitting in on this, giving it police credibility.

"Frankly, we don't want Colombian psychopaths in the UK," the man continued candidly.

Francis flinched at the description of his wife.

"You can fight her defense in France, of course, and her extradition there from here; there are procedures. But she will be held in remand, she won't get bail. I am assured of that, I think, given the photographs we have of Rousseau's remains.

"Alternatively, we can simply deport her back to Colombia; revoke her right of residence in the UK as a foreign national who has confessed to a criminal activity."

Francis saw where this was going.

He said, "What criminal activity you have in mind, may I ask?"

He could think of a number of things Daniella had been involved in that the Milnes would have to fight tooth and nail; they would bring others into the frame both here and overseas.

"Given the information we have obtained from Niall Irvin, we are thinking of forgery; she participated in a conspiracy to buy and re-sell a fake painting for the purposes of deception and illegal profit. A painting like that one, I think."

He pointed to the Cadell bought at the Edinburgh

auction.

"Now we can prove that, I think, with our witness. It is all homegrown, no messiness about overseas stuff. And no-one else involved who will be prosecuted. It doesn't even show off her nasty side, either."

He let it sink in.

"If we have her confession she could be out of the UK in short order, back to Colombia. But be aware, Mr. Milne, she won't coming back into this country, ever. And she will have to take her chances with any country she chooses to reside in that the French won't extradite her, if they later decide to do so. We just want her on her way."

"We have two children," said Francis.

The man sounded completely unsympathetic. "Sophie Rousseau had one; the child's grandmother is now raising her."

Francis looked at Strachan, who had said nothing so far. This man hadn't even provided a name.

Superintendent Strachan said, "We thought you might want to talk to your wife before we charge her and interview her. It could save time and help us in the course of our enquiries. We will give you time, and you can take your lawyer in with you, also. If you have one, that is."

Steve was sitting in the living room when Francis finally got to his brother's home much later, after talking with Daniella. The choice had been no choice at all.

Steve looked equally exhausted and Joan wouldn't speak to Francis.

"Your stupid wife," was all she said, as she saw him in the hall. Then she went into the home theatre and closed the door.

Steve offered Francis a drink. "You will need it; a lot

has been screwed up for us since Connolly's operation went under. Their grief doesn't make it easier for us to do business."

Francis told him the situation with Daniella.

Steve said, "No solicitor will take us on. Niall spread the word that Connolly and Daniella are people who would do serious harm to their own defense counsel. He told a junior at his former law firm that Daniella went over to France to ensure Rousseau suffered, but they are treating that as 'privileged', thank God. They mentioned it to Connolly as part of the explanation why they would no longer act for him. He passed it on to me. We have the plague, it seems."

Francis said, "There won't even be a trial, Steve; she is just being deported to Colombia, residence rights revoked based on her statement about the painting. They say they can do that, ship her out. I have no idea what to tell the kids. There ought to be a way to fight it; she has kids here, right?"

Steve shook his head, "I don't know. The rules we play by in our business normally don't seem to apply here and we have no real legal expertise to turn to, it seems, until I find someone to take us on. But if she has signed something, I very much doubt it. It will be a done deal."

Secretly he hoped that they would put Daniella on the next plane out, given the trouble she had caused. He was starting to worry about bigger things, trying to work out how much Niall Irvin actually knew about the Milne operations, factual things that he could testify to in court. They really needed a good lawyer now.

38 HEATHROW

Jian Li said, "I was so upset saying goodbye to 'The Gwyns' and Andrea. I hope I will get to see them again although we will all stay in touch, of course. But now I know I will be seeing you in four months, so this does not feel all bad."

She had been talking about their various Bangor friends.

It was now late June. Catrin was seeing Li off at Heathrow airport. Li's year of study at Bangor was over. She had a good course transcript plus her work on a maritime law project to take back with her to Hong Kong. It would provide a good base for her final year of study towards a law degree. Her year had been an academic success after the turmoil of the search for her lost brother and the events at Craig Y Don Road.

During the exam period Catrin had been keeping in touch with her friend daily, hearing about how things had gone. Afterwards, Jian Li had come down to London for a visit and then had returned to Bangor for some sailing; she had developed good friendships in the Sailing Club there.

They had come out to Terminal Three at Heathrow on the Tube and Li did not have a lot of luggage with her. 'I had things shipped' was her explanation, which surprised Catrin. Most students took all they could with them, as much as their baggage allowance permitted.

"I am looking forward to the trip to Hong Kong; it really is exciting," said Catrin. "This will be travelling overseas, not just a short trip to France. I'm trying to think what to bring for your parents other than pottery; something Welsh perhaps."

"Or from London, they will appreciate anything, I know," said Li. "They are looking forward to meeting you. Perhaps something you find in the gift shop at St. Paul's Cathedral, now you are going there more regularly."

She smiled. "Cho will get you a staff discount and my parents, as you know, are very religious."

She laughed at her own joke and Catrin could see Li was nervous and emotional, as affected by this parting as much as she was.

Li's parents and grandparents had ties back to mainland China in the days of the evangelical missions there; Catrin knew they were devout Methodists. Catrin and Li had met with Cho, the former lover of Li's brother, Han, during Li's last visit. He was one of the people she had wanted to say farewell to. He still worked in the gift shop at St. Paul's.

Cho had been easier with Catrin in Li's presence than when he had seen her outside St. Paul's Cathedral on a previous visit. She had smiled and he had nodded but had moved on. The first time he had met Catrin Sayer was when she waved her warrant card in his face and had told him he was being taken in for questioning. So on seeing her again, she thought, it was natural that he was steering clear.

The evening before the flight Jean and Melanie had cooked dinner for the four of them and had given Li a small dish that they had made. Catrin gave her one of her pieces that she had reserved for this day some time ago. In return, Li had surprised them with an ornate set of Chinese chopsticks in a beautiful lacquer box that she had asked her mother to choose and send over.

Jean was as taken with the beauty of the decoration on the box as with the chopsticks themselves.

"There is only one box but it has enough chopsticks for 12 dinner guests, so you can use them whenever you eat together and with others." said Li.

Helen had said Li could have her bed for the night, which Catrin much appreciated. Helen was staying over at her new boyfriend's place. The two friends talked into the early hours about everything; from when they first met to Li's plans for Catrin's visit to Hong Kong.

The one new item of news that Li had for Catrin was that on her return she was going to work part-time for LinTan Shipping in their legal department, beginning her training in maritime law issues, as well as complete her final year of her degree. Starting work was the reason that was taking her back now.

Catrin knew of Mr. Lin, of course, head of a large shipping company based in Hong Kong. He had become involved in the Han Yeung affair and got out of his depth, she thought.

Catrin had been struck, as they talked, how Li had changed from the quiet, hesitant student she first knew in Bangor to a more self-assured young woman. The year had been good to her in that sense, despite the loss of her brother and a short-lived relationship with another student.

So at the airport there was little else to say. Catrin gave her a big hug. Li touched the side of Catrin's face with the scar as she pulled back and said, "See you soon."

She headed into the 'Priority' security line pulling her small carry-on suitcase; a business woman off on travels, it seemed, more than a student heading home. She looked back once and waved. It only took a few seconds and Jian Li Yeung was gone.

39 KENTALLEN

There is a channel off the main flow of Loch Linnhe near Glencoe that leads into Loch Leven. Onich is on one side, not that far from where Malcolm Drummond took in the view and had his last smoke and cup of coffee. The village of Kentallen sits on the other. It's not a very large village, with its various buildings on the edge of the loch or perched on the hillside, but it hosts a resort hotel and a world class seafood restaurant.

Away from the restaurant and hotel area, though, it is a quiet village often blessed with spectacular sunsets off the west coast. High on the hillside sit a row of new cottages. They had been built six years ago but in this village they would be the 'New Cottages' until someone built some more elsewhere that took over the title.

The estate agent dealing with the resale of Number Four of the New Cottages was the same man who had sold Ken and Amelia Nicholson their own, Number Two, five years ago. Seeing Ken in the street he waved and walked over to catch up.

"The Selby couple didn't stay long, I see," said Ken. They had the place only eight months.

"No, unfortunately, the 'half a week in Glasgow, half a week here' for the wife didn't pan out. It's the modern world, Mr. Nicholson, living part-time in one place, working in another. Are you and Mrs. Nicholson still happy here?"

"We are well-settled, so no more estate fees for you until we are carried out or put in a home, Mr. Aitken."

The estate agent laughed; a potential sale was not totally off his radar but, in truth, he was happy to see properties well-maintained and developed. The Nicholsons had looked after their cottage very well over the past five years; their garden was beautiful.

Other than create a lot of redecoration issues inside with wiring taken out recently, the Selby couple hadn't done anything with Number Four.

He didn't say anything to the neighbour, it was an issue of professional discretion, but there had been talk about the fact that when the wife left on the Sunday evening each week a man, the same man, came and stayed until the Thursday, when the wife returned. There was salacious gossip about it but he didn't really know what to make of it.

If he had asked Ken about it, he would have had a reply along the lines that he kept himself to himself, so didn't see much. In fact, a retired military policeman, Ken Nicholson saw a lot and drew his own conclusions.

Such as the fact that Mrs. Selby went around armed with a concealed sidearm. It was the clothes that gave it away as much as the walk and balance; and the occasional adjustment she made at the waist. He had carried a service firearm himself for long enough to know. She didn't handle herself or carry her firearm like a criminal; she was in his line, had his training.

One time her jacket had blown open in the wind and he, looking out the window at the time, saw her pull it closed, but not quite fast enough.

The other man had the Monday to Thursday shift, she had the remainder of the week and the weekend, he surmised.

The vehicle accident at the bottom of the hill last month, a tourist watching the scenery rather than the road and hitting a delivery van, had brought a fast and, some said, over-the-top police response. In the pub that night someone joked that it must have been coincidence; emergency response by police and ambulance into the villages was not like in the city, it was patchy. Ken thought it might be rather good while the neighbour in Number Four was around.

He had only met the Selby 'couple' once to talk to. He and Amelia were taking their normal hillside walk one Sunday and came across them on the same path. Amelia had been talking about meeting them sometime, although their shared neighbours in the house between said that they weren't that friendly. On the hillside path Amelia did most of the talking.

They seemed friendly enough. He had a cultured Scottish accent and said he was from Dumfries and his wife was from Glasgow. Ken kept his eyes on the man, trying not to look at the woman and find a cop eyeing a retired cop. That she knew the lives and backgrounds of everyone in the block of cottages was a given to him.

Selby had been in local government, education he said, but health reasons had forced him to finish. "The strain," he said. Ken knew about that and could certainly see strain on this man's face.

"And yourself?" he asked.

"Retired five years ago, a police officer in the RAF," he said. Now his 'wife' was avoiding looking at him, Ken saw.

Amelia said that they must come over and chat, have some tea. They made pleasant noises about it but Ken did not think it would happen, somehow.

When they left it was without warning or saying goodbye to any of the neighbours. The day following a removal van came, followed by a communications van. Nobody recognized the logo on the communications vehicle, someone remarked afterwards; it wasn't the company that installed and repaired the local internet service. The same day a 'For Sale' sign went up.

A day or so later Ken walked along the front walkway linking all the cottages and went up the path for a second or two to confirm his suspicions. The door had a Chubb lock and two deadbolts. The windows had deadbolts too and he could see the tell-tale marks of the alarm system.

Amelia had a habit of commenting on items in the newspaper each morning and, from past practice, always picked up anything of criminal interest to tell Ken. He had told her he was retired now but it didn't stop her.

She remarked a couple of days later that there had been a breakthrough in a large drug gang trial in Glasgow, something to do with an issue about the legality of evidence provided by a gang member turned Queen's Evidence. It had been holding up proceedings pending a judicial ruling as to what was allowable. When she had finished the paper he read the article himself and then went on-line.

The Selbys had moved in to Number Four just two

weeks after a major drug bust of the Dominic Connolly gang. They had moved out the day of the ruling that a particular witness could finally give evidence in a series of related trials. The witness couldn't be named, said the article, but it was a major breakthrough for the Crown, felt the reporter.

It could be just coincidence, thought Ken, knowing deep down, with a working life as a police officer behind him, that it probably wasn't.

He had heard rumours from a chat with one of his old colleagues that there was an interesting legal case not too far from him, in Glasgow. His friend had retired to the south coast; Glasgow and Loch Linnhe seemed close enough to him.

It was an issue about whether a lawyer privy to criminal activities could become a prosecution witness. Something about differentiating between the privileged information received while acting in a legal capacity from information received while participating in criminal activities. A ruling was bogging things down.

Not for much longer, Ken thought, thinking that the witness in question had been living not far from him under the name Selby.

EPILOGUE
CALA EN BOSC

The plain-clothes officer of the National Police of Minorca parked his car in the shade and waited outside the complex of holiday homes. His guest, a visiting British police officer, had entered the second floor apartment. She was inside about twenty minutes and then emerged with a suitcase, closing her mobile phone.

"There has been a slight change in plans, Detective Madero. I will now stay over for the evening, so I will need to make a reservation at a hotel. I told my Administrative Officer I would do that locally and she will change my flight back to London for tomorrow morning."

He smiled. "That is wonderful, Sergeant Sayer. Hotels on the island of Minorca are not hard to find and I know one I am sure will please you. Would you be free for dinner this evening, perhaps?"

"Thank you but no, an early dinner meeting is the reason I am staying over."

Catrin had caught a 6.30 a.m. tourist flight from

Gatwick into Mahón. It was still only late morning.

"But perhaps lunch and an opportunity to see something of your beautiful island would be possible, if you have the time, of course?"

"I would be delighted, Senorita." He had quite taken to this young police officer with a scar on her face. "We will make the time."

John Dalton had been co-operative when Catrin went in. After all, he had eventually been covered by Niall Irvin under his immunity deal so he faced no charges in the UK. Why Niall had chosen to do that, he didn't know; no-one else seemed to get out of his betrayal. Perhaps, like Dominic, he had a soft spot for him from the past, from life in the Gorbals. John knew he could have returned to Berwick-on-Tweed or Glasgow if he wanted, but he had chosen to stay in Minorca.

It was a year after the Connolly gang arrests and some of the trials were in progress. He occasionally saw a news item about people he knew, generally getting convicted. Connolly's case hadn't come to court yet, he had heard, but it was imminent, the news reports said.

During the inventory work on the Gault paintings conducted by the Kelvingrove Museum it became clear that two of the fourteen paintings that had started this case were still missing. Irvin had been re-questioned and that led them again to Dalton. When contacted, John Dalton confirmed they were with him, unaltered, properly stored with a third painting by Gault also provided by Irvin. They were welcome to them.

Neville Coltrane had then been approached about getting them back. Strachan thought it needed someone within the police service who could deal with the security aspects but also have an artist's eye, to spot any 'funny stuff' that Dalton may try to pull; after all, his record for forgery was well-known.

Given the current circumstances, Coltrane had proposed that the newly-promoted Detective Sergeant Catrin Sayer should make the trip and DCI Worsley had readily agreed. On the flight down south from Gatwick, the mayhem caused by the Irvin operation came back fully to her as she focused on the day's work rather than the various 'live' cases she had to handle at present.

Her barely-concealed hostility towards Dalton tempered a little when she saw the painting on the easel. It was a near-complete head and shoulders portrait of an older woman. She was smiling, at ease, sitting wearing a silk blouse and nice jewellery, framed in late afternoon light on the balcony Catrin could see through the French doors. It was an excellent painting. She knew from experience recreating silk well on canvas was challenging but he had caught the material and the skin tones beautifully.

"This is Miriam, a friend of mine. She retired here around the same time as I did. It's her birthday present."

He gestured to the other paintings around. "The others are for the tourists, for some reason they love Picasso-style copies rather than my local scenes – but they all have my signature, no-one else's. I have a street license now and they sell quite well."

"You have talent Mr. Dalton, it's…" Catrin said.

"… a pity I wasted it. I know." smiled John Dalton. "You have no idea when you start what talent is, what you should do. I just wanted to get out of the Gorbals, of Glasgow. And now I'm sixty-eight, soon to be sixty-nine. I am not looking back. Just enjoying what I have left, buying paint and painting for myself."

She picked up the suitcase. They had already looked at the Gault paintings together and re-packed them. She had been satisfied that they were the genuine article. Dalton's comment had been, "They are good, but I don't rate them as being Colourist standard myself, not Cadell or Fergusson paintings. Frankly, I am surprised the Kelvingrove is making a fuss about him."

As she turned to leave he said, "I am done with forgery, Sergeant Sayer, but if you have the time I will tell you about the world of fronts and backs of paintings from a forger's perspective. Neville Coltrane and some of his people will know a lot of it, I know, but it would be first-hand information for you. I won't drop anyone I know in it, I am not an informer, but it will clear the air a little, perhaps?"

He had seen the scar, a white line on her cheek, and felt the tension. Frankly, he felt, her injury was nothing to do with him.

Catrin thought about it and nodded. "I would appreciate that." She started to put the case and her shoulder bag down.

"It will have to be this evening, though. I am going to Miriam's now, to read to her. It's my daily chore... she doesn't have too long left really, so I don't miss the middle part of the day with her, it is her best time." He didn't expand on it.

Catrin thought. "I will stay over then. Can I record our conversation?"

"By all means, please do. I will see you back here at, say, five p.m.? I will have some soft drinks and wine, some hors d'oeuvres. We can talk and then perhaps have dinner nearby afterwards, if you wish."

"Perhaps we can, but no guarantees, Mr. Dalton. We will see."

She took the paintings with her anyway and called Aina to let her know the change in plans.

Much later that evening as Dalton finished his discourse on forgery she switched off the recorder function on her iPhone. She played back the last segment and it was as clear as the test they had done at the beginning.

"Thank you Mr. Dalton, that was very enlightening for me. I made a comment this morning about your talent. I said, 'It's a pity -' and you interrupted me to say that you had wasted it. What I was going to say was, "it's a pity that your creativity didn't channel itself into the art directly, but into forgery, and ask you why that was? What you have told me this evening just brings home how creative you can be."

Dalton thought about her question and replied honestly.

"I think great painters put their creativity into works they will do whether they make a fortune out of them or end up destitute. They are driven to do it. I was driven by the desire to make money and in the end I wasted a lot of my life in gaol."

She nodded, apparently having reached a similar conclusion herself.

"Shall we have dinner now, Sergeant Sayer? We eat late in Spain," Dalton asked.

"No, Mr. Dalton, I think not. I was on a flight from Gatwick at 6.30 this morning and I had what would be for me a late and heavy lunch with my colleague from the police service here. But thank you for the offer and for the juice and hors d'oeuvres. But I really need to get some sleep."

He looked disappointed.

Catrin thought, 'tough for him'. She wanted to get out.

"I do have some advice for you, though, in fair exchange," Catrin said. "Daniella Ramires Milne is now living in Portugal, with her father. She, as I think you know now, was Niall Irvin's target. She and Francis Milne are separated and in the process of finalising a divorce; she uses her maiden name Ramires now.

"She has not, as far as we can tell, let go of her wish for vengeance against Niall Irvin and Dominic Connolly. There was an attack on Connolly in prison recently we believe to be attributable to her. In fact, he was unhurt but he injured his assailant.

"Your role and name has carefully been kept out of any public materials and court proceedings and we have taken steps to ensure that your identity has been protected. Even the choice of flight I took this morning was selected to help maintain your anonymity. You have my real name. The passport I travelled on this morning is in another name, because my real identity is known to Ramires and others, thanks to your friend Niall Irvin. So we are honouring fully our side of the immunity deal with Irvin."

She continued, "Have either Irvin or Connolly been in touch with you or, perhaps I should ask first, would you tell me if either of them had been in touch?"

Dalton was fully alert now, no longer lost in his reminiscences.

"Sergeant Sayer, if they had been in touch I would not tell you what they said to me. But I can say truthfully that neither of them has communicated with me since I arrived here."

She nodded. "They both seem to want to protect you,

then."

John Dalton said softly, "I have known them since they were boys."

She nodded but said nothing and stood up to leave.

"So you need to be careful, Mr. Dalton. You may have been simply the technician in the deception of Daniella Ramires but we have no idea how broad her aim is in this vendetta."

She looked over at his paintings.

"You may even want to change your signature, for example. A nickname might work."

His face clouded over. She thought he was probably thinking about how many he had sold and were any purchasers visiting from Portugal.

"Now I must leave. That Guardia Civil patrol car sitting outside is to take me back to my hotel. Good evening."

Catrin left without shaking John Dalton's proffered hand. She wanted some air, some exercise, a shower and a sleep. To her, John Dalton, Colin Cheney, Niall Irvin and Dominic Connolly were all the same, to differing degrees; sleazy men who would see innocent people injured in one way or another to make illegal money. She had no time for any of them.

NOTES

The 'Scottish Colourists'; John Duncan Fergusson, Francis Cadell, Samuel Peploe and Leslie Hunter lived and painted in the latter of the nineteenth century and the early part of the twentieth century. Some of their paintings are at the Kelvingrove Museum and Art Gallery but the descriptions of paintings in this novel are entirely fictitious.

The Metropolitan Police do have an Art and Antiques Unit within its Specialist Crime Command, established back in 1969. However, its people and activities described herein are entirely my own creation. The 'Art Crime Unit' in the Metropolitan Police in this novel is an invention that has no real-life counterpart.

ABOUT THE AUTHOR

Allan Jones lives in Ontario, Canada. He was born and grew up in Merseyside, England. By profession an industrial chemist, he worked for many years as a consultant on international chemical regulation. He has lived in or travelled to most of the regions featured in the Catrin Sayer novels.